HOPE

HOPE

Love & Disaster Book 3

Tara L. Roi

BEE BOOKS

NEW HAVEN

HOPE: Love & Disaster Trilogy Book 3
Copyright ©2022 by Tara L. Roí

E ISBN: 978-1-7353484-7-6
Hardcover ISBN: 978-1-7353484-8-3
Paperback ISBN: 978-1-7353484-9-0
First edition: December 2023

For information, visit BeeBooks.org
Book layout: R. L. Fraser
Cover design: R. L. Fraser and MacKenzie Coffman
Author Photo: DeCarlo Photo Studio

Content Warning

Dear Reader,

Writing a second chance, redemption romance means delving to the core of some tough topics. I began this book with two goals:

1. To serve women who have experienced infidelity and chosen to work things out with their partner, and

2. To write a book that explores wildfire from the perspective of people living through it and from the perspective of a scientist trying to prevent more wildfires from happening.

Please note this novel includes:

Vague references to the suicide of a family member,

Verbal abuse from a mother to a son,

Wildfire and the aftermath of wildfires,

Discussions of infidelity and its emotional consequences,

Misogynistic language (from characters we don't like), and

Infertility.

I have taken great care to address each of these topics with sensitivity. As the title implies, I have done my best to weave each of these issues into a storyline that focuses on repair and healing and will leave you with a sense of hope.

Still, if you feel triggered by any of the topics above, this may not be the book for you.

I encourage you to take care of your heart. If that means turning the page, enjoy the ride and let me know what you think. If that means closing the book, I understand. Thank you for taking care of yourself.

xoxo
Tara

As always, for MacKenzie.

Prologue

October 6 - Wildbranch, CA

Celeste

As soon as the envelope disappears into the slot and clunks at the bottom of the mailbox, my stomach tightens. I've made a huge mistake. Shit. Shit. Shit. Shit. How can I get the letter back? My fingers are thin but not thin enough to fit into the slot.

Possibilities:

Fishing line?
Coat hanger?
Bra strap? Damn these new mailboxes that no one can break into. Not that I ever knew how or wanted to get into an old one. It's a felony to tamper with the mail. Why isn't infidelity a felony?

My handwritten words flash through my mind: "You implanted this idea in him... Not all men cheat... All those times you disparaged men in front of Josh..."

I cringe.

That's right, folks: it's Celeste Cairan, the great relationship coach, who, after discovering her soulmate's infidelity, wrote a scathing letter to his mother. Yes, Celeste Cairan, who ignored the loving relationship she shared with her soulmate's mother and instead blamed the woman for having raised him wrong. I'll have some new openings in my schedule when my existing clients realize I'm a complete fraud. Can't keep a man. Can't sustain a relationship for more than seven years. What's the refrain? Those who can't do, teach. Yup.

Ash falls from the wildfires in the mountains, coating my arms with a sticky gray pallor. What are the chances the fire will snake a path through the mountains directly to this mailbox and turn that letter to dust without scorching anything else?

Or... better fantasy for everyone: it rains, washing away the ash, stopping the fires, running the ink on my handwritten diatribe. The letter could get lost in the mail. One can only hope.

Damn it! Why must I always speak my mind? What good can possibly come from this?

I drop my forehead on the mailbox. The heat of absorbed sunlight is remarkably soothing. I'll just stay here for a while. Maybe the heat will transfer some of the mailbox's blue paint onto my skin, marking me. A cobalt blue reminder to all who cross my path, like The Scarlet Letter. Instead of A for adulterous, B for bitter.

"Excuse me. Are you done here? I need to mail something," a soft voice says to my right.

I roll my head toward the sound. Sunlight silhouettes a tall figure.

"Sorry." I step away from the mailbox, recognizing its defeat over my better intentions.

"Hey." Her voice perks up. "Didn't I just see you in *California Inspiration Magazine*?"

How did she recognize me behind the n95 mask and goggles? "That was me." A real inspiration.

"You're that relationship coach with the book... I love that book: *Nonjudgmental Relating: the Path to Love and Reunion*."

"Thank you. My editor chose the title." Now would be a good time for a targeted earthquake to open the sidewalk and swallow me whole.

"Gosh, my husband and I sure could use your help."

I highly doubt it.

"Do you have room in your schedule?"

"I'm not sure. All my appointments get created through the calendar on my website."

"Hey, we're stoked about the workbook. When's that coming out?"

After I write it. If I can write it. "Probably sometime next year," I say, trying to sound lighter than I feel. "Listen, I've gotta run. The smell of burning plastic is killing me. Lovely meeting you. What's your name?"

She says it. I repeat it and promptly forget it as I walk away.

Another gem from the letter I just mailed springs to mind:

"What choice did Josh have but to live down to your expectations?" That one's a doozy. On the plus side, I told Ellen she's like a mother to me. Maybe she'll focus on that and forget the rest.

Josh

THE REPORT MAKES NO FUCKING SENSE. I SEE IT SAYS THE FIRE retardant caused toxic contamination of the soil, but how? Silica comes from sand. Cellulose comes from wood. Water is water. Ammonium phosphate is something we're eating all the time. And these are not the compounds in this toxicology report.

I take a swig of water. All this wildfire smoke parches my throat—a mild side-effect, all things considered. Is it possible our formulation reacted with something already in the soil to create the benzene and cadmium that's showing up in the reports?

I look into Julio's wide face, replay our first trip to the test site in my mind, see us gathering samples, bringing them to the lab.

"Is my memory going?" I ask. "We tested the soil before, right?"

He nods with his full body.

"This was supposed to be a clean site. No public access. No hiking, planting, dumping…"

Julio shrugs. "State can't control people's actions."

"Back to square fucking one."

"You think something else is contaminating it?" Julio asks.

"Must be, but…"

"What if we bring soil into the lab and apply the hydrogel here? Simulate rainfall here. Control the process start to finish, like we do with the fume hood tests."

I clap. "Yes. Simple. Elegant."

"To be extra sure, we could also run it on potting soil. It's gotta be clean coming in packaged, right, boss?"

"Right. I'll—" Celeste's text tone jogs me into another reality.

I'm out. Left a note on the counter.

I sigh, text back:

Wish you'd reconsider.

I stare at the phone a moment too long, waiting for a reply I already know will never come. Damn it all.

"You okay, Josh?" Julio asks. "Listen, I'll pick up the potting soil after work. I know you're dealing with..." He clears his throat. "Sorry."

I school my face to neutral and meet his gaze. No judgement in his expression at all. How rare is that?

"Much appreciated," I say, imagining Celeste putting the last of her boxes into her car, driving away, ash falling all around her. Ash. Holy shit. Of course. "Julio."

"What?"

"What happened between the time we took the clean soil samples, put the retardant down, then collected the second samples?"

"First, it rained, which shouldn't have washed it into the soil but did, meaning we need to adjust the viscosity so it stays put longer."

"Yes, and we know that because about a week later?"

He looks up, thinking, then his face brightens. "The Reservoir Fire."

"Exactly! Three days, 128 acres burned to ash."

"The ash contaminated the soil."

"It wasn't us at all. Well, maybe, but I doubt it. Let's review those toxicology reports out of Fort Collins, see what they've been finding. I'm willing to bet it's some of the same compounds."

Rachel pops her head into my office. "It's eight. I'm heading home."

"Good night, Rachel," Julio and I say in unison.

"I'm gonna head out, too, boss," Julio says. "See if I can make it to Garden Supply before it closes."

I have no desire to go home, but I'm beat. Ash falls on me as I ride my bike through the city. How did it not occur to me that our soil sites would be contaminated? That's cute. Real cute. Almost as cute as Celeste deciding to move out over one fucking mistake. One mistake. I wasn't even sober.

The motion detector turns the spotlight on my driveway, illuminating my Jeep and the empty spot where Celeste parks. Parked. Foolish of me to think her car might be here. Hope springs eternal.

I carry the bicycle to the back porch, lock it against the railing, and stroll inside through our bedroom, removing my riding goggles and respirator. Her picture's gone. "Damn it, Celeste," I say aloud like she's here, wishing she was. "That was on my nightstand. Bad enough you left all these empty nails on the walls where our decorations used to hang. But that picture was mine."

I stride down the hall into the kitchen, wondering what I have for dinner. Did Celeste take the food? Never figured her for petty. I guess I misjudged. The envelope catches my eye, propped up against the vase of roses I bought her, a last-ditch attempt to apologize.

Wait a minute. What happened to the roses? The stems are there, but the flowers are gone. "Jesus, Celeste." Well, she's creative. I'll give her that.

I'll read her note after I eat. Luckily, she did leave food in the fridge, and I'm going to assume she didn't poison it. I pull out a bowl of marinating tofu and mushrooms, a red pepper, some bok choy, and broccoli, bringing everything out to the deck. With ash falling like snow, I'm appreciating the overhang I built out here, which protects the grill from God knows how many toxins that ash contains. She'd insist we cook inside. She's not here.

My phone trills with Amira's ringtone. I answer the video call. She's almost unrecognizable without her dreads. "Hey, Sis. What happened to your hair?"

She runs a hand over her shaved head, opens her mouth, then chokes out a sob. Shit.

"Uh, oh. What's happening?"

"Why do you do it? Why do men cheat?"

"Nice to see you, too. And you're what? Ruminating on your ex-husband after eleven years of divorce because...?"

"No," she says, defensive. "It's Derek."

"Who's Derek? You're dating someone?" I turn on the grill as my stomach rumbles.

"Not dating. He's been doing a female fast."

"A what?"

"Google it."

"Hang on..." I tap the phrase into my search engine. "Okay, wow. He's dieting and you're upset?"

She sighs and fills me in on the details and progression of her "situationship" with this dude Derek. They met when he was two months into some program where he doesn't date, flirt, or have sex with anyone for three months. All I can think is: Why? But my little sister's on her own trip, and I try to catch up before she loses me.

"It seemed like we were moving toward a relationship. I thought he shared my feelings, until I caught him downtown hugging some blonde. I don't get it. He seemed so into me."

"How do you know he isn't?" I ask.

"I know what I saw." She wipes her nose.

"You sure? Maybe the guy was clearing unfinished business with someone."

"No. He never dates anyone more than three times."

"Sounds like a real winner."

"Shut up." She sniffles, blows her nose. "He is. Derek saves lives. He's kind and sweet, and he doesn't want shallow sex anymore. He wants something real."

"Hmmm. I don't know, sis. Impulse control issues?"

"Why did you cheat on Celeste?"

Jesus, Celeste. I thought we agreed to keep family and friends out of this. "I take it she told you, huh?"

"No, but last time we talked, you said you broke up. That's how you end every relationship."

"Harsh!"

"True."

I sigh. "I hate that you're right."

"So, why do it?" she asks. "Why not use your words? Say, 'I don't want you anymore.'"

Leave it to my sister to ask the hard questions. I blow out a puff of air. "It just happens."

"Every time, Josh. It's a pretty shitty M.O."

"Thanks for the attack, Amira."

"Sorry." She sighs, chokes out another sob, tries to speak, sobs more. This guy better be worth it. Amira inhales a shaky breath and sputters, "I need to understand, and right now, you're the representative of all men who cheat."

Nice. I growl and search again for the program my sister's talking about. Here it is.

Amira sniffles. "What is wrong with your species?"

God, grant me patience. I search the dark sky for help. On a normal night, I'd have a superb view of the moon and stars. Instead, ash falls, illuminated by floodlights. "You know, kid, the only reason I haven't hung up on you is because you're my sister, and you're a fucking basket case right now."

"Love you, too."

"I could ask you why women are so damn high-maintenance."

Amira snorts. "By high-maintenance, I assume you mean recognizing our worth and expecting to be treated well?"

"Hey, this fast he's doing looks interesting."

"He says he's rising from the sewer of toxic masculinity. I thought—"

"Really? Rising from the sewer... he says that?" What a self-important douche.

"I was being poetic, Josh."

"Good, because any guy who's that full of himself—"

"Today he called me a gold digger."

"Ouch."

"Do you know how hard it was for me to accept help from him?"

I laugh. "I can imagine. You hate receiving gifts."

"That's not true!"

"Mmmm."

"Of course, I like gifts!"

I purse my lips. No need to make Amira feel worse than she already does.

"Really? Is it that bad?" she asks.

Since she's asking, I tell Amira about that time Celeste got her a beautiful Christmas gift and Amira's response was so rude, Celeste cried. My sister's mouth falls open.

"If this dude's helping you, paying for things, offering you more, more, more, and you're acting like he's wrong for giving, maybe he feels unappreciated. Some women actually like that shit."

Amira groans. Though she's thirty-three, I'm hearing her teenage self crying about being teased. "What do I do, Josh?"

"You're still at his house, and he left?"

"Yeah. To meet that woman."

"If that's the case, why is he letting you stay there?"

"Because he likes to take care of me."

I raise my eyebrows, give her my big brotherly stare. "Mm-hmm."

"Oh."

"And you think he's putting eggs in other baskets? Things aren't always what they seem." For example, a guy can fuck up with another woman and still love his girlfriend.

"It could've been a misunderstanding, I guess."

"Occasionally, you are wrong."

She doesn't take the bait. Instead, her puffy eyes plead at me. "How do I make up to him, Josh? Derek is the first guy I've actually loved."

I drop the phone, then hurry to pick it up again. "Sorry, sis. Love, huh?"

"Yeah," she says with an exhale.

"That's a big deal." My stomach growls, louder this time, reminding me why I came outside. I prop the phone at an angle, grab my chef's knife, and make quick work of chopping the veggies.

"Where are you?" she asks.

"In the backyard grilling tofu and veggies."

"At... what time is it there?"

"Nine-ish. Long day at work. Listen, you want him? Apologize. Make it abundantly clear you see and appreciate everything Derek's done for you. From where I'm sitting, it doesn't sound like you appreciate him. And if I were him, I might be looking for an exit."

"Oh." The heartbreak in Amira's voice mirrors my current emotional state. She thanks me and ends the call.

I finish chopping the veggies, pop them onto skewers with cubes of tofu and mushrooms, then baste the kabobs with the marinade and lay them on the grill. Female fast. What would possess a man to take such a drastic step?

While the kabobs cook, I walk into the kitchen. For what? I don't recall. Celeste's note commands my attention. Do I want to open it? No. I'm bone tired and have had enough of emotions for one day. But it's staring me in the face, a Band-Aid I need to rip off.

Josh,

I don't understand your choice. I thought what we had was beautiful.

"It was, Celeste," I say to the notecard, imagining her brown eyes.

I thought I was special to you.

I glance at the beheaded roses in the vase. "How many ways do you need me to demonstrate you are special to me?"

I thought our relationship could heal us both. I believed you gave me roses to declare your love, knowing they've always been my favorite flower. Now, I have to wonder: were all those bouquets meant to assuage your guilt? Did each one represent a different woman?

"No. God. There were no other women. Why don't you believe me?"

I believed our roots ran deep, nourished by the rich soil of our shared history. Now, I don't know what was real. Should I take comfort knowing I wasn't the first woman you cheated on because you couldn't handle your feelings? Why am I bothering?

You'd like me to reconsider? I cannot reconsider anything when I trust nothing. Empty apologies don't move me. Maybe, as you say, you weren't trying to end us. But you did. Sorry to bring your daughter into this, but you're setting a poor example. If you hope she'll start taking your calls again, try learning how to respect women. You need help, Josh, and I hope—for everyone's sake—you get it.

~ Celeste

The air leaves my lungs. "Low blow, babe."

I crack open a beer and trudge to the deck to flip the kebabs, texting Terry:

Ever hear of a female fast?

He responds with a phone call, which I take as I recline on a deck chair, staring into the woods behind the house. "Yo, Ter."

"Yo, brah!" He sounds so cheerful. "Celeste moved out today, right? Come on over. Let's celebrate your freedom with some primo indica."

Celebrate?

"Indica sounds perfect, but I'm not feeling the celebration right now. My speed is food, shower, bed. Tomorrow's looking intense at work."

"This weekend, then."

"Sure. And a hike," I suggest, and take a long pull from my Modelo Negra. Hits the spot.

"I'm in. We'll get the crew together. By the way, no clue what a female fast is."

I open the site on my phone and read him the description of the three-month program designed to help, "...change how you handle sexual energy for more fulfilling relationships."

"And it means you can't flirt, date, or have sex for three months?"

"The six-month program is even more demanding."

Terry's cackle comes through my phone, loud and clear. "Why in hell would anyone wanna do that?"

"I don't know. Maybe..." *so they can have more fulfilling relationships.* No sense telling Terry that, nor admitting I find this whole *changing your relationship to sexual energy* idea intriguing.

"I've got better medicine for you, Josh. It's called a hike, a bong, and a night out. I'll play wingman."

"If you mean a night out shooting pool, hearing a band, yes. If you mean a night out trying to pick up women, no thanks. It's too soon, man."

Besides, there's only one woman I want. Granted, she ditched me this afternoon, and the chances of her returning look unpromising. But... maybe with time? Maybe in a month or two Celeste will see I wasn't trying to end us. It was a mistake. I was drunk off my ass. I'd never cause her pain like that again.

You are cordially invited
to witness
Sage Ellen DesChamps &
Wesley Williams
unite in marriage
at their home in New Haven, CT
New Years' Day ~ 1:30 PM

After the ceremony, please join the celebration
K-Gallery on Chapel Street
across from Yale's Old Campus.

1

New Haven, CT

Celeste

Travel always saps my energy. Now, as I close my eyes and let the elevator wall hold me upright, the sound of an all-too-familiar voice fills me with dread.

"Hold the elevator!"

The whoosh of the closing doors is aborted with a clunk. I open my eyes. The sexy, muscular forearm that stopped the doors in their tracks pokes through the opening. Ballsy. Impatient. Josh.

My heart pounds. Time slows as the elevator doors slide open to reveal the man I haven't seen in almost three months.

The burgundy scarf I knit hangs loose inside the turned-up collar of his charcoal overcoat. The one I bought for Christmas last year. He has some nerve. He knows it flatters his height and makes his auburn curls pop. Dark denim hugs his thighs, and…

You must be kidding. Does Josh honestly have the gall to wear the gray vegetable-tanned leather Chelsea boots I had custom-made? He knows what they do to me.

Yes, Josh, you and your damn manipulative outfit are making me all hot and bothered, but I'll have you know my blood is running cold.

"What are you doing here?" I ask.

The sweetest smile lifts Josh's already high cheekbones as he punches the button to my floor. "We RSVP'd yes. Remember?"

"*Before* we broke up," I say.

His hazel eyes radiate genuine love.

How many times have I seen that look? How many times did I believe that look? How many times over the last seven years did that look let me know I was finally home, safe, cherished? Now, all I can see is the lie in that look.

The doors slide closed. Is it too late to get out? Can I climb seven flights of stairs with this gargantuan suitcase? For once, I wish I had remembered Josh's repeated mantra to pack less.

The elevator jerks into motion. I'm stuck riding up with him. I position myself right in front of the doors because, damn it, I'm leaving this trap first. The numbers on the wall change at the pace of molasses. I will the machine to move faster because I feel Josh's eyes caressing the length of my back. It makes me shiver.

Images flash through my mind: the fantasy we often spun together. In it, I hit the emergency stop button, grab him by his tight auburn curls, pull his face to me, and bite that plush bottom lip. He plasters me against the wall, lowers his tasty mouth to mine. We consume each other like wildfire, all heat and light and intense energy. He slides my dress above my hips, growls when he discovers I've gone commando. I undo his pants and force them down, wrap a long leg around his waist. His ready staff springs through the opening in his boxers. No point slipping those off. He can enter paradise just as he is, and my Garden of Eden is fresh with dew.

But the snake in this Garden of Eden isn't Josh's cock. It's Lucinda. That fucking bitch. The now familiar sensations return. Roiling stomach. Stabbing, wrenching chest pain. Empty lungs that won't take air despite my gasping.

I look at him over my shoulder and sneer. "I thought you'd have the decency not to come."

The light in his eyes weakens, then goes out. "Sage said she wanted me here," he murmurs. "She said I'm like family."

"Yeah, the relative who makes you need therapy." I turn back to face the door.

"Cute." His tone tells me he's amused.

I'll show him cute. When the elevator reaches my floor, I stride out without looking back.

"Celeste," he calls, at the same moment I realize I left my stupid suitcase.

Josh could just push the door-open button. Instead, the 'hero' holds the damn thing open with his muscular arm. Well, I'm not looking.

I ignore his seductive woodsy scent and reach past him for my bag. Of course, its wheels get stuck in the threshold.

"Let me help you." Josh reaches for it.

"I don't need your help," I snap, trying to tug the thing free.

"Clearly, you've got it all under control." More amusement from him?

Hell, no. I lift and yank with all my strength. Too hard. The suitcase rolls into the hall without a care, while I land on my ass.

Josh throws his garment bag on the floor and rushes to my side. I stop him with a glare. He holds his hands up and backs away, giving me room to rise. On my own, thank you very much. I take my shred of remaining dignity and walk down the hall, hopefully in the right direction because I need to shower before the rehearsal dinner.

2

New Year's Day

Celeste

UNTIL LAST NIGHT'S REHEARSAL, IT HAD BEEN TWENTY-plus years since I set foot inside one of the fancy arts and crafts style homes in this neighborhood. Then, I was babysitting a professor's kid, and after I put her to bed, I'd eat all their snacks while pretending it was my home. I'd lounge in the wicker furniture on the wide front porch, gaze at the leaded glass windows, lost in the way they caught the light.

I used to imagine Josh coming up the stairs, sitting beside me in the porch swing, holding my hand, explaining organic chemistry. We barely knew each other then, only saw each other a few times before graduating and losing our connection, but he appeared in my fantasies routinely.

He was smart, but didn't lord it over people. Handsome, but seemed unaware of it. Strong and caring. He'd take the bus from MIT in Cambridge to New Haven to visit Amira.

She was just nine then, and since Sage babysat her every day after school, she often hung out in our dorm on Yale's Old Campus. Our suite was huge, with its own living room and bay window overlooking the street. When she knew Josh was coming, Amira would sit in the window seat and watch for his arrival. Sometimes I joined her. When he knocked, she'd run to the door, and he'd swing her into the air.

The gentleness in his voice when he spoke to her sparked my dreams about raising children with him. I'd hope he didn't catch me staring. Reconnecting with him seven years ago was a dream come true.

Now, Josh is ruining Sage's magical event. Even when I was upstairs helping her get ready, I felt his presence killing the enchanting vibe, infecting the whole house. Luckily, the candles and firelight, plus the special blend of sacred herbs Sage's sister Amy threw into the fireplace are dispelling some of Josh's ick, so we can all enjoy this dreamy ceremony.

The string quartet switches from Brahms to reggae, our cue. I lead the way down the wide chestnut stairway, followed closely by my three best friends, one of whom is about to marry the man of her dreams. I pause at the landing, as we rehearsed, and nod to the groom.

Why did Sage want Josh here, anyway? So, they stayed in touch after college, their work dovetailing as she photographed him in the lab and in the field. So, she featured him in her environmental heroes exhibit. So, she and his sister grew super close in adulthood. So what? Sage and Wesley kept the wedding small-ish. Couldn't she have made an excuse?

I'm being selfish. This is my best friend's special day. She gets to have whomever she wants at her wedding, and I have to deal.

Josh

Maybe I shouldn't have come. After what Celeste said in the elevator yesterday and now, with the shade she's throwing me, I wonder. When Sage and I spoke on the phone last month, she said she'd feel hurt if I skipped her wedding. Technically, I shouldn't be socializing with women, but a long-time friend's wedding is a reasonable exception. No one in the program gave me shit for it.

Only one person has made me question my choice, and she's leading the bridal procession down the stairway, smiling through tears. Emotional over her best friend getting married? Or upset I'm here? She keeps looking my way, sniffling, looking away.

Until this moment, I felt welcome.

Here I am, seeing a therapist weekly, doing the six-month female fast, trying to grow, and she's treating me like enemy number one. Not that I told her about the program. I thought Amira or Sage might, though. Maybe Celeste is oblivious to what I'm doing.

Maybe I deserve a little shade right now. Maybe I can live with it. Hell, I'd rather stand in Celeste's shade than in another woman's low-wattage light.

But for the next four months, I have a clear M.O. No flirting. No dating. No sex. Weekly check-ins with my accountability buddy. Workshops. Classes. Daily meditation and journaling. These last two months, the hardest part has been avoiding Celeste when I'm dying to make up for how I hurt her.

I need to focus on something else, like that stunning dark wood mantlepiece and the built-in bookshelves flanking it. Are the leaded glass bookshelf doors original to the house?

When I pulled up out front, I could tell someone had loving-ly restored the home. Amira said the groom did some of the work.

Impressive. Now, watching him stand erect by the brick fireplace, votive candles along the mantle casting a glow on his eager smile, my thoughts drift.

I imagine I'm in his place, waiting for Celeste. She stops at the landing, graceful, and surveys the room. I imagine she's gazing at me with love, rather than looking through me. In my fantasy, those tears express joy. In reality, her sorrow hits me like a stab to the chest.

Look at me, Celeste, like you used to when you believed in us.

This train of thought is not helping.

Celeste looks stunning, in a dark blue shimmery getup that accentuates her long legs and gentle curves. The top highlights her perfect full cleavage. I've been missing that cleavage.

A new fantasy forms, so visceral it feels real: her skin soft under my touch, sexy asymmetrical collar bone warm under my lips, strong, thin fingers gripping my hips as she stands on tip-toe to nuzzle my ear...

Whoa. I need to calm down, get hold of my mind. Data. Wildfire stats. 1,975,086 acres burned in California last year. $148 million in damages. 24,226 structures destroyed. One hundred people and thousands of animals killed.

If our solution works, can we bring wildfire deaths to zero, save people's homes, worksites, and places of worship? Speaking of worship...

My amber-skinned angel turns and begins the last part of her descent. Has the string quartet been playing reggae all along? I'm noticing now because Wesley's singing the lyrics to Chronixx's "Majesty," a personal favorite.

If Celeste were meeting me at the altar, I'd sing Jimi Hendrix's "Angel."

Celeste

THE GROOM, A TALL, THIN WHITE GUY WITH BLACK CURLS AND tropical blue eyes, beams a smile and sings something about Sage being his queen. Wesley's warm tenor is a siren call luring us down the last few steps. As if Sage needs more enticement. Still, she waits on the landing while we three bridesmaids take our places in front of the bookshelves beside the roaring fire. Wesley begins the last verse of the song, Sage's cue to descend toward her man.

Even with a baby bump the size of Alaska, she looks like a tan Aphrodite wafting down the stairs on her father's arm. Her dark brown curls stand out against the butter-colored silk shantung. The empire waist gown is beautiful on her. She reaches the fireplace, kisses her dad on his copper cheek, and takes Wesley's hand as he sings the final notes.

The string quartet stops. Amy, the mirror image of Sage but with salt-and-pepper hair, a few more laugh lines, and a hippy-style dress, opens the ceremony with a reiki gesture, blessing all of us. Amy's presence makes me happy. But as she talks about marriage, my mind spins in unpleasant directions.

I thought Josh and I would be married by now. If by some miracle, I find an honest man, a man who'll stay, I'll be the last person in our college class to tie the knot.

Celeste, snap out of it. For a few hours, can you simply be happy for Sage?

In my mind, I see her when we met, smiling nervously, bouncing on her toes. I could tell instantly that she was one of the kindest, most genuine people in the world. Although she's been through a lot, she never let it dim her sparkle. I wish I could say the same about myself.

But I'm staring at the latest instrument of my destruction, trying to send him a telepathic message to go home. Just when I finally thought I was getting it together, Josh came and set my life ablaze. I've become a bitter, nasty woman, a fraud. I have no right to coach people about relationships or write books about love. I'm filled with hate.

3

Josh

THEY PULLED OUT ALL THE STOPS FOR THIS WEDDING reception. The art gallery is decked out with candles and flowers on the high cafe tables and strings of lights all over the walls. Huge photos of the bride and groom with family and friends adorn the walls. There's Celeste and me with Sage and Amira. Celeste and I are beaming at each other. A punch to the gut. I need to get away before I lose my shit.

On the back wall, a big screen plays videos on a loop. Sage and Wesley from childhood to now. Here's the meme and the video that went viral. According to Sage, that ridiculous footage from the so-called "fainting proposal" nearly broke them up, but now they're watching the video, laughing, holding each other tightly.

Sometime in the future, Celeste and I could be at our wedding reception, laughing about this trial. Joking about how Celeste hated me, how I took to groveling. Will it come to groveling? If that's what it takes to get through this, I'll do it. Life without Celeste is not an option. No way can I go on for the rest of my days like I have these past two months. I cannot—will not—lose her.

I've never met a woman, not even the mother of my child, who compares to Celeste. Only Celeste understands my research. She keeps up when I talk about polymers, then can switch gears and get me laughing at some stupid joke, then shift to talking about her own work. And she holds me in sway with her strategies for helping couples. We share a mission to help people, though our methods aren't remotely similar. Celeste sees patterns in how couples relate and sabotage themselves on their way to happiness. She says it's predictable. Every couple goes through something. Why can't she see that's all that's happening with us now?

Celeste dances across the floor, oblivious to me, champagne flute in one hand, the other waving to the rhythm of the hip hop the DJ's spinning. For a fleeting moment, I can almost feel her dancing in my arms. But she drifts out of view, and it feels like a part of my body is missing.

Celeste

The twinkling lights, delicious vegan canapés, music, and all these people have me tipsy. The champagne probably helps, too. I take another glass from a traveling caterer and dance my way across the room to hang with Amira, Sage, and Kath. My girls. My posse. Why do I live so far from these people? I've been going through hell all alone. Just me and the ashes falling from the sky out there in wildfire country.

I throw my arms around these beautiful women. "Hey look! We match!"

"That's because you're all my bridesmaids," Sage says, kissing my cheek. "How you holding up, Cece?"

"Grrrreat!" I attempt to imitate the tiger in the old cereal commercials we grew up with.

Sage, Amira, and Kath exchange a look. Even buzzed, I can read people. They're concerned about me. Not for long.

I refuse to draw attention to my problems on my friend's wedding day. I may be tipsy, but I still remember that adage that got me through freshman year of college: fake it til you make it.

"Thanks for inviting so many hot single guys, Sage," I say.

She smirks. "Wes has a lot of friends from the epidemiologist community, the lab, and the Acro yoga circle."

"Yeah, speaking of yoga, that instructor's cute."

"And bad news. We dated, remember?"

"That's right. Well, there's always Elijah—"

"A doll," Kath interrupts. "Just like in college, everyone has it bad for Eli, but…" She hitches a shoulder.

Sage finishes her thought. "He's still grieving, and honestly, I'm starting to wonder if he'll ever date again. Sometimes it seems like a tiny part of him died with Farrah."

"Oh."

Kath grips my shoulder. "Never fear, darling. This is a wedding. We'll find you a man for the rebound."

"The rebound?" Amira asks.

Kath nods definitively. "It's too soon for Mr. Right. But Mr. Right Now? Perfect to 'jumpstart' a woman's healing."

"Yes," Sage and Amira smile at Kath, then at each other.

Slowly, all three turn to me, a family of Cheshire cats, plotting a conspiracy. Not sure I love where this is going, I smile anyway, hoping it hides the tension gripping my stomach. I appreciate a little eye candy, but the thought of anyone touching me makes me shiver. I need to love a man to want his hands on me.

I guess I relate to Elijah. The part of me that knew how to trust a man died when I learned about Josh and that awful woman. How can I ever give anyone my heart again?

Josh

CELESTE LEANS IN AND TILTS HER HEAD TOWARD HER FRIENDS, giving them her undivided attention. They're blooming in her light. She has that effect on people. Unfortunately, attention is Celeste's superpower and her kryptonite. Not everyone loves being the center of intense focus. It freaked my buddies out.

An argument flashes through my mind.

Celeste's whipping pancake batter with more force than necessary, no idea how fucking cute she is. Then she opens her mouth and the accusations start. "Why are your friends so unwelcoming? They act like they own you, like I have no right to be around."

"Chill out and you might find them inviting you to more things."

"Excuse me?" Her already tense voice rises a notch.

"You intimidate them," I explain. "Back off. Be patient. Stop trying so hard."

"I'm being myself," she huffs, then points the whisk at me, dripping batter all over the floor. "You should defend me."

It's hard to tell someone whose intensity scares people that no one, not even I, can believe she needs defending. I said it though—another dick move on my part—and she gave me that same look she fired at me in the elevator yesterday. A scowl marred her beautiful face and weirdly turned me on.

If I could take back what I did… But I can't. As soon as Lucinda and I were naked, I knew I was making a mistake. But who can stop a freight train in motion? Not me.

When I came clean, I thought Celeste would forgive me, understand the shame I felt after screwing up. Why can't she see, she's not like the other girlfriends I cheated on? Why couldn't she hear that I wasn't trying to end us? She'd been pressuring me, and I didn't handle it well. Didn't handle it well? *Way to play down your accountability, Josh.* Gonna have to journal about that.

Now, I watch Celeste float around the room, greeting my step-mom, my sister and her fiancé, my niece, other people I vaguely remember. Must be old friends from college. Everywhere Celeste goes, she lights the room. Everyone she touches winds up beaming. This is her crowd. These people appreciate her.

I appreciate her, but I haven't always. Watching her, I feel lit, like Celeste is igniting me from the inside out. Except whenever I catch her eye, her rage sends flames straight at my heart and reduces me to ash.

The bride approaches, radiant. Despite my sadness and confusion, I can't resist returning her broad smile. Sage opens her arms as she nears. "Josh, I'm so glad you came."

"A pleasure to witness your nuptials, Sage!" I squeeze her around the shoulders. "Seeing you so happy, and how Wes responds to you, it's clear you've got a good guy there."

"I do! How's the big, exciting world of hydrogels?"

"Great. We're testing a—"

Celeste walks behind Sage and hugs some big blonde guy. Must be six-four. Who the hell is that? Why is she smiling at him like that? And he's smiling back at her, like—

"Josh?" Sage puts her hand on my shoulder. The gentle pressure of her touch brings me back to the wedding. "Are you alright? You were saying something about your research and then stopped mid-sentence."

My cheeks get hot. "Sorry! Yeah, it's good. I'll be happy to share more when we have some definitive proof."

"Keep me in the loop. I always enjoy photographing your work in and out of the lab."

"Thank God. You've probably helped us get more funding than anyone."

"You give me too much credit," she says.

"No joke. When foundations and government funders see our work has media attention, it gives them more reasons to support it."

Sage claps. "Well, la dee da. The world needs your research."

"I dunno about the world, but thanks." I bow, embarrassed. Also proud. I've worked hard for this period in my career, where my work is finally coming close to making a difference. Fuck, now what is Celeste doing? First the blond, now some new guy?

Derek comes over, throws his arm around my shoulder. "Hey man, how you doing? Looking a little distracted and distressed."

"Is it that obvious?"

Sage squeaks. "Kind of. I'm sorry. Breakups are hard."

Humiliated, I press my fingers to my temples. "I've never felt like this before."

"It's rough." Derek looks me straight in the eyes, like he needs me to understand. "Especially when you realize your actions pushed the relationship over the edge." Damn. Straight to the heart.

If the man didn't ooze sincerity and concern, I might not be able to hear his words. Fact is, Derek's been here. Not that he cheated on anyone, but Amira thought he was cheating on her, and his shame and pride kept him from telling her what was really going on. He almost lost her because of it.

I take Sage's hand. "This is your special day. I don't mean to ruin it."

The woman's face is all compassion, and I can't take it. Through her kindness, I see the truth I've been avoiding. I'm a complete asshole. I don't deserve Celeste's forgiveness.

But we always forgive each other. We've gotten past every argument. I am an asshole, but I can't believe this is the end. I won't believe it, so I share my intentions with Sage and Derek. "I don't deserve her now, but I'm gonna make things right. When I finish this fast, we'll get back together."

Sage widens her eyes. "Hmm. Okay."

Derek pats me between the shoulder blades. "I know how much you want that."

They don't believe me. Fine. But I've created magic in my lab; I can do it in my life. The only person I need to believe me is Celeste.

"Weddings are a wicked good time to practice what you're learning in the program," Derek says.

"In theory," I say. "Most guys... Hell, even Josh-circa-2013 would see all these women and salivate. Josh today? One temptation and one alone."

At the moment, my temptress is flirting with yet another man. This one's Asian and hot as hell. I'm gonna be sick. If I was into men, I'd wanna flirt with him, too. It'd be great if Celeste was a little less tempted by the free-floating men at this shindig.

"Most guys would tell you to get over Celeste the good old-fashioned way," Derek says.

I cringe. "Gross." No, I do not intend to get under someone else. Even if I wasn't being celibate for six months.

"Right? Your journal's gonna be your best friend tonight." Derek laughs. He must be thinking what I'm thinking, but neither one of us is about to say it in front of the bride. It's not my journal I'll be stroking tonight.

Sage interrupts my train of thought. "One thing I don't get about this whole female fast... how can you tell who to avoid? Just because someone looks like a woman doesn't mean they are."

"True," Derek says. "And not all females want men." He gestures to Sage's other bridesmaid and her wife, two very fine women who are clearly into each other.

I add, "The point is to check your romantic and sexual impulses. You know, because we all have a masculine and a feminine side. Luckily, there is one female I can spend time with this evening, if she's willing."

"Your sister?" Derek asks.

"Her too, but I meant my niece. Where is your soon-to-be step-child, Derek?"

"I think she's with her grandmother." He gestures with his head.

Sage kisses my cheek, lays her hand on my shoulder. "I'm gonna circulate. Hang in there, Josh."

She disappears into a cluster of wedding guests, and I follow Derek in the opposite direction.

"You ready for step-parenting?" I ask.

"I think so."

"Good for you, man. I couldn't do it."

"Went into pediatrics for a reason. Kids have always been special to me. Hell, I was a camp counselor for four years," Derek says.

"No kidding."

"Wesley's dad sent us to this Episcopal Church camp out in central Mass. Camp Bement. It was great, so when I got too old to be a camper, I went as a counselor-in-training. Soon as I was old enough, I got a job. I was the only Black kid there, of course, and that was weird, but I was used to being outnumbered at school and in our neighborhood."

"I know that story. Growing up in western Mass, I never fit in."

"Pretty White out there, huh?"

"Very. And I love my mom, but being White she couldn't possibly understand what it's like to be Biracial in a White world. Everyone always trying to figure out what label to pin on me. Is he Black? Puerto Rican? Some other thing we should shun?"

"Brutal," Derek says.

One thing I love about Derek is how he can see different sides of things. Too many people would say something stupid, like "at least you can pass for White," which is bullshit. If it were true, then White people wouldn't always be trying to figure out my heritage. It's also flat out offensive. Like passing is a goal? Derek's one of those rare GenX-ers who recognizes that striving to pass is self-hate. For decades, my goal was to be accepted as-is, not to pass for something I'm not. Somewhere along the way, I stopped caring. Those who get me, cool. Those who don't can kiss my ethnically ambiguous behind.

Derek wraps an arm around my shoulders as we approach my niece Lila and her grandmother Tania. Tania, my step-mom, is an amazing woman. She always welcomed me, even though I was her husband's first child from another woman. When Dad up and left Tania, she kept welcoming me into her home. If not for that, Amira and I might not have the relationship we do today.

"Tania." I open my arms and embrace the petite woman warmly.

Contrary to stereotypes, all Black men do not want white women. However, my father definitely has a type: pale skin, green eyes, and brown or red hair. My mom's the redhead. Tania's the brunette, though I think that lustrous brown comes from a bottle these days.

"Joshua, it is wonderful to see you." Tania squeezes me tight.

"Hi, Uncle Josh," Lila says, interrupting. She snakes her way between her grandmother and me for a hug. I kiss the top of her head.

"There's the little girl I was coming to see."

"Excuse me." Lila pulls away. "I'm not a little girl. I'm old enough to wear makeup!"

"That's why your face is sparkling, huh? I also hear at the ripe old age of twelve, you, Lila MacKenzie, are single-handedly restoring Louisiana's coastline."

"Single-handedly?"

"Did I exaggerate that?"

"Mama says you're always exaggerating."

"She says that, huh? How's this? I could see you single-handedly restoring the coastline of your state and the entire nation."

"I like that vision." Lila beams up at me, the spitting image of Amira, except Lila's skin is lighter, like her dad's.

"How's your life?" I ask.

"Better, now that mama and Derek are engaged."

If pride were a physical thing, Derek would be wearing it like a cape. I've only known the man a couple months, but that's the biggest smile I've seen on his face, other than when he and Amira told me about their engagement.

I wink at Derek, then ask, "What's so great about that?"

"Mama is happier than I've ever seen her. Plus, Derek's fun."

"Thanks, kiddo," Derek says.

"How's school?" I ask.

"Straight A's this semester."

"Again?" I hold my hand up for a high-five, and she meets it easily.

Lila must be five-six. She towers over her grandmother and, now that Amira's heading our way, I see how much taller Lila is than her mother, as well.

My niece continues, "We're planning new coastal restoration projects to plant cypress trees and native grasses. And I think we're gonna try oyster seeding."

Tania laughs. "Oyster seeding? Like plants?"

"It's a scientific term, Nana."

Tania cups Lila's face in her hands. "I could listen to you all day. I learn from you."

The DJ announces the bride and groom's first dance. Knowing Sage, this will be adorable. We turn to face the center of the room, but Lila nudges me, then holds my attention with her old-soul gaze. "Uncle Josh, when are you gonna marry Celeste?"

The question opens my chest like a knife. A low growl emerges from Derek's throat.

"Did I say something wrong? You just went pale."

I swallow hard. "Honey, I... we broke up a few months ago."

"No! I wanted her as my aunt."

Sage and Wesley take each other's hands in the center of the room.

Derek says, "You won't lose Celeste, Lila. But she and Josh have to work out their own stuff."

"If I have my way, Lila, we'll get back together."

The music begins. What the hell is this? Some weird mashup of reggae, Grateful Dead, and... yoga music? Sage and Wesley move together slowly at first, strangely. Nervous titters fill the room. Now, bride and groom go all out, gesturing bizarrely, combining every silly dance move from the 1970s, 80s, and 90s, and the nervous titters turn into full on guffaws. Sage always has had a unique way of putting her guests at ease.

I'm laughing for the first time in too long, laughing so hard, I almost don't notice my phone vibrating in my pocket. Who could that be on New Year's Day? I pull it out. A western Mass area code flashes across the screen, but it's not my mother's number. At first, the caller ID says Unknown, then it flashes Springfield Hospital. The laughter dies in my throat.

4

Josh

EXCUSE MYSELF AND ANSWER AS I BEELINE FOR THE QUIET restroom. A nurse tells me they admitted my mother to the ICU.

"Intensive care?" My heart's ripped from my chest and thrown onto the floor.

The nasal voice on the other end of the line explains my mother was in a car accident and something about emergency surgery revealing diabetic kidney disease. Now, she's in kidney failure. "The address we have in her emergency contact info says you live in California. Can you get on a flight? We're trying to keep her stable."

"Is she conscious?"

"Yes, but she's sedated. She was panicking when she woke."

"I'm in Connecticut for a wedding. Please tell her I'm on my way. I'll be there tonight."

I confirm they have my daughter's number on Mom's emergency contact list and ask them to get in touch with her, too. Not that I won't try to reach her. I'll try. And fail. Satya hasn't taken a call from me in four years, two months, and fifteen days. I end the call, open the door to the restroom, and run smack into Celeste. Dread and hope fill me at once. Of all the moments for this to happen.

"Are you okay?" Celeste's eyes open wide. "You don't look well."

"My mom's in the ICU up in Springfield. They said I should go say goodbye."

"Oh, honey." Her voice exudes compassion, like it used to when she loved me, and she pulls me into a tight hug. "I'm sorry. Is there anything I can do?"

I want to melt in her arms, but that's off limits. "I... uh..." Need to pull it together. The last thing I want is to cling to Celeste's pity or walk through a wedding reception with tears streaming down my face.

"You're trembling. Listen, you're in no shape to drive. I'll take you."

"You're gonna skip out on your best friend's wedding?" I brave a glance into Celeste's eyes. Kindness, concern. Can she see the need in my eyes right now? "No way. Can't let you do that."

"Ellen needs us, Josh." Celeste flinches. "I mean, you. She needs you, and you're too shaky to drive."

"Putting other people ahead of yourself, as always, Angel." As soon as I say the word, I regret it. Oh, it's true. But calling her by my special name for her, like we're a couple? "Sorry."

"Where's your car? The hotel?"

I nod, the movement a tremendous effort.

"Let me tell Sage and Amira what's happening," she says, stepping away.

I catch her shoulder. "Hold up. You're slurring. How much have you had to drink?" I examine her face.

Her cheeks redden and her volume increases over the pumping bass in the background. "Too much to think straight." She looks down, clearly ashamed.

"Car accident got my mom into the hospital. Let's not have one on our way to see her there."

"You still want me to come?"

My heart lurches. I made a huge assumption that she'd want to go with me. What if I have to face this alone?

Celeste looks up at me, softness in her eyes, as she steps back. "I don't mean to impose. I just... Since my nana died, Ellen's the closest thing I've had to a mom. And I... well, I hope the doctors are wrong, but... I couldn't live with myself if I didn't go with you now."

"Then you should come. I mean, not should. I want you to come."

"If she... not knowing what she meant to me... If she thought I..." Celeste's voice trails off on the last few words, but it sounded like she said, was still mad.

I cock my head, wondering. Mad about what?

Who cares? We need to step on it. "You go talk to Sage and Amira. I'll wait for you outside."

We part. I plaster a smile on my face and sneak out of the reception. Alone in the icy darkness, I double over, gasping and gripping my knees for stability. Light from old fashioned street lanterns bounces off clean piles of snow and stained glass windows on the Yale dorm across the street.

Now that I've caught my breath, I'm ready to go. Where's Celeste? I love the woman, but damn, she moves like molasses. I can't go back inside looking for her. I'd have to face all those people again, pretend everything's fine so I don't spoil the revelry.

Please hurry, Celeste. Please. For the love of God. Step it up. Time is not our friend tonight. My thoughts are racing a light-year a minute. How long have I been pacing, waiting? Didn't check my watch when I came out, but it's 5:17 now. When did they call? The call log on my phone says 4:58. Nineteen minutes ago. Okay. Alright. That's not horrible. If nineteen minutes makes the difference between... Oh, God. Don't go there. I blow out a puff of air. *Woman, please!*

At 5:21, Celeste emerges, wrapped in her favorite blue coat and extends her hand. "Poor thing, you must be freezing. Here." She holds out my overcoat. "Sorry. It took a while to find."

I slip it on, and relax into the warmth. So wrapped up in my head, I didn't realize I was cold until this moment. "Still taking care of me." I smile.

"You know I always take care of the people I—Anyway... Thanks for appreciating me."

She didn't mean that as a dig, but the fact she mentioned it reminds me how often I complained about her maternal nature. Like her caring for me was an insult, a critique of my ability to fend for myself. *Another dick move, Josh.*

She's toeing the dusting of snow on the sidewalk.

I should say, Thank you for your thoughtfulness. Instead, I clear my throat to get her attention and offer my arm. She takes it. The weight of her hand in the crook of my elbow helps me breathe easier as we walk the two-and-a-half blocks past the New Haven green, with its classic brick church, and turn right onto College Street. All the shops and restaurants are dark for the holiday. Strings of lights arch across the street, illuminating the gentle snowflakes landing in Celeste's hair. Snowflakes sprinkle themselves across her nose and eyelashes, too, a sight that fills me with longing.

Why is my mind going there?

"Fuck, I hope the road conditions don't slow us down too much," I say. "Usually, a light snowfall here means a heavy, wet snow up in western Mass."

We pass through the brass revolving doors of the fancy hotel. Never could've stayed at a place like this growing up. Now, it's not such a big deal.

"Good chance plows won't even be out, with it being New Year's Day."

"We'll get there on time," she says.

There she goes again, trying to help me relax. It's all I can do to not wrap my arm around her as we reach the valet. I give the guy my parking stub. A few minutes later, he returns and hands me the keys. I open the passenger door for Celeste. The shock on her face reminds me how long it's been since I showed her this level of care. It's a small gesture, opening a door for someone. Why did I stop? Once she's settled in her seat, I close the door and go around to my side. I slip behind the wheel, wondering where else I signaled to the people I love that they weren't worth my time and effort.

"I know it'll mean a lot to my mom to see you. You're the only woman she—" I stop myself. If I finish that sentence, Celeste will get even more wound up than I feel. I finish the train of thought in my mind: the only woman she ever wanted me to marry.

Celeste

THE SPEEDOMETER READS FIFTY MILES PER HOUR. JOSH IS DRIVING well below the speed limit on the highway, being careful because of the snow. Still, between our speed and the dizzying effect of the snowflakes flying at the windshield, I feel woozy. The alcohol is probably magnifying the effects.

"You didn't drink at all tonight?" I ask.

He shakes his head, keeping his gaze on the road. "Because of the fast."

"The what?" I close my eyes to block the snow globe effect, too late to prevent a headache.

"Amira didn't tell you?"

"Amira and I have been friends for twenty-five years, Josh. We talk about things besides my relationship with her brother."

He clears his throat. "Right." That wounded tone in his voice. God.

I sigh. I could've been less snarky. I massage my temples to ease the headache. "Are you doing the same program Derek did?"

"Yeah, but longer. He's my accountability buddy."

"Which means…"

"I call him or text him if anything comes up that I need help processing. He's the designated person to encourage me, help me think things through."

"But he finished the fast months ago, right?"

"Correct. Accountability buddy is the next phase, a way to give back and reinforce what someone worked on during their fast," Josh explains.

"I see, but what does that have to do with alcohol?"

"We examine how we numb ourselves to avoid feeling, how it plays into unhealthy relationship dynamics. Some of us choose to fast from our go-to numbing strategies, whether it's porn, TV, gaming, shopping, or substance use."

"I never thought you had a drinking problem."

"It's not about addiction. We're building mindfulness."

God knows, he could use help in that department.

"I was drinking and smoking pot to stuff my feelings. I used sex that way, too."

I'm not sure I want to hear more.

He continues. "You know, I wasn't trying to end our relationship, Celeste."

"We don't have to talk about this," I say.

"I think we need to."

Way to miss the hint, Josh.

"I wasn't trying to end us. I didn't intend to get together with her. It was an accident."

A vision of Josh and Lucinda fills my mind. I've imagined it so many times, you'd think I caught them in the act. Thank God, I didn't. Still, every time I replay the scene, I hear someone screaming in my brain. I guess it's me.

"I knew it was a mistake as soon as we started, but I didn't know how to stop it," he says.

My stomach cramps, and I groan, not even trying to stifle it like I normally might. He touches my leg, making me shiver and open my eyes. His eyes are on me instead of where they should be—the road. He exudes concern, but misses my pointed, obvious hint to shut the hell up. "Fact is, we'd been in a rough place. You know?" Josh returns his gaze to the snow-covered highway and continues. "We were arguing a lot. You wanted a baby. I didn't want another kid, and—"

"Well, that's a moot point now."

"Okay?"

I don't bother to explain that the week after we broke up the OB/GYN let me know that one: I didn't catch an STI from Josh, and two: I can't have children. Twenty years of undiagnosed endometriosis robbed me of my chance to have what I wanted more than anything else, besides a happy life married to Josh.

"What I'm saying is I wasn't trying to end it."

"You've said that a few times now. I get it."

"I'm sorry. I didn't know how to deal with the feelings, and I was drinking more and smoking more pot. Checking out."

"Yeah. I always hated when you withdrew, but can we stop talking about this? It's upsetting me, and I'm trying to stay calm so I can be nice to you during this stressful time."

Josh sighs and grips the steering wheel harder. He's working his jaw, which tells me he's wrestling internally. He wants to say more—which is rare—and I just cut him off. But seriously, what's the point of this conversation? Am I his damn confessional? If he unburdens his sins on me will he feel pure when he visits his mom? It's not like she'll let him off the hook, unless she's unconscious when we arrive.

Shit. I'd better tell him about the letter before she does. She will not be kind.

I close my eyes, trying not to feel the vehicle moving. Inhale to a count of eight, hold the breath for eight, exhale for the same count, then hold the breath out for that long, and repeat the cycle again. After a few rounds of box breathing, Josh asks, "Hey, you alright over there?"

"Mm-hmm." I keep the breath pattern going, trying to get hold of my physical sensations.

"We ran into each other at Dawson's Pub, and Lucin—she was telling me how much she loves your work and has so much respect for you."

"Right. Her deep respect for me made her want to sleep with you."

Josh sighs. "I see now that she was trying to find a way into my bed."

"You mean, our bed."

Tonight, when I saw Josh's face, felt him shaking with the news about his mom, my heart broke wide open and love poured out. It almost felt good, like it might be safe to give this man my compassion. Now, envisioning him with... I shake my head to clear the images. Too late.

My freshly opened heart feels the familiar stabbing sensation, which expands into a gaping black hole in the middle of my chest. Damn it. I'm trapped with my emotions and the man who generated them until we get to the hospital. Now, all I can do is resume box breathing.

"Celeste, if I could take it back, I would. I would never make that choice again. I should have come to you with my struggles. I needed someone to talk to. You were at that conference. She was there. She has that accountability group. She suggested, we could hold each other accountable."

"For what?" My cynical laugh makes him cringe.

"I don't remember. By the time she walked into the bar, I was already on my third scotch."

"Maybe the worst part is that you took her into our bed."

"I know." The muscles in his jaw clench. I close my eyes, press my lips into a tight line and keep breathing. He says, "You asked why I wasn't drinking tonight. That's why."

"Makes sense."

"Good thing, too, because if I had been, I wouldn't be able to get to my mother now."

A mission that matters to both of us. We each have air to clear with Ellen, so she can go in peace and we can relieve our consciences. I force a gentle tone. "Funny how things work out."

"Here's your lucky building," Josh says, changing the subject.

I open my eyes and look for the pointed dome that rises from the Hartford cityscape. Its chocolate kiss shape, dark blue color and golden stars remind me of a genie.

"I'm making three wishes. Are you?" he asks.

"Of course." I wish to be free of this anger and heartache. I wish for Ellen to heal quickly or pass peacefully. I wish for Josh and Ellen to resolve the emotional distance between them before she dies. It's caused each of them so much pain.

"What did you wish?" he asks.

"If I tell you, they won't come true."

"You always say that."

"And you always tell me your wishes, and then they don't come true."

"Have yours?"

"Probably not, but I keep hoping this time will be different." Kind of like the start of every relationship.

"Celeste, it's really kind of you to come with me. Your support means more than you could know." Josh lays his hand between the seats, palm up like always, an invitation I choose to ignore. I don't want to hold his hand. I'm here to apologize to Ellen. If Josh knew my reason for joining him, he might not be so grateful.

I pat his hand and put mine in my lap. A compromise. A mistake. That minuscule touch shoots electricity up my arm, making my body ache with need. Not need. Not even desire. Pain. I do not want Josh Albright. I should've stayed at the wedding reception.

I need to look into Ellen's eyes one last time, to apologize. I cannot let another mother die with the weight of my words on her heart.

Similar words took my mother to her grave. Then, I didn't know what I was saying. This time, I chose my words carefully. I needed to blame someone for my loss, needed to be right. I was so sure that if Ellen had been kind to her son, he might have been faithful to me. Ellen never wrote back, which is probably a blessing. I hope to God she doesn't use my letter against Josh tonight. For all he's done, he doesn't deserve to have his last moments with his mother be caustic. What a destructive cycle.

Like the cycle of trauma my therapist is always bringing into our conversations. If my dad and grandpa hadn't died fighting that forest fire… then my mom wouldn't have become despondent… and she wouldn't have… left me… and I wouldn't be blaming myself and attracting emotionally unavailable men.

We cross the state line into Massachusetts in awkward silence.

As he pulls off the highway to follow the H signs, I ask, "So how's your fast going?"

"Great! I've never been so self-reflective in my life, and I think it's paying off."

"Good for you, Josh."

"I'm not supposed to say this. I'm doing the program to heal and grow. I want a healthier relationship with myself and all the women in my life—my mom, my sister, my daughter." He pauses, as if waiting for me to chastise him. Instead, I listen. "And I'm doing this for you, too, for us. I hope to earn back your trust and respect."

A tear slides down my cheek. I make no effort to hide it or wipe it away. I desperately want to believe Josh, to trust him again, to take that hope he's offering and grow it into the relationship I always believed we had. But what I thought was real, was a mirage. I still haven't made peace with that simple fact. Hope? If I hope, I open the door to hurt again.

My stomach clenches. That old story roils around in there. If I were coaching someone, I'd tell them to not believe the story. I've tried, but the story keeps coming back with more mounds of evidence to back it up. It's not safe to hope, because life keeps showing me that I'm the kind of person people leave.

5

Josh

THE CONVERSATION IN THE CAR KEPT MY FEAR AT BAY, but as we step through the sliding glass doors into the hospital lobby, a wave of dread crashes over me. I'm tempted to just turn around and run.

"You okay?" Celeste's light touch on my shoulder brings me back to reality.

"I haven't talked to Mom in a long time."

"You told her we broke up, right?"

I cringe.

"Oh, Josh! Haven't you spoken with her at all in the last three months?"

"I let her calls go to voicemail, and when I call her back, I dial the landline when I know she won't be home."

"Oh, Josh." Celeste shakes her head.

"It's just—"

"May I help you?" the receptionist asks.

People walk around us, giving us looks. Am I the only person who'd rather stand still in the lobby than rush to the bedside of his mother? Celeste places her hand on my upper back, her touch giving me courage to move with the gentle forward pressure she applies. I give the receptionist my mother's name and she gives us the room number and points us toward the bay of elevators that lead to the ICU.

I push the button and wait. "It's never been easy between Mom and me, you know?"

"I know," she murmurs.

"And I didn't..." I can't say I didn't want to let her know I'd failed the one woman she actually wanted me to marry. "I knew she'd be upset that we broke up, and I didn't wanna deal with it."

"But you saw her at Christmas?"

"You know her friends always invite her. She has fun with them."

Disappointment crosses Celeste's face. Fact is, she always made sure we flew back here to see Mom, or we paid her airfare to see us. Celeste always said, "Ellen might enjoy friends, but she needs family." My last chance at Christmas with Mom and I blew it. My stomach lurches.

Now, Celeste says, "Josh," again, her voice laden with pity, disappointment, and something else that I can't place.

"What's up?" I ask.

"I might have let her know we broke up."

"You've been talking to her?"

"No, but I..." Celeste takes a deep breath and lets the words fall out. "...sent her a letter."

The elevator finally arrives and we pause our conversation while a large family and a couple of doctors exit. A woman reeking of cigarettes slips past us into the elevator, followed by a young couple and a nurse with a cart. All these people were beside us the whole time, and I failed to notice them? We squeeze inside. The doors slide closed, and the elevator begins its ascent, bringing me closer to one thing I wish I could avoid.

Celeste taps my shoulder. She has that look on her face that lets me know the urgency of what she needs to say. Eyes wide and intense, upper lip sucked between her teeth. I hate having private conversations in public. The fact we just said as much as we did in front of all these people without me noticing makes me sick.

She stands on tiptoes and whispers, her breath warm in my ear. "I was upset when I wrote the letter. So, full transparency, I came to apologize. I couldn't bear Ellen going to her grave thinking—" She gasps. "I'm sorry. I shouldn't have said that." She lowers her heels, looks down like she did something wrong.

Takes me a minute to register that word: grave.

When the hospital called, they didn't mince words. I caught their drift, accepted it without thinking. Part of me did, anyway. The elevator stops. Thank God, cigarette girl leaves. We've got another three floors.

"Josh? You okay? I'm sorry."

I glance at the young couple, who are either actively ignoring us or pretending not to eavesdrop.

"I... yeah. Everything happened so fast. Guess I was thinking the same thing on one level. But hearing the word out loud. It sounds different from: get here ASAP. Definitive."

"I'm sorry, Josh. It's hard enough to lose a loved one when everything's great between you. I can't imagine..."

"Haven't lost her yet."

Celeste clears her throat. "True. And now you'll get the chance to work things out with the two most important women in your life."

"You and my mom?" I ask, hopeful.

"Your daughter and your mom. Satya's coming, right?"

"I think so. I called and left a message, asked the hospital to call." How do I tell Celeste that for five years, she's been my closest family? Satya will always be my little girl, but she shut me out of her life.

The elevator reaches the ICU floor, and we step out, scan the hall for room numbers. The acrid smell of disinfectant and illness makes me shudder, glad I didn't pursue medicine.

Celeste puts her hand on my upper back again and guides me past the nurses' station, down the hall to the room with the dry erase board with Albright handwritten in black ink. "I hope you're not mad," she murmurs.

"About what?"

"About me coming to apologize instead of just support you."

"I appreciate you care enough to give Mom some peace before she... in her time of need."

At the door to the room, Celeste stops. "I'll wait out here."

My already pounding heart takes off like a racehorse. It's hard to breathe. "Can you come with me?"

She quirks an eyebrow.

"I need you now." I cringe. I betrayed her. Yet I have the gall to demand she support me? Her worried face softens into compassion. Our eyes meet. Celeste takes my arm, and we enter as one.

I am unprepared for this. My mother in a hospital bed, puffy face, normally pale skin as washed out as her silver hair. Is she with us?

"Mom?" I choke out.

She moans. Thank God. I rush to her bedside, take her hand between both of mine. Feeling the pulse in her wrist softens the pounding in my heart. "Mom!"

"Josh." Her voice is weak, but her eyes flutter open as she turns her head to smile at me. "Sweetheart, you came."

"As soon as I found out, Mom." I sit on the bed next to her. "We were in Connecticut for Sage's wedding."

"Mmm," she says in acknowledgement. "We?"

"Celeste is here."

I thought that might make her happy. Her eyes light up. "Celeste? Where?"

"Ellen." Celeste rushes to stand beside me. "I'm so sorry."

Mom shakes her head. "It's alright."

"No, for the letter. I'm sorry. I was cruel."

"You were right," my mother whispers.

"No! I was in pain and I took it out on you."

I look between them. My mother's face exudes love—honestly, an expression I've always wished she'd bestow upon me. Celeste's face twists in remorse. Maybe this letter was worse than I imagined.

I want to ask what she wrote, but her eyes are fixed on my mom's.

"Ellen, it's important you know. You... you've been like a mother to me."

"You are a gift... Your letter..." Mom pauses for breath.

"I shouldn't have said those things."

"I needed to know. Thank you."

"I don't deserve your thanks."

"Celeste, you helped me understand..."

Celeste gasps and puts a hand on her heart. This conversation is damn cryptic. What in hell did Celeste write in that letter?

"I know you two need time alone," Celeste says. "I only needed to... May I hug you?"

Mom nods.

I step out of the way so Celeste can lean in and hug my mom. My mother's too weak to respond, but moves her swollen hands as close to Celeste as possible, patting the space around her. Celeste places a gentle kiss on mom's cheek. Mom murmurs something to her. Celeste squeaks, kisses her cheek again, then turns, her face wet with tears.

"I'll be in the waiting room." She blows Mom a kiss and strides out of the room.

I return to my mother's bedside, unsure what to expect, what to do. I sit on the bed. "Is this okay?"

Mom nods. "I'm proud of you, Joshua."

"For what?"

"Everything."

She wouldn't say that if she knew how I hurt Celeste.

"I was awful," Mom admits. "I'm sorry."

"Mom, no. Why would you say that?"

She pats my hand and speaks between labored breaths. "You rose above it... Celeste explained how badly I hurt you. You kept your distance because... I was horrible."

"What?" My jaw tightens.

"I blamed you." She shakes her head. "Not your fault."

"Blamed me?"

"Your father cheated..." Mom pauses for breath. "...and left. That was his problem."

"I know. Save your strength, Mom."

"I tried to make it yours."

Her words land in my heart, but instead of detonating like usual, they settle.

A nurse comes in and introduces herself, verifies I'm Ellen's son. I step aside so she can check Mom's vital signs and assess the bags of fluids attached to IVs. She asks Mom how she's doing, if she's happy I'm here.

Mom smiles. "Very."

The nurse smiles at me and leaves. I return to Mom's side, sitting in the empty space on her bed.

"Josh, I loved your father."

"Mom, you don't have to—

"He was creative, brilliant, sweet, funny. We used to laugh, Josh." She smiles and her gaze seems to travel back in time. "Then he left me for Tania." Mom closes her eyes for a minute.

I lay my palm underneath hers, so she'll feel my touch without the added weight. Her hands are so swollen, they must hurt, unless one of those IV bags is filled with morphine.

"Joshua." Her eyes snap open and she holds my gaze, willing me to pay attention. "I didn't know how to grieve." She winces at a memory. "I said don't be like..."

I hear it now, as I did then. "Don't be like him." I'm ten years old, standing by the front door, watching my father leave, suitcase in hand. I turn to my mother for comfort, but rage and anguish contort her face. Instead of consoling me, she says, "Don't be like him."

I'm twelve. Mom catches me self-pleasuring. She says I better learn to control myself.

I'm thirteen, and fifteen, nineteen, twenty-three... I see the end of every relationship, the inevitable moment when I tell Mom I broke another girl's heart. "You're just like your father," she says, in disgust. All the feelings of shame and self-hatred return for an instant, leaving me numb, until Mom pats my knee. The unfamiliar comfort feeds a hunger I'd completely detached from, or maybe tried to fill in other ways. I see her again, as she is now, making up for lost time as much as one can from a hospital bed.

The doctor comes in and introduces himself as Doctor Fisk. He looks about Mom's age; with salt and pepper hair, a warm face. I stay beside Mom. Doctor Fisk drops his gaze to our clasped hands, smiles, looks at the monitors, asks Mom how she's doing.

She gives him a weak smile. "My son is here," she says, filling my eyes with water again. I squeeze her hand, bite the insides of my cheeks to keep myself together.

Doctor Fisk lets us know they're doing everything they can, but it's a hospice situation now. "Kidney function is at one percent."

Data. That undeniable fact brings up a wave of nausea that I swallow and breathe through, so I can be here for my mom this once.

"In another situation, we might be searching for an emergency kidney donor."

"We're the same blood type, right, Mom? I could give—"

"No, sweetheart."

"Yes, we are." I look frantically between Mom and Doctor Fisk. "B-positive, right? I can—"

"Your mother has a Do Not Resuscitate order in place, Josh. No extreme measures."

"Mom?" I croak.

She nods and squeezes my hand faintly. I hear a thousand dinner conversations in my mind, the debates about medical advances and life support. Mom always stood on the side of minimal intervention. In theory, I thought it was fine. But now... fuck. My chest is gonna explode.

"What about dialysis?" I ask, desperate, already knowing her answer.

She quirks an eyebrow.

The doctor oozes sympathy. "Ellen, is there anything we can do to make you more comfortable?" he asks.

She shakes her head and gestures toward me, smiling. "My son is here," she repeats.

As if my presence is all she needs. Guilt.

Doctor Fisk nods and smiles sympathetically.

I turn to him. "My daughter, Satya Albright, is probably on her way from Boston. I don't know if it's past visiting hours, but can you please make an exception?"

"Of course. I'll make sure her name's on the admit list."

"Thank you."

The doctor leaves.

I stroke Mom's hair and forehead, worried this might be her last breath. She takes a labored, raspy inhale and looks at me with something that resembles compassion, loosening tension I've held in my body for three decades.

"You cheated on Celeste."

Guess I misread Mom's expression and soft voice. She softened me with kind words, but now it's back to business. I steel myself for the attack.

"Her letter... said you cheat because I... taught you to live down to my expectations."

Goddamn it, Celeste. My breath leaves and anger fills its place. "It's not your fault. I'm the one—"

"She was right. I wounded you." Mom's eyes meet mine with desperate intensity. "You deserved better, Josh. If I could've done better, I would have. I didn't know I was hurting you."

"It's okay."

She shakes her head. "No. I'll regret it until I die. So, not much longer." She smirks.

I chuckle. "You and your sick sense of humor." Mom could always make me laugh. Now, my laughter turns to sobs. "I'm sorry, Mom. I'm sorry I left you alone." I slip my arms under her torso, mindful of the tubes, and pull her close. "I'm sorry, Mom."

"I love you, son."

"I love you, Mom."

"She loves you, too."

"Not anymore."

"She's here. Isn't she?"

For you, Mom. I keep that to myself. Why take my dying mother's fantasy away? I'm grateful Celeste left her best friend's wedding to make peace with my mom.

"She came to you wounded, Josh," Mom whispers. "You didn't know how to heal each other."

"You're right," I say, thinking of the toll it took on Celeste to lose her father before she could form solid memories of him and then to lose her mother a few years later. Unlike me, Celeste never used her pain to hurt others. Until I cheated on her, she was kind and giving.

Mom continues, "I know the rage that made her write that letter, Josh. I lived it for thirty-three years. Take care of her. Help her heal, and she will help you heal."

6

Celeste

A WAVE OF EXHAUSTION OVERTAKES ME AS I ENTER THE empty ICU waiting room. The gray and orange couch looks uninviting, but I drop into it anyway, grateful for a place to rest. For the last few hours, I've ignored the text alerts buzzing on my phone.

Now, I see thirty messages from Amira and Kath, who created a thread for us three. Lots of heart emojis and urgent questions. Do they really want me to FaceTime them at 1:00 AM? I hope so because all this stuff with Josh and Ellen has me spinning. And now that I have closure with Ellen, I need to start planning my future.

"You look exhausted, Darling," Kath says, concern shining through the purple cat-eye glasses, her face free of its usual dramatic makeup.

"It's been a long night, but we got Josh to his mom, and I got to say goodbye."

"How'd that go?" Kath's brows arch over her glasses.

"Good."

"Good?" Kath asks.

"Then why are you wrinkling your nose and rubbing your ear?" Amira asks.

I sigh. Do I want to rehash what just happened? My throat tightens, signaling my body wants a subject change. I massage it. "Believe it or not, she thanked me for my letter. She said I was right, and it helped her understand why Josh had shut her out."

"Damn. Ellen actually thanked you for sending that letter?" Amira asks.

"All Celeste did was lay a little **bell hooks** on the woman," Derek says. "Did you read *The Will to Change*, Celeste?"

"Sure did. It resonates. Her idea that toxic masculinity is a problem created by men who hate themselves and perpetuated by women who hate themselves."

"I love how bell hooks calls on mothers, aunties, grandmas, and sisters to give their sons safe space to cry, encourage them to tap into their femininity."

"This sounds like a book I need to read," Amira says. "Maybe share with the parents I counsel."

"Ellen was a perfect example. She couldn't show her son how to be vulnerable and real, and she raised a toxic man."

Derek says, "It's a communal problem. Too many of my species believe being a man means acting angry, belligerent, maybe violent, and unfaithful."

"Mm-hmm," I agree. "Women and men need to train their sons to be loyal. It doesn't happen by accident."

Amira's wiggling around like she's wrestling with something. Where is she? A water sound comes through the line. "Sorry for peeing while we talk. I'll mute myself."

Kath shakes her head, laughing silently.

"We can still hear you, Mimi." I smirk.

"Sorry. One sec. Just need to finish. Derek can you hold this? Muting myself again." There's a blur of motion on the screen, then Derek's smiling face. He waves.

"It's cute how you share your intimate moments with us," I deadpan.

Kath giggles. "Honestly, Darling. There's such a thing as preserving the mystery."

Amira re-enters the frame, face covered with suds. "Once you have a kid, privacy becomes a fantasy. Right Derek?"

He yawns. "Learning that real fast, though at least as the stepparent, Lila doesn't walk in on me in the bathroom. Where are you now, Celeste? ICU waiting room?"

"Yeah. Coming here tonight reinforced what I've been feeling for the last few months. I need to move back East. My nana's gone. Josh and I are through. What's left for me in California? Wildfires and drought?"

"You can write books anywhere," Derek says. "But don't you see clients in person?"

"I can see them online, and I'll find new clients."

"With the notoriety you've gained in the last year, that should be easy," Kath says. "We'd love to have you closer, wouldn't we, Lauren?" Kath turns to her wife, whose blonde curls fill the screen before her face.

"Yes, we would!"

"I could babysit Sage and Wesley's baby." The thought brings a smile to my face, even as it hits me in the gut. Since I can't have a child, the only way to have one in my life is to babysit.

"Nothing says 'I love you,' like watching someone's infant." Amira's on the move again, heading down the stairs and into her mother's kitchen. "Want apple pie, Derek?"

"Just tea, hon."

"I'm hungry all the time lately." She holds a forkful of pie aloft. My mouth waters, missing that pie. Tanya used to bring apple pie to our dorm room as an extra thank-you for watching Amira. Her apple pie helped college feel more like home. Did I pass a vending machine in the hall? Amira continues, "Anyway, Celeste, I know you wanted to make amends with Ellen and stuff, but why now?"

I give her my you're joking look. "What choice did I have? She's dying."

"Can't control time of death," Derek says.

"Sorry. What I'm really asking is, are you helping my brother because you're hoping to reunite?"

I wish I was better at changing the subject. "Definitely not, but after everything we meant to each other, how could I leave him to deal with it alone?" I'm glad there's no one around to hear us. Still, I wish I'd grabbed my earbuds and some comfy clothes from my room before we left New Haven.

Kath and Lauren have a silent conversation. The way these two interact, so in tune with each other, inspires me. They finish and Kath says, "Some people would say handling this situation alone would be the best medicine for him."

Lauren looks into the screen. "Agreed. The only way Josh will understand your true value is if he has to handle all this stuff alone and wish you were by his side. Then he might recognize the value you bring to his life."

I ponder Kath and Lauren's words, scanning the array of magazines on the coffee table.

"...Love," Amira says.

"What? Sorry, I got distracted by another alien sighting article—"

"I said, that's tough love, what Kath and Lauren are suggesting."

"Listen, if my agenda was to get Josh back or even to make him suffer, I would've stayed in New Haven tonight, let him wallow in his pain. I've had a lot of revenge fantasies." Images flash through my mind:

Keying Josh's car.

Letting the air out of his mountain bike tires.

Throwing that heart-shaped crystal he gave me through his bedroom window and it hitting Lucinda in the third eye.

Now, I look at my hands, ashamed.

"Revenge fantasies are normal. As long as you don't become obsessed with the ideas," Amira says. "You're not obsessing, right?"

"The vindictive thoughts were fading until I saw him in New Haven. They reignited and were burning bright until I saw his face after he got off the phone with the hospital." I shrug. "My heart cracked open."

Another silent conversation occurs, this time between Kath, Lauren, Amira and Derek.

"It doesn't mean I'm pining for him," I say.

They all look at me, incredulous.

"Fine. I admit I've daydreamed. I can't help if he sneaks into my mind on occasion."

"Uh, oh," Kath says. "Her voice went up a notch. Celeste is running defense."

I purse my lips, ignoring the comment. Sometimes, it's annoying how well these people know me. "Having the occasional," *x-rated,* "fantasy is not the same as scheming for his return."

Amira nods. "I'm glad to hear you say that, Cece. Offering your kindness with a result in mind could backfire big time."

"I know." I clear my throat. "Josh may be incapable of fidelity. I doubt I'm capable of trusting him, even if he can be faithful. Still, he's a human who deserves love. I realized tonight, to my surprise, I still love him."

"Uh, oh," Kath says.

"No worries. I refuse to act on it. And I refuse to shame myself for feeling love."

"I felt similar when my ex-wife came to make amends," Derek says.

I exhale, the validation helping me relax.

He continues, "No chance I wanted her in my life again, but when she apologized and told me she was dying, I realized, after ten years, I still cared for her. Owning that brought relief I didn't know was possible. That's when my real healing began."

Amira wraps her arm around Derek's shoulder. He lays his head on hers. Josh and I used to be romantic like that. *Enough, Celeste. There's more to life than romance.*

"You've got a good man, Amira. When are you guys getting married?"

"October 10th. Save the date." Amira leans against him and yawns. "I'm ready for bed. Call us when you know your plans for the week, Cece. Josh, too. If he needs anything…"

I flash a thumbs up. "Quick question. The last time I lived in New Haven, I lived on campus. Where should I look now?"

"It would be self-sabotage to move now," Kath says.

"Agreed." Lauren pops into the screen next to Kath.

"Didn't you guys say you'd love to have me back?"

"It would suit us, but I think it's best for you to wait," Lauren says.

"You have too much to clear up first," Amira says. "Are you in therapy right now, Cece?"

"When haven't I been in therapy?"

"Good point. So, take a vacation. Go on a retreat or something. Get away without throwing your whole life into upheaval. Kay?"

I frown. "I guess that makes sense."

"Get some sleep. You don't have to decide tonight."

We make kissy faces at each other and end the call. I groan into the empty room. They're probably right. I fall back on the hard couch and tuck my legs under my coat. Since things fell apart in October, I've felt out of place, discombobulated. I've been struggling to think straight. How much longer can I go on like this? Something has to change.

7

Josh

MY MOTHER MOANS. I FOLLOW HER GAZE TO THE door and see my child, all grown up. My daughter is a lovely young woman. Despite the electric blue curls and olive eyes, Satya looks the spitting image of photos of my mother at that age, when she was still taking care of herself. Fit. Dressed in a similar hippie style.

Seeing Satya after so long fills me with warmth, lifts my cheeks into an uncontrollable smile. Tears well up in my eyes. I stand and open my arms, even though I haven't released mom's hand. Satya dips her head in acknowledgement and walks directly to the other side of my mother's bed. Crushed, I sit.

"Oh, Grammy." She kisses her forehead. "What did you do?"

Mom moans again. Did she use her last words for me? Is there nothing left for her granddaughter? Guilt sets in.

We sit in silence for a bit. I watch my daughter's face, trying to soak up everything I've missed in the four years we've spent apart. Satya looks at me warily, whispers in mom's ear, eliciting a smile from her. Mom looks into Satya's eyes, then mine. "You two have things to work out."

"You don't need to worry about us, Gram."

"I won't be here to worry about you for much longer."

Satya gasps.

"Mom." I wince, feeling my daughter's discomfort. If only it were so easy that my mother's dying wish could make Satya speak to me. I'd give anything to know why my daughter cut me out of her life.

She's watching me now, trying to convey something with her eyes. I think she's asking for time alone with her grandmother. But I just promised Mom I'd never leave her again. What if she dies while I'm gone?

Though it pains me to leave my mother for one second in this situation, they deserve their private goodbye. "Mom, I'm gonna step into the hall for a minute. Okay?"

Mom squeezes my hand. Satya looks at me with less coolness than before. I kiss Mom's cheek, slip my hand from hers and walk out the door, praying she'll still be with us when I return.

Celeste

Eyelids drooping, I scroll through the real estate app absent-mindedly, not noticing the listings in New Haven, Amherst, or Boston. I want to make a plan and explore my options over the next couple of weeks, so when I go back to Wildbranch, I can tie up loose ends and get out. I am done with that town.

A light touch on my knee sends heat streaking up my thigh, jolting me awake. Josh. Hoping to calm the sexual charge, I take his hand. Wrong move. Now, I'm pulsing with need, tired, and confused.

I slip from his grasp, so neither of us will get the wrong idea. Away from Josh, I know I'm better off without him. In his presence, I forget important facts as his energy draws me into his orbit.

"Satya's here," he says.

"She made it. I'm so glad."

"My daughter barely acknowledged me, Celeste. I opened my arms, and she walked right past me."

"Ouch."

Josh puts his head in his hands. "I'm losing them both at once."

"Satya's here. You haven't lost her."

He needs comfort. Every one of my nerve endings responds. Usually, my body's signals push me in the right direction. Not with Josh. It hurts to see him looking so broken, but it's not my job to fix him. I refuse to engage, even though guilt wells up inside me.

Why should I feel bad? For being unresponsive? *Fuck you, Guilt.* He's the one who said he's not supposed to have physical contact with women. I won't mess up his fast by rubbing his back.

It was bad enough when he blamed me for his infidelity, like going to a conference is a license to cheat. I won't be blamed for— *Stop it, Celeste. This isn't helpful.*

I take a deep breath and stare out the window at the falling snow. "I'm sorry to be insensitive, Josh, but we have practical stuff to consider, like flights."

"Shit. Mine is tomorrow afternoon. Think it's too late to change it?" He pulls his phone from his suit jacket and opens the airline app. "When do you go home?"

"I extended my trip another week."

"Oh?"

"It feels good to be out of California, have a change of scenery. I might hang with Kath."

"I don't mean to hold you up," he says.

"You're not," I say.

"I'm supposed to check out of the hotel tomorrow, but there's no way I'm leaving my mother. Shoulda grabbed my stuff before we left. Now I'll get charged for another day or more."

"Amira said if you need anything to call. Maybe she can clear out the hotel room?"

He looks at me with appreciation. "You always think of the important details."

I swallow hard. For seven years, I craved Josh's affirmation. He used to razz me for planning and considering everything that might go wrong. Now, he's praising me, teasing my heart open again.

Foolish heart, all it takes is a few kind words for you to bloom? Don't you feel the danger here?

Luckily, I have boring logistics to distract me. "You need to extend your rental car, too, right?"

"Thanks for the reminder. What about you?"

"I took a ride share from the airport. I need my clothes, though. If Amtrak is running over the holidays, I can take the train down tomorrow, get my stuff, and figure out my next move."

Josh looks like he's waging a battle behind his eyes. Finally, he says, "Or, you could take my rental car, do what you need, then come back."

"I hate to intrude on your super important family time."

"You're not."

"Josh," I protest.

He strokes my cheek, an excruciating reminder of what I thought we were, and tilts my face until our eyes meet. "Celeste, you are family."

Everything in me screams, kiss him, but I resist. He's doing his female fast. I'm consumed with anger, resentment, and confusion.

I love him. I hate him. I want to help him. I want to move. It seems like I need to choose between helping him and looking for a new community. Tears of frustration well up and spill over.

8

Josh

THEY BRING A COT INTO THE ROOM, BUT NEITHER SATYA nor I want to release Mom's hand. Satya crawls into bed with her. I put the cot right next to the bed, so I can hold my mother's hand while I rest. Despite my exhaustion, I will stay awake for her. If death is scary, I won't let her face it alone.

The warmth of the morning sun on my face wakes me, a contrast to the cold, stiff hand in mine. Please, no.

I open my eyes. My mother's hand is gray. "Mom?" I slide my gaze to her face. Drained of color, mouth and eyes open. "Mom," I say, knowing there's no possibility of waking her. "Mom." I squeeze her stiff hand. I failed.

"Dad," Satya murmurs, leaning forward in the big armchair on the other side of the bed. "She passed around four-thirty."

"You were awake?"

"Yeah."

"Did she say anything?"

Satya shakes her head no. "Just took a long final breath. I saw something float above her, like her spirit was leaving her body."

I slide my gaze from Satya's face to Mom's. My mother's once brilliant green eyes are now as black as night. "Her eyes…"

"I know," Satya says. "Bizarre, huh?"

As horrible as I feel about losing my mother, I can't help celebrating a little about my daughter speaking to me. Please let this continue.

"Was it awful watching her die?" I ask.

She shakes her head no. Probably would've freaked me out. Guess it's good I was asleep.

"Satya, I'm sorry you had to see Grammy die, but I'm glad you made it to say goodbye."

"The roads were a mess. It took three hours from Amherst, but I wanted to be here when she passed."

Amherst? Did she move? I thought she was in Boston. Now's not the time to press for details. I'm more concerned that Satya isn't crying. "Are you okay?" I ask.

She nods yes, but her eyes radiate pain.

"What time is it?" I ask.

"Five-fifteen?"

"You've been sitting here all this time?"

"I didn't wanna wake you, and I figured if I called the nurses, you'd lose your chance to say goodbye before they took her away."

"Aww, honey. Thank you." I want to reach for my daughter's hand, but I'm afraid to break this tenuous moment of peace between us by pushing. I gesture to the call button. "You ready now?"

"Yeah."

I press the red button by the bed.

A nurse enters and comes to my side, whispers. "How're we doing?"

"Mom passed about an hour ago."

"Mm-hmm. We saw that on the monitor at the nurse's station and didn't want to disturb you. Have you said your goodbyes?"

I nod. "What happens now?"

"We'll clean her, drape her with a sheet, and take her to the morgue in the basement. Have you selected a funeral home?"

I shake my head, overwhelmed already. Funeral home. The nurse continues, but my brain is swimming. I want to ask her to hold that thought while I run and get Celeste. Nice, Josh. What kind of man takes advantage of the kindness of the woman he betrayed because he can't handle a simple thing like hearing about a funeral home?

"Sir, did you hear me?"

I look sheepishly at the nurse. To her credit, she's offering a gentle smile, not scolding. I take a deep breath. "Sorry. No. I, uh…"

"That's alright. Your wife's in the waiting room, right? We'll give her the info sheet about local mortuaries and options for burial or cremation."

My wife. I'm gonna be sick. She might've been my wife if I hadn't acted just like my father. Mom's apology rings in my head.

I am not Jason. I can make things right. I manage a weak smile for the nurse. "Thank you. I'll take the sheet."

9

Josh

Despite the arctic temperatures, I crank open the casement windows to clear the cloying blend of scented candle and cat litter from Mom's bedroom. Mom hasn't had a cat in years, but the damn shag carpeting she was so attached to holds a shitload of unpleasant smells.

Satya sits on my mother's bed, folding clothes and sorting them into piles. One to keep for herself, another for charity, and a pile to bring to Amherst's next fabric recycling event. "Gee, Dad," she says, as I return to the stack of mementos I've been combing through on the floor. "I'm surprised you're not rushing through this like you normally do."

It hurts that she's right. I never have been one for dealing with emotions. "Yeah, this is tough, huh?"

Maybe on some level, I knew my mom was proud of me. Still, when she said it last night, I thought it was… I don't know, a lovely parting gift. Now, I see the evidence all over the house. Photos of me in all stages of my life. She has—had—a binder filled with my science project reports from fourth grade through high school.

All the ephemera reminds me that Mom was always there. It's Dad who rarely showed up. And I thought she hated me. That's the power of a poorly chosen word, I guess.

"How are you holding up, kid?" I ask.

She looks out the window. I follow her gaze to a vista that's almost the same as it was in my childhood. Snow weighs down the branches of the tall pines and sugar maples, catches the sunlight like so many sparkling jewels.

"Dad, why didn't you talk to Grammy?"

"I thought she hated me. Every time she saw me, she criticized me. Seemed like my entire existence was a burden and a disappointment."

"Ouch," Satya says.

"Yeah. Now I see all these things she saved. I have no clue how she got half of these. Printouts from news releases the university posted last year? I never sent these to her."

"I did." Celeste comes into the room with a tray of steaming mugs, bringing the aroma of cocoa, cinnamon, and spice.

"Mmm. Celeste's famous hot cocoa," Satya says. "I've missed this."

"Josh, your mom was extremely proud of you. She just didn't know how to express it," Celeste says. "She had no idea how to separate her pride and love from all her resentment and hurt. That had nothing to do with you. You know that, right?"

I take a long sip of the hot cocoa, enjoy the hint of cinnamon and vanilla filling my senses, and ponder Celeste's words. I guess I'll have to let the idea sink in for a while.

"Thanks for saying that." I brave a glance at her.

Her gaze is all compassion. "It's true. Find anything you like, Satya?"

My daughter points to a pile of sweaters. "Grandma sweaters are in right now. I won't have to shop for a year."

"Nice. Would you like me to bag up the other stuff, sweetie?"

"I don't know what this family would do without you, Celeste."

Neither do I.

The heat in my chest makes my heart puddle. Celeste has obviously said nothing to Satya, and I haven't had the guts. Does it really matter if we tell her?

Unfortunately, Satya is highly perceptive. Is it my sudden interest in the shag rug underneath my jeans, or Celeste's famous heart-on-sleeve facial expression that makes my daughter groan?

"Oh, no. You guys aren't together anymore, are you?"

Keeping my focus on the floor, I shake my head and whisper, "No."

Celeste

Josh stares at the worn shag rug, his shame palpable. I look from him to Satya, in time to catch her expression change from appreciation to disappointment. She purses her lips in that same pouty way she did when she was sixteen, then blows air through them so forcefully she sounds like a horse.

"Did he cheat on you, too?" Satya asks, her voice taking on an acid tone.

I inhale slowly and deeply and let the words fall with my exhale. I will not drag her into the mess we created. "What happened isn't important."

"He did, though. I can tell by the way your lips are trembling. Damn it, Dad! Celeste was the best thing that ever happened to you."

"No, sweetie." I hold her gaze, needing her to understand. "You were, are, and always will be the very best thing that ever happened to your father."

Tears spring to Satya's eyes. Josh sniffles and wipes his cheeks, looking at his daughter with a blend of hope and sadness. I clear my throat to catch his attention. It doesn't work. He needs to get off the floor and go to his daughter right now, but he sits there, frozen, like he always does when he's confronted. Josh is not a fighter. First he freezes, then he flees, sometimes into himself, sometimes actually leaving the space to go for a run or a bike ride.

Don't withdraw now, Josh. Go to her!

I know this is hard for him. It's the most his daughter has spoken to him in four years, and what she's saying is that he fucked up. Again.

"Wait," Satya says. "If you guys broke up, why are you here now, Celeste?"

I explain what we mean to each other and how I could never leave him to handle this alone. "Not that he is alone. I mean, you're here."

"I know what you mean," Satya says.

"Anyway..." I try to force a lightness into my voice that I don't feel. "This is what we do for the people we care about, right? We make sacrifices sometimes."

I can tell Satya's not buying it.

"Would you two like a moment alone?" I ask.

"No," Satya says.

Josh looks up at me, as if to say: please don't.

"Or... Josh, I see you're going through the old photos and photo albums. I can't imagine there's anything in there you wouldn't want to keep."

"Guess you're right. Satya and I can divvy this up. Huh, Rainbow?"

"Yup," Satya says, grimly.

I say, "I found some companies that will take the furniture. Is there anything either of you want?"

"Nah. It's all pretty cheap," Josh and Satya say in unison.

"They're coming tomorrow. Maybe we should clear out your mother's desk and hutch and make sure there's nothing in her nightstand before they come take the furniture. Pack the dishes and things?"

"Sure. You okay in here alone, Satya?"

"Yes, Dad," she says, as if Josh is the biggest idiot in the world.

He looks at me, pain radiating from his eyes. The same pain I used to see during visits to his mom. Inevitably, she would say something hurtful, and his heart would break in front of her. If she noticed, she ignored it. I'm sure she had no idea the damage she was doing.

Seeing that expression on his face now makes me want to take him into my arms and hold him close. Bad idea, though. Very bad idea. Josh needs comfort; that's clear, but I cannot be the one to offer it. He'll have to do what I've been doing these last few months—self-soothe.

10

Josh

Iᴛ'ꜱ ᴏᴠᴇʀᴡʜᴇʟᴍɪɴɢ. Aʟʟ ᴛʜᴇꜱᴇ ᴘᴇᴏᴘʟᴇ. Aʟʟ ᴛʜᴇꜱᴇ perfumes and the god-awful air freshener. Maybe it's the chemist in me; I'd rather smell embalming fluid. I'm dying to get out of this funeral home. Instead, I'm making the rounds, accepting condolences from mom's cousins and friends.

Satya and I opted out of having a receiving line. It's a small town. We know everyone here, at least by sight, though I barely recognize some of my old high school friends. We lost touch years ago. I missed the last several reunions. That these people showed up for me today adds to my emotional soup.

Everything seems hazy and confusing. One face morphs into another as I make the rounds. The hushed tones of gossiping voices swirl around me, filling my ears like they're amplified.

"Jason didn't come."

"Jason should've come."

"Never treated Ellen with the respect she deserved."

"At least Josh showed up for this."

"Too bad he never showed up for his mother when she was alive."

"Is that why Satya stopped talking to him?"

"She's the spitting image of Ellen."

No respect for the wicked, I guess.

I appreciate that Mrs. Meers is here. Her round face and watery blue eyes send me empathy, so I stop and sit with her. She takes my hand in her papery one. We offer each other condolences. She was Mom's best friend for forty years. I know she's hurting, but when I ask how she's holding up, she waves away the concern.

"Josh, I've wanted to tell you this for a long time. One of the hardest things as Ellen's friend was to watch how she spoke to you and say nothing. I didn't know what to say, and I'm sorry for that."

I'm stunned. "You noticed."

"Of course. But you know, back then our culture had different ideas about raising children. Parents blamed their children for everything. I didn't believe in it myself, but I didn't know how to go up against an entire society, so I raised Dominic and Michael differently."

"How are they doing?"

"Michael's on his way here. And Dominic's doing great out in Hawaii. Three kids now. Real estate business is treating them good. Happy wife, happy life."

"Yup," I say, though I never understood the concept until now.

"All that pain between you and your mom saddened me. I'm grateful you told me Ellen had the chance to apologize to you, and that you got to say goodbye."

Fuck. A lump forms in my throat. My lip is quivering. Pressure builds behind my eyes and I squeeze them shut, trying to stop what's coming. The scent of coconut lotion envelops me as Mrs. Meers encircles me in her warm arms. I can't help it; I'm bawling like a baby. "I'm sorry, Mrs. Meers."

"It's alright, dear." Her voice trembles as she breaks down. "Go ahead and cry."

There's something no one's ever said to me, not outside the men's group, anyway. For a flash, I see a possibility for a different version of myself; the self I could've been if my mother had told me it was okay to cry when Dad left.

When I'm able to hold my shit together, I pat Mrs. Meers' back. We pull apart, meet each other's gaze, a new understanding and respect between us. "You go circulate, dear. We'll talk at the luncheon. Yes?"

"Alright." I stand and look for Satya, but find myself staring into the face of my child's mother. I freeze. Lynn's mouth moves. Shallow condolences, blah, blah, blah. The words are right, but the scowl chills me. Lynn is definitely not sorry for my loss. She's here for Satya. Why she bothered to find me is a mystery. Stunned, I force my chin to dip in acknowledgement as I will her to move on. When she finally steps aside, I feel a hand on each shoulder. Terry to my left, blond hair piled on his head in a man bun, like he just rolled out of bed. Brent in a skullcap that covers his bald head.

"Hey, what are you guys doing here?"

"We were skiing up at Stowe. Heard the news and came down to support," Brent says, tapping a fist to his chest.

This is why I could never leave NorCal. With friends like Brent and Terry in my corner for twenty years, and a great job, why would I leave?

"You look like you need an escape," Terry says.

"Do I?"

"Let's go. We've got some primo Sativa."

"Not right now."

"Then keep us company."

What's the harm in getting a bit of fresh air? "I could use a break. Let me just reassure my kid I'm not jumping ship."

"She'll be fine," Terry says. The only other dad in our friend group, he probably knows better than I what a young woman needs in a situation like this.

Still, given the tenuousness of my connection with Satya, I'm not taking any chances. "You guys go ahead. I'll meet you out there."

I find Satya standing with the Ice Queen, my sister, Derek, and Celeste. I know literally nothing about fashion, but come on—who wears all white to a memorial? Lynn always would do anything to stand out in a crowd, even if it meant offending people. I do my due diligence and inform everyone where I'm going. Damn if my sister doesn't shoot me the evil eye.

"Got a problem, sis?"

"You do you, bro."

"Feeling a little overwhelmed right now." I hold my hand out to Satya. "Join us?"

"Thanks, Dad. I'm not looking to get high at my grandmother's memorial."

"Neither am I. Just getting some air. What they do is up to them."

"True dat," Derek says, but even he's throwing me a warning look that I don't love.

Someone clears their throat, and I realize Brent and Terry are waiting for me by the door. I follow them outside. We're not even off the porch when they light up. "Jesus, not out in the open. We're in Massachusetts, not California. I don't know if it's legal in public places."

Brent takes a hit and hands me the joint. I shake my head and back away. Etiquette says I should take the joint and hand it to Terry, but I'm not in that world right now. Things are different here.

Celeste

NANA WAS THE LAST PERSON IN HER FAMILY TO GO. OUR FAMILY was small to begin with. Her nephews, my uncles, had all died years before her. Not one of them had kids, which makes me the last of the Cairans. So our service was tiny. She had several close friends, and my close friends came. It was basically a love fest.

Ellen's memorial is tense. Between the gossip flying around the room and Lynn showing up... She always put Satya on a plane alone, so Lynn and I had never met before today. Now, I see what a blessing that was. She is every bit the cold bitch Josh described. It's stunning, especially given Satya's warm and sweet nature. Lynn's coldness toward Josh at his mother's memorial blows me away. Does she think she's masking her feelings? She forces her face to make sympathetic expressions, but her tone of voice and icy stare directed at him make me shiver. I can only imagine how it makes Josh feel. I glance between him and Satya. Maybe they're used to it, or unaffected because they're already in so much pain. He holds his hand out to Satya, but she refuses to join him and his friends outside.

As soon as he walks away, Satya says, "That pretty much sums up my childhood with Dad."

All eyes dart to her. She shakes her head and looks down.

"Those guys are jerks," Amira says.

"Yup," Satya says.

"Seriously, what's the appeal?" Amira asks.

I've always felt the same way, but I don't wanna pile on Josh right now.

"I have half a mind to go out there and tell that fool to get back inside where he belongs. You don't abandon your mother's memorial," Amira says.

"This place is pretty overwhelming with fragrances, and you know how sensitive Josh is. Besides, it's been a tough week," I say.

Derek strokes Amira's back. "Maybe you're being a little hard on him."

Their eyes meet and Amira concedes. "You're right."

I won't share too much in front of Lynn, but I have to defend poor Josh. Was this a dick move? Sure. But... "He and Ellen had a real reckoning at the hospital. He's been kinda different ever since." I glance between Amira, Derek, Satya, and Lynn, hoping they'll get the message to ease up. Derek's with me. Amira's waffling. Satya and Lynn? I doubt it. "Anyway, all this opening and closing of the door let the cold air in. I left my sweater in the car. I'll be right back." I squeeze Satya's hand.

"Drag that bonehead in when you're out there," Amira says.

I hitch a shoulder. "He's an adult."

Outside, I fish the keys from my purse and go directly to the car. The scent of skunk lets me know they're all getting high, though I'm not sure where they are until I hear that idiot surfer with his blond man bun. "Dude, you gave up boning, you gave up smoking bones, and you gave up alcohol. What the hell are you doing with yourself?"

"Jesus," Josh says.

The snake murmurs something I can't decipher. Did he say, "we're concerned about you?" Bullshit. I'm sure Brent is giving Josh his mesmeric stare, like Caw from *Jungle Book*. I've watched Brent in action at parties. He fixes his hypnotic gaze on someone, plants a suggestion, and they go along with him.

Now, he intones, "It seems like you're punishing yourself for something. Why would you give up all of life's pleasures? What good is that?"

Surfer idiot adds, "What's one hit gonna do, but help you relax?"

Josh forces a laugh. "Seriously guys, I don't need or want it right now. I'm trying to feel my feelings and get through this."

"Feel your feelings," Caw croons. "Nothing wrong with feeling relaxed."

You'd think he was trying to make a sale. Maybe he is. I've heard he sells a variety of substances. The legal ones go to his therapy patients. The illegal ones go to his friends.

Sounds like Josh is staying strong, though. "...more pleasures in life than sex, drugs, and alcohol."

"If you say so, Brah," Terry says. "What the hell is that bitch doing here?"

"She's the mother of my child."

"Not her."

"Who are you talking about?" Josh asks.

"Celeste."

A low growl rumbles through the air, a sound I've heard Josh make on very few occasions. "Excuse me?"

"She broke up with you months ago, cut you out of her life completely. Now, she's here? What's her endgame?"

"No game. Celeste is here supporting me out of love and concern, nothing more."

"Is that what that is?" Caw asks. "Looks to me like a play to get you back into her clutches."

"I appreciate you interrupted your ski vacation to come down here. I'm going back inside to grieve with my family."

"We're always here for you, brah," Surfer says, sounding completely fake. "Family 'til the end."

"Mm-hmm." Josh says.

Say what you want about Josh. He just stood up to his friends for me. He said I'm here supporting him. In the past, he would've said, "She's my girlfriend. She should be here," without acknowledging what I offer him. Anyway, I'm not his girlfriend. I shouldn't be here, at least not more than anyone else. But he didn't give them the satisfaction of dissing me. *Thank you, Josh, for finally standing up for me.* I sneak back to the porch, hoping they don't see me.

Josh

THE FUNERAL HOME DOOR THUDS CLOSED BEHIND ME. COLD, dry air assaults my skin and freezes my lungs as I inhale. The urn weighs heavy in my hands. How is it that the muted colors of winter seem more vibrant than they did two hours ago? I scan the near-empty parking lot. Celeste leans against the car in intense conversation with my daughter, Amira, and Derek. Moving toward them, I drink in the view of my little girl. People can be gone in an instant.

Satya has been standoffish this morning. I hope she'll be willing to connect now, and include me in the conversation. Maybe I can convince her to join us at the luncheon Mom's friends organized in the basement of the town hall. Hope fills me as I stride across the parking lot, feeling the crunch of gravel and snow under my boots as I cross the parking lot to my family. As soon as I reach the group, Satya says, "I gotta go."

"Satya." I reach for her. She moves out of grasp. "Are you coming to the luncheon?"

"I gotta get home." She gets into her little orange car, waves and drives away.

I stare at my daughter's vehicle as it turns from the parking lot onto the road. It disappears, leaving in its place a trail of exhaust vapor suspended in mid-air by the cold. An icepick drives through the top of my head. Numb, I force words out. "I thought she might want Mom's ashes."

Amira pulls me into a hug. "Give her time."

Derek pats my back. "See you at the church, Josh. Celeste, you riding with us?"

"Nah, I'm good." She smiles.

Amira and Derek look surprised but climb into their rental SUV and drive away.

Celeste takes the urn from me and gets into the passenger seat.

"Thought we were starting to reconnect, but since Satya realized I cheated on you, it's like I don't even exist."

"They say girls model their romantic relationships after how their fathers treat their mothers, or surrogate mothers. If she's going by what she's witnessed, maybe she assumes her father thinks she's unworthy of loyalty."

The words hit like a punch to the gut. "I probably needed to hear that." I sigh, pop the car into reverse and back out of the parking spot. "Thanks."

"I doubt she'll come around on her own. You'll have to work to regain her trust because, unfortunately, Satya thinks she's better off without you."

"If she'd tell me what I did, that'd be easier."

"Then part of your work is to figure out how you hurt her."

If it wasn't so easy for me to relate to what Celeste is saying, I'd probably be really pissed at her right now. Instead, I'm aggravated with myself and this whole damn situation. Yeah, Mom apologized. Yeah, it brought closure. And guilt, and grief, and... something I'm not supposed to be feeling right now. Resentment. Because if things had been different... If Mom had been different, like Mrs. Meers, like Celeste. If Dad hadn't left to begin with and put her in that tailspin. My muscles are tensing by the second. I pull onto the street, and everything in me wants to punch the car up to eighty, take this anger and stress out while driving.

I resist. I'm not seventeen anymore.

"This luncheon ought to be fun. All Mom's friends who think I abandoned her, which I did."

"Yeah, the gossip wasn't subtle. Ever notice how old people whisper at full volume?"

"Question is: have they forgotten they lost their hearing? Or are they pretending because they really want to be heard?"

"The stealth approach to gossip. Interesting theory." Celeste's giggle eases my mind. Leave it to her to pull me out of my pity party.

"Some of them were practically yelling," I add. "Hoarsely, so we'd think they think they're keeping it on the down low."

Celeste giggles harder, which sets me off, which makes her laugh so hard, she snorts. "It's not even that funny," she chortles. "But…"

The harder she laughs, the harder I laugh and soon my face is wet with tears.

"Oh, Josh." She puts her hand on my thigh, then lifts it away quickly, like it's on fire. It is now. The heat of her touch travels straight to… damnit, a part of my body I do not need to be thinking about right now.

She sighs. "Sorry. The one thing I loved about my Nana's memorial and reception was learning stuff about her that I didn't know before. It was comforting to be with people who cared about her. Once I went back to my life, there was no one around me who could relate."

"Makes sense. Connecting with Mrs. Meers and my buddy Michael was great, I have to say…" Anyway, it's not the gossip that bothers me as much as it is the fact that most of it is spot on. "You really think being a poor role model was enough to drive Satya away?"

"I don't know. She mentioned something about your friends, too."

"Did she?"

"A cryptic comment she refused to explain. I wonder what it was like for her to grow up with her parents on different sides of the country."

"I know what it was like. I lived it, with Dad in Los Angeles and Mom here."

"That's what it was like for you. Satya's not you. Plus, her mother is not your mother and you are not your father."

"I know, but—"

"Why assume you understand what someone else is going through because you had a similar experience?"

"Jesus, that never occurred to me."

"You're not alone. Most people make similar assumptions. I did, until I went through coaching training. And people, especially children, make up stories to explain what happened to them, and sometimes the stories in their head are light years from what anyone would think of as reality. Then they carry them into adulthood and make decisions based on them. I wonder what Satya's been telling herself."

"Good question."

"Maybe if Satya feels safe telling you what drove her away, then you can rebuild trust with her."

I park outside the old town hall, stare at the tower with its wrought iron bell, reflecting on the lecture I just received. "You really are insightful." I turn to her, catch her eye. "I can see why people love your coaching."

"Thanks." She looks down, like I said something wrong. I was complimenting her. What's wrong with that?

11

Celeste

OES JOSH FEEL AS EMOTIONALLY DRAINED AS I FEEL right now? Despite all the drama between him and his mom, we had good times with her, too. Sharing happy memories with Ellen's friends was like standing under a waterfall, cleansing and healing. I learned Ellen showed my letter to her closest friends. They helped her process it and recognize that I had given her an amazing gift—the chance to make amends with her son. An amazing gift. Wow.

I could have left after she died, gone home feeling satisfied by the last words we shared. This extra whatever-you-wanna-call-it brings me a new level of closure. I didn't realize how much I needed this, too.

Holidays at Ellen's had their share of tension. Witnessing her trying and failing to connect with her son pained me. Watching

Satya trying to diffuse the ticking bomb between her father and grandmother: excruciating. Invariably, Ellen would tire of Josh evading questions about his life, so she'd share some story from his childhood that painted him as flawed. That would push him further away to another room, the front yard, the car, where she would follow, accusing him of being like his father. She never saw the differences between the men, how Josh chose to use science for altruism rather than for personal gain. Josh would get so frustrated. Peace came on drives like this: riding on quiet back roads, gazing out the window at bare trees and quaint New England homes.

"Shit." Josh says as he pulls into the driveway of his childhood home. "She doesn't waste time."

I follow his gaze to the realtor's sign planted in the yard. We get out of the car, stand in the driveway, and stare at the For Sale sign. "Oh, honey, I'm sorry."

"I thought this would happen after we left. I wouldn't have to see it."

"You don't have to sell, you know."

He lifts a brow, gives me a side-eye, and trudges up the short cement walk into Ellen's little Cape Cod-style house. It's happening again. He's withdrawing. Heaviness settles in my heart. Damn it, why do I think I should comfort him? Why do I feel compelled to reach out? He lays the urn on the laminate kitchen counter. I place my hand on his back. Moving away from my touch, he shrugs off his coat and throws it onto a dining chair, grumbles something unintelligible and stalks down the hall into the bathroom. The sound of the shower running fills the room.

I stand in the middle of the kitchen, helpless, confused, suddenly exhausted. It's only four o'clock. How do I help him through this last painful piece of saying goodbye to his mother?

When Josh emerges from the bathroom, muscular chest bare and a towel slung low around his hips, I'm still standing in the same place. I drink in the view, envisioning a variety of ways to comfort him. All paths lead to disaster. I kill the fantasy in my mind, return my gaze to his face.

He scans my body but averts his eyes quickly, a look of disgust on his face. "You taking off your coat?"

"Wanna join me on a walk?"

"Nah. I'm gonna lie down."

It's not his job to comfort me. He's the one who lost his mother. But suddenly, he can't stand the sight of me? I shouldn't have tried to touch him, I guess. Learning about his tryst with Lucinda should have been clue enough that he no longer finds me desirable.

"Well, I'm going." I tug my hat low on my head.

He grunts in response, and I open the door wide so he can feel the blast of cold air as I leave. Passive-aggressive, I know. Sometimes, I can't help myself. I'm tired of feeling rejected.

The snow-covered yard glistens in the moonlight. I stride across it, my boots crunching through the hard crust and sinking an inch into the soft layer of snow below.

Why do I feel rejected? I'm telling myself a tale; several actually. The worst one, currently bubbling up and making it hard for me to breathe, is the one I've been repeating in my head these last few months. Josh cheated, not only because his mother inadvertently trained him to, but also because that's what I deserve. I'm the kind of person people leave, and one way or another I'll always end up alone.

A doozy. Can I un-believe it? Maybe I could tell myself it isn't true, but life keeps showing me otherwise. How can I ignore that story when there's so much proof to back it up? Is there?

My dad and grandfather risked their lives fighting fires, but didn't intentionally abandon me. Mom could've stayed. She had a choice. She chose grief over me, but if I hadn't said those awful words, would she have felt so despondent?

I hate this train of thought. Why am I doing this to myself?

I take a deep breath, remember what my therapist said to do when I sense I'm about to spin out. "Where are my feet?" I ask myself aloud. They're on the paved country road, illuminated only by the moon and the stars.

Out here in the middle of nowhere, with no light pollution, the stars are brighter and more plentiful. Back home, there's no escape from light pollution. And with the wildfire smoke blanketing our region so often, blocking our view of the sky, it's easy to forget stars exist. Here, they're vibrant. Maybe this is where I need to be.

12

Josh

AS WE STEP FROM THE RENTAL COMPANY VAN TO THE departures area in front of the terminal, it hits me: this is the end of our journey together for a while. After this, I have no reason to see her, no excuse to spend time with her, which is fine. This past week, Celeste has shown me more kindness than I deserve. Her presence made it possible for me to get through Mom's death and memorial.

Now, I need to get my head on straight, get back to business in more ways than one. I fell off the wagon this week, letting her touch me, reaching for her hand, even hugging her, inhaling her scent.

I'm doing it again. Can't stop myself nor the relief I feel as her special blend of lavender, rose, and cedar fills my nostrils. My pants feel tighter.

I carry both of our bags to the TSA line.

"I guess this is goodbye," she says. She gives me that look that says she wants physical contact. One last time? A goodbye kiss? I imagine the chaste brush of her lips. We can't stop there. Our kiss turns passionate and I lift Celeste onto my hips. Her long legs wrap around my waist. No. Not going there right now.

Those beautiful brown eyes ask so many questions, questions I can't answer today. Keeping a good six inches between us, I say, "Celeste, you've been amazing this week. I hope you know how much I appreciate your support, your guidance, your help. Couldn't have gotten through this without you."

"Thanks, Josh." A shy smile lights her face.

I want to kiss those dimples. The look in her eyes says she wants me, too. It takes everything I have not to reach for her. The light in her eyes dims.

I try to reignite it with an explanation. "It'll be weird not to see you when we get home. Our physical contact this past week violated my female fast. Under the circumstances, I needed it, but now I can't indulge. You understand. Right?"

Honoring my commitment to the fast shows Celeste she can trust me. Why does it feel like an epic fail?

The curl of her supple lips, the way she swallows hard and drops her gaze to the floor tells me I hurt her. Again. She doesn't trust me more.

I lean in to convey my sincerity. "I love you."

A tear slides down her face. She sniffles, "goodbye, Josh," and turns away.

Pain and relief mingle in my chest, and I'm in no shape to figure out why. One thing is clear: standing side-by-side in line will torture us both. Instead, once I see her enter the security scanner, I'll take my place in the queue.

Celeste moves through the winding security line. I stay still, letting people flow around me and fill the gap between us.

13

Josh

I THOUGHT I'D BE ABLE TO CLOSE THE TOMB OF THOSE painful memories, give the realtor the keys, and drive away without looking back. I thought I'd use this time on the flight home to journal about Celeste, think about moving forward, or maybe rest. But the past keeps playing in my ears. Mom screams accusations... Somehow it's my fault because I'm just like my dad. Mom's bloated face, the gray pallor, her quiet acknowledgement of her failings. Apologies. Why is this still coming up?

I play the action-adventure film offered on the flight, but see my mother and me try to find common ground, searching for some way to enjoy our relationship, year after year. Staring out the tiny airplane window, I watch resignation building inside my younger self, see myself giving up hope of a healthy relationship with mom. Our last moments together play out before me, filled with confessions and sorrow and regret.

After that long-ass flight and the endless drive home from San Francisco International Airport, I thought coming home would be a relief. Instead, I open the door, and shafts of evening sunlight illuminate the empty spaces Celeste used to occupy. The kitchen island, where she nibbles a cookie and writes her relationship book. In front of the sink, where she washes veggies. In front of the blender, which she fills with ingredients for one of those green smoothies she adores. On the couch, where Celeste curls up, folding her long, sumptuous legs under her, cozy like a cat, hair twisted into a bun. Or where she sprawls out, legs stretched across my lap, and tips her head back in delight as I massage her feet. On a blanket in front of the gas fireplace, she reads poetry aloud to me and opens her mouth to receive a grape from my fingers. She "accidentally" nibbles my fingertips, a sparkle in her eye.

I drop my bags by the door, hit the shower, and rinse away the day, the week, the last three months. I emerge refreshed until the spot where her toothbrush used to sit catches my eye. The ghost of her reflection in the mirror winks at me. Her beautiful mouth is covered in toothpaste foam because, for some reason, she never could keep it all in her mouth.

She kept other things in her mouth, though. Now, I'm throbbing below with the sense memory of her glorious lips wrapped around me, tongue pulsing. Her eyes shower me with so much love I can't bear it. I don't deserve it. Especially not now.

I wish I could erase the memories of how she responded when I came clean. More than that, I wish I could undo the actions that filled her gentle eyes with shock, turned her face into a mask of revulsion. She backed away like she was facing a monster. And I casually said, "You're making too big a deal of this. It was an accident. I didn't plan those times. It only happened that one weekend you were away."

"Those Times? Plural?! I thought you said it happened once! You're changing the story already."

"Twice that weekend, but only because she spent the night. If she hadn't been here in the morning..."

Celeste vomited all over the carpet. Right there. That spot. I scrubbed for hours but couldn't get the stain out completely. She packed and screamed and sobbed and said she could never sleep in our bed again because I hadn't just cheated on her but had brought the woman into our bed. Funny how it didn't occur to me she'd take issue with the location of my infidelity. Not funny. Pathetic. Disgusting. Callous.

My body feels heavy again, defeated by my foolishness. Confused by everything. Why would I think she'd want me back? What will I do without her?

I can't stand these feelings, which means, according to the program, this is a perfect time to journal. I brew a cup of yerba maté, sit at the kitchen island and write. It doesn't help. I'm not staring down temptation. It's my memories that are breaking me.

I send Derek a video chat request. His face lights the screen with a welcoming smile. "Josh. Made it home alright?"

"If by alright you mean averted temptation, then yes."

"How's Celeste?"

"We said goodbye at the airport. Now, I'm home and all I feel is confused and overwhelmed by grief. How do I move forward?"

"You've been through a lot this week. First and foremost, be gentle with yourself."

"What does that even mean?" I pace the kitchen.

"Don't beat up on yourself."

"Everywhere I look, I'm reminded of my failings."

"Shit. Maybe use a softer word than failings. Tell me more."

"This house. Every time I move, I see Celeste. Now she's gone, and I'm the ass who made her leave."

"You can't change the consequences. Can't take back the choices you made that led to those consequences. Next best thing to do is face them."

"How? Journaling works for temptations, but it's not doing shit to clear these memories from my mind. I know I can't call her. I don't even want to. I want her to see I'm trustworthy. If I call her, she won't believe me."

"Congratulations. You're a step ahead of where you were last month."

"Am I?"

A text rolls in.

"Buddy, when you started the program, you couldn't seem to wrap your head around why you needed to steer clear of her or give her space. Now you understand. That's big."

"Doesn't change the situation, though."

"True dat. If the results are a mirror of your beliefs, what does that consequence tell you about what you believe about yourself and what you deserve?"

"It tells me I created the situation because deep down, I believe I deserve to be alone."

"And why would you deserve to be alone?"

My phone dings. Marty texting me an invitation out to drinks in honor of my mom.

"One sec, Derek." I reply to Marty.

Not drinking RN. Female fast.

WTF does female fast have to do with drinking? Grapevine says Josh needs to chill.

Truth! But not drinking. Plus early work day tomorrow. Dinner later?

You got it.

"Josh?" Derek asks, sounding annoyed.

"Sorry. Because I'm not worthy of love."

"Because...."

"Like my mother said growing up, I was just like my father."

"Ouch."

"I had some healing around that," I say, propping the phone on my dresser so Derek and I can see each other as I unpack. "Because of Celeste, my mother realized she had hurt me and that she was wrong. She said I'm not my father, and she created a problem for me that didn't have to be there."

"Your mom said that? Damn."

"Mm-hmm." I lift my garment bag onto the bed and unzip the shoe compartment.

"What are you feeling in your body right now?" he asks.

"A black hole in my chest that only one person can fill."

"Celeste?"

"Yup." I remove my dress shoes and sneakers and put them in my closet.

"Been there. Truth is, Josh, you're the only person who can fill that hole, and that's what this work is about. Recognize what you need to do for yourself. Without numbing out or seeking the company of others to make you feel any kind of way. Friends, family, partners... they can't fill the hole inside you. You have to recognize you're worthy of love."

"Come on," I scoff, removing my shave kit and bringing it and my phone into the bathroom. "You think every married person feels a rush of self-love and worthiness before they—"

"Fifty percent divorce rate indicates that's a 'no'. But you'll have a better shot at a healthy romantic relationship with someone—"

"The only romantic relationship I want is with Celeste."

"Hey, if that can work out for you and be good for her, I fully support it. It's not your reality now, though. I know you want to avoid pain. But the only way out is through. Gotta sit with it. Stop resisting the hurt."

I cock an eyebrow at him, annoyed, especially because he's right.

"Go meditate. Let yourself dive into those emotions. That's how you fill that black hole. If you run, distract yourself, numb out, blame anybody else, you'll miss this chance to grow."

"I hear you."

"See these feelings as precious jewels. You get to hold them a little while until they dissolve and the energy moves through you and out."

"Precious jewels. You sound like my sister."

He chuckles. "Amira's poetic soul is rubbing off on me. You get my point. As you sit with the emotions and let them dissolve, nourishment will slowly fill the emptiness. Not in one sitting."

"This is not remotely what I wanted to hear."

"I know."

"But I know it's what I need. Thanks, man."

Derek's smile is so wide it seems to take up the whole screen. "Let me know how it goes."

We end the call and I finish my tea. I go to my favorite spot under the skylight in the bedroom, sit cross-legged on the floor, set the timer, and begin my silent meditation. I acknowledge my feelings without judging them, or judging myself for having them. I let everything be present. It's an interesting practice, not trying to change feeling like crap, not being cynical about it, just accepting it, accepting my humanity. After thirty minutes, I feel a little lighter, a little stronger. The confusion that I had been feeling slipped away at some point. The grief is still there, but it's released its tight hold around my neck.

Now, I'm thinking about what I found at Mom's house, thinking about Celeste. When I write in my journal, it doesn't help.

But when I write to her, insights reveal themselves, like we're talking. I've written her a few letters since I started the program, all unsent. With all these thoughts bubbling up, I need to write another one. Maybe when I finish the fast, I'll send her all the letters.

January 10th

Dear Celeste,

I didn't tell you this when we were clearing out Mom's house, but I found the letter you wrote her. It was tear-stained. With her tears or yours?

Damn, girl, you held nothing back. I'd be mad, except your letter inspired Mom to make amends with me. Because of what you said, Mom got to leave this world in peace, knowing I forgave her.

More importantly, though your words were harsh, you showed Mom something I don't think anyone else, including me, ever did before: she mattered.

It's funny I'm just seeing it now: the message cheating sends someone is that they don't matter. How many women have I sent that message to? The toxic cycle you described in your letter is real. I'm grateful to have found a therapist and a program with all these spirit brothers to help me break the toxic cycle in my relationships.

I see now; my mother emotionally abused me. Not when I was little. Back then she directed her anger at the cause—Dad. Once he left, I became the vessel for her fury. At first, it stunned me, but kids are adaptable. After a while, her berating felt normal. In a twisted way, it showed me I mattered. I must be important because, like my dad, I had the power to distort Mom's face into a horrific mask.

Eventually, I could only take so much of her anger, so, like my dad, I abandoned her, and sent her the message she'd already internalized: she didn't matter.

Thank you for opening a door to a new reality for Mom. Yes, it filled her with regret. But it also showed her she had the power to change her world. Luckily, she got the chance before it was too late.

Thank you for planting seeds in my heart, as well. Leaving me and leaving that note about my failure to respect women... your rage was clear. And it was righteous. Your words called me to grow, even if I couldn't acknowledge their wisdom at first.

My mind is exploding right now, as I put all these pieces together. Because you left me and left that note, I wondered whether I had a problem relating to women. That led me to do the female fast. Thanks to the program, I had the wherewithal to be emotionally present at my mother's deathbed. Without it, I would've shown up at the hospital, kissed Mom goodbye, maybe shed tears, but with no clarity or love. I would've heard her apology without internalizing it, and no healing would have occurred.

Even in your rage, you shower love. You're like Aphrodite. Everywhere you go, flowers bloom under your feet. You humble me, Celeste.

Can I ever be worthy of you? I'll spend the rest of my life trying.

All my love,

Josh

P.S. Over the holidays, I made flower-themed foods, thinking of you and your passion for roses. You've added such a sweet fragrance to my life.

14

Celeste

Home. Cozy. Delightful. Safe. My sanctuary.

I love returning from a trip. My soothing homemade lavender-rose-cedar potpourri greets me when I push the door open. Heaven. But before I can take a deep breath and revel in the scent, a tidal wave of loneliness crashes over my soul, almost knocking me over.

My heart rate goes into overdrive.

Do not panic. This is just a feeling. It's like being swallowed in a cave. That one time I went spelunking. The darkness. The confusion. *Do not panic. You're okay, Cece. You're safe. Turn on the light.*

It's dark. That's the problem. I run my hand along the wall to my left, feeling for the light switch. I flip it up, and everything is illuminated. *See? Safe.*

Too late. When a tidal wave crashes over you, you get soaked through. Light can't stop you drowning. Loneliness fills my lungs and heart, my cells. I can't escape what's inside me.

With everything illuminated, I'm confronted by bare walls, boxes I never unpacked. When I left Josh and found this place, I told myself it was a temporary landing pad. I hated him, but hoped he'd fix us. Only a little bit of me hates him now. Still, realizing I love him doesn't mean I can be with him. Too many obstacles stand in our way. His friends' words replay in my head.

Snake's accusations about why I went to Ellen's memorial: "… a play to get you back into her clutches."

Surfer jerk: "We're always here for you, brah. Family 'til the end."

Seriously. Brah? What an ass.

I could turn around, get in the car and find somewhere else to sleep. Now that the loneliness is inhabiting me, what difference will it make to leave? I'll just bring it. Do I plan to stand in the doorway all night? Sleep on the threshold?

"You okay, Ma'am?"

A kid stands under the spotlight in my driveway. Maybe fifteen, non-binary or still figuring things out, judging by their appearance. Concern in their expression. "I passed by fifteen minutes ago and saw you standing there. Doesn't look like you've moved. Is your bag too heavy or something? Do you need help?"

Aww. People give teenagers such a bad rap.

My voice sticks in my throat, so I shake my head no, clearing my throat. Finally, I croak, "All set. Thanks. Just thinking."

"Okay. My name's Gem. I live two houses that way." They point toward the mountain. "If you ever need anything, knock on the door. Usually someone in my family's there."

"Aren't you sweet."

Gem flashes a lopsided smile. "We're all just walking each other home, right?"

Quoting Ram Das. Why am I surprised? This is Northern California, after all. Before the tech gurus infiltrated, this was land of new agers, yoga instructors, homesteaders, and spiritual intellectuals.

"Thanks, Gem. I'm Celeste. I'm kind of in transit, but feel free to knock on my door, too."

"Good night, Celeste." Gem strides away.

So much for sleeping in the threshold. I close the door behind me, roll my suitcase down the undecorated hall into my bedroom. Bed, pillows, nightstand, comfy chair. The adorable architecture and built-in cabinets and bookshelves sold me on the home. This place exudes charm, wants only a loving touch. Aside from the mini-rose bushes I've planted in large pots in every room, I've brought nothing to this space. The only meaningful touches here are inside cardboard boxes piled against the guest room walls.

Pandora's boxes, filled with memories I could totally face if I wanted to. But why do that to myself? Unpacking those boxes in my guest room will unleash chaos. To what end? To stare at pictures of the mirage that was my life?

My therapist agrees I need to bring order to chaos wherever it shows up in my life. Right now, that's my suitcase, so I unpack quickly, start a load of laundry, prepare a bag of items for the dry cleaner, put away all my toiletries, and shove the bag into the closet.

Still overrun by thoughts.

What I need right now is a list. Lists make everything better. I bring my journal to the kitchen table, brew a cup of relaxing Tulsi Rose tea, and jot down the attributes I want in a new community:

A strong co-working culture, so I can easily connect with other professionals who work independently;

A strong arts community, because communities that support their artists are more compassionate and vital places to live;

A place where education is prioritized and funded. (So I'll never have kids. A community that doesn't educate all its children is a community that's destined to fail when those children grow up and take over the government but don't understand the essential elements of a working community. Elements like safe roads and walking paths, the necessity of access to fresh, healthy food, equal access to quality health care. How can anyone expect children who weren't taught about infrastructure to understand how to run a town?)

I want to live in a city with easy access to nature, or in a quiet town outside a vibrant small city. New Haven? Providence? Boston? Too big. Way too expensive. I add, "affordable," to my list. Northampton? Amherst?

Ellen lived twenty minutes from Amherst. But her friends said she only went there to work, shop, and eat out. Her social life was in town, where she was one of a few unmarried women, always excluded from dinner parties and couples' outings. Ellen's isolation embittered her more. All her girlfriends have someone to hold each night and wake beside in the morning, to share all the things that make life sweet. Ellen was the only one who was alone. I would hate to be in that situation. I add, "vibrant community for single people," to my list. Older single people. I'm not trying to hook up with twenty-somethings. I'm not trying to hook up with anyone. I want a real relationship with a real man who won't leave.

There's only one problem: me. If I'm the kind of woman men leave, how can I expect any man to stay and be faithful?

15

Josh

THE DOOR SNAPS CLOSED BEHIND ME. OUR EQUIPMENT'S whirring, buzzing and knocking welcome me home, along with hip-hop music bouncing off the walls. Someone else might take a few extra days off work to recuperate from a parent's death. Me? I need to work, especially now, when so much is riding on our success or failure. If today's experiments go like I expect, then we'll be one step closer to a wildfire prevention solution.

Judging by the music, Tony got here first. Rachel would be torturing us with Lana Del Rey or something equally depressing. Julio would be blasting something by Gabriel Fauré, or, if he and his partner were arguing, the love songs of Brazilian duo Elis and Tom. I'm cool with all of it. As soon as I'm working, the sounds will fade into white noise.

I got into science because it made sense to me and I loved it. Meeting Celeste reaffirmed what I already suspected. The true value of our work in the Albright Lab doesn't lie in producing eco-friendly items people can buy at Shop Smart. We're saving lives, preventing trauma, preventing chronic and life-threatening illnesses. At least, that's the goal. If today's tests prove successful, we'll be closer to achieving that goal and can move on to Phase Four.

Used to be, I'd see news of a wildfire and envision a charred forest. Sad, for sure. But the real cost is the people we lose and the emotional havoc endured by their survivors, like Celeste and her mom and grandmother.

Whatever else is happening in my life, being in my lab, surrounded by creative energy, knowing I get to use science to make life better brings my body and mind into a state of bliss. It's almost like a trance, except my brain is fully online, amped to solve problems.

Today, Julio and I will test the new and hopefully improved hydrogel. We believe we've found the right flowability and slip to allow long-term retention of the fire retardant most foresters use on plants. We need this to succeed.

I make a point of stopping by each lab bench to connect with the folks who are hard at work so early on a Monday morning. At every damn bench, I receive condolences, concern about my loss, empathy. Exactly what I do not want to deal with right now. Work is my escape from all the heavy emotional lifting I've been doing these last few months. Now that I'm here, and everyone's bringing it up, walking on eggshells, I realize how damn exhausted all that grieving has made me. All the difficulties the female fast has raised regarding my relationships seem like child's play compared to what went down in that hospital room. Give me a pleasant work distraction, please.

I step to the middle of the lab and raise my voice. "Yo, listen up. Happy holidays. Welcome back. All that. I appreciate your well-wishes and sympathies. But like I always say, we wanna keep this lab safe, we need to leave our problems at the door. Myself included. I'm happy to commiserate over a beer after work, but in here, I need to focus. Clear?"

A chorus of seven chemists and biologists shouts, "Clear." Hopefully, they'll inform the other nine members of the lab as they trickle back from their vacations in the next week.

At one bench, I stop to sniff the ethyl acetate, appreciating its sweet, fruity smell. Then I move to Julio's bench. He's strapping the go-pro to his forehead. "Big day ahead, Julio. You ready?"

"Ready and primed." Julio does a little shadow boxing to prove his point. He whistles his excitement.

"Fantastic. If Phases Two and Three go well, which they will, then we'll call CalFire." I throw him a high five. "Catch up with you in a minute."

At Rachel's lab bench, I receive a micro-gaze and a nano-smile before she redirects her attention to the microscope. "Josh, you're putting in an order with Sigma Aldrich today. Right?"

"Yup. Over lunch."

"I emailed you, but also want you to hear I need more supplies for my biomimetic soil cleanup project."

"Right. Hydroxyethylcellulose—"

"Yes. Also methylcellulose and ludox."

"Got it. How's the project?"

"Close, but not quite there." Frustration tightens her voice and the muscles around her mouth.

"Sounds like progress, Rachel. Take your time. There's no rush."

"Except my funding's running out."

"We'll take care of that together, alright?"

She rears away from the scope, stares at me like I have three heads.

"You're doing great. Don't be so hard on yourself."

"You look like my boss. You sound almost like my boss. But this... softer, gentler version..."

I groan. "Damn. Have I been that hard to work with?"

She squeaks, quirks a brow. "I've definitely worked with bigger ass—" She presses her lips together.

Assholes? I want to crawl under a rock, but I force myself to look directly at her. "Wow. Shit. Put a pin in that because this is a conversation we definitely need to have, maybe as a group. For now, let me apologize. I'm sorry for any pain my words or general attitude have caused you. Okay?"

She looks up, finally meeting my gaze, exuding vulnerability. How did I not catch this before? The woman listens to Lana Del Rey for Christ's sake. She nods and turns back to her lab bench.

Finished making the rounds, I retrieve the hydrogel materials from the chemical safety cabinet and return to Julio, who's setting up the tripod in front of the chemical fume hood looming on his workbench. Have I been an asshole to him, too? To everyone? His resting cheerful face and open expression make him look relaxed. Is that how he actually feels?

Julio turns on the body-cam and the camera he placed on the tripod. I hold a pile of hay in front of my chest and explain the process. "In Phase Two of our experiment, we're using fire and bedding hay. Hay is a good proxy for dried grass, which you'd find on any roadside, hiking trail, or yard. We'll be conducting the experiment in this chemical fume hood, but first, we need to prepare the samples outside."

Julio rolls his eyes at my dramatic tone of voice, so I lay it on thicker, like they do on reality TV shows. I explain our process as he follows me outside, the go-pro camera rolling. I spread a clean tarp across the cement, followed by twelve piles of hay, and use a standard garden sprayer to apply the fire retardants. Half the hay gets our hydrogel. The other half, I douse with the product our forest service uses. With a third garden sprayer, I simulate a half-inch of rain.

Meanwhile, I narrate, "The retardants firefighters use now work great if there's no rain between the application and ignition. But rain, heavy dew, even high winds will flush that material into the soil where it can't do any good. When someone throws a burning cigarette onto the roadside, or pulls their overheating car off the road, the grass ignites. We designed our hydrogel to stay put through the whole fire season, even when it rains."

But will it? When we tried last fall, it washed right into the soil. I banish that memory, dry the hay samples, and focus on this experiment, narrating my actions as I place treated hay into four small burn chambers. "Recognize this?" I ask the hypothetical viewer. "Looks suspiciously like the charcoal chimney starter you use to get your grill going, right? Same hollow metal cylinder with holes on both ends. Same small wire grate inside. The only difference is what we're putting inside. We're using hay and chemicals."

Julio follows me as I bring the chambers back inside the lab. I put two with pink hay on the left side of the fume hood and two with our gel on the right. "Our burn hood ensures any smoke is vented outside. Not that we'll have any smoke. This also guarantees any toxic fumes will be filtered and vented outside. Of course, even if the hay burns, there shouldn't be any toxins."

To illustrate the non-toxicity of our product, I hold a dropper bottle in front of my face like we practiced. In the past, I shoved products at the camera, which Julio said threw the image out of focus.

"Our hydrogel is made from silica (basically sand) and cellulose (sugar polymers that come from wood or cotton). Cosmetics and food manufacturers modify viscosity with hydrogels. Our product also contains ammonium phosphate, the key ingredient in the fire retardant the US Forest service has used for seventy years. Ammonium phosphate is so non-toxic, it's even used in baking. Still, we put extra safety measures in place. We have twelve canisters to run three rounds of tests. We filled six chambers with hay treated with our clear hydrogel. See how it gives the hay a gloss? We treated the hay in the other chambers with the commonly used fire retardant. It's pink because firefighters drop this stuff from planes. The color shows the pilots where they dropped it."

Inside the burn hood, we have four metal stands with gas lines and ignitors underneath. I put the first four chambers inside the chemical fume hood, turn on the ventilation, and start the fire. The black metal chambers glow orange as they get hotter, and the analyzers on the bench across from the fume hood show the temperature rising. My temperature is also rising, and my body hums with excitement. With each round of tests, the hum inside me increases. We're using simple metrics. In three rounds of tests, the pink hay is engulfed almost immediately after flame exposure. But even after ten minutes of exposure to fire, the hay treated with our gel doesn't burn.

I'm ready to spontaneously combust with joy.

Before we move onto phase three, we need to finish recording the data. I try not to look over Julio's shoulder as he completes the task, but I'm so excited I can't resist. Still, I apologize.

Julio shrugs. "Whatever, Josh. I'm used to you."

Ugh. Guess I've been an ass to everyone.

We break for lunch, and when we return, we begin Phase Three.

We're outside, wearing protective gear, preparing all the samples at the same time and storing some for later to make sure everything is consistent in each round of burns. Outside, we have bigger hay samples, and use a standard garden sprayer to apply the fire retardants, simulate rainfall with another garden sprayer, and let everything dry, then light the fires with a blowtorch. Watching my product perform better than the pink stuff again, I'm unable to keep the jubilance out of my voice as I speak into the camera. "Again, our gel outperforms the traditional fire retardant."

These lab results prove my work could save countless human lives and God knows how many species of wild creatures. It could save our pets, forests, homes, our places of worship. On top of that, it could keep our water and farm fields clean. How do I know? Because all the research happening right now, mostly in Colorado and California, reveals when wildfires spread to communities and burn homes, commercial buildings, and cars, those vinyl sidings, paints, tires, electronics, lawn furniture, and plastic toys create toxic ash. It falls into our waterways and onto our soil, creates massive pollution that we end up eating, drinking, and bathing in. How much of that might be prevented with our product?

I raise my hand to Julio. "I need a moment." I blow a puff of air and drop into a forward fold, elbows on my knees, head hanging loose.

Two hours later, I'm celebrating the biggest success of my career over dinner with Julio. Neither of us can stop smiling. "What are we gonna call this, boss?"

"I hate to name it before we run the field tests."

"Come on, Josh. After today, you know that's just a formality. We're golden."

"Golden," I repeat, dazed, elated, simultaneously unsurprised and completely blown away. We're golden. Golden, except for the dark hole inside me. I always envisioned celebrating moments like this with Celeste, but I can't call her, text, or even send an email. I take a long pull from the craft kombucha. Of all my projects, this one excited Celeste most. She's always hated fire. If her dad and grandfather hadn't responded to the 8-Eagle Canyon Fire, they might still be alive. And her mom... Celeste's whole life would've been different. Today's success will mean a lot to her. I drum the table. Julio waves his beer in my face. "Boss! Yoohoo."

"Sorry, Jules." I shake my head to clear it. "What were you saying?"

There is one other person I need to share this news with. She may not answer my call, but if nothing else, I can leave a voicemail.

I may have failed to be the role model Satya needed in relationships, but we share a passion for science, and at least I can be the role model she needs in her career.

16

Josh

TEN PM EAST COAST TIME. IS IT TOO LATE TO CALL MY daughter? We're family, not strangers. If she's willing to hear from me, I doubt she'll quibble about the time. Besides, if she's anything like I was, she still habitually stays up well past midnight.

I look at the reflection in the sliding glass door. "Quit hemming and hawing Josh. Make the call." I walk onto the deck, dial the number.

Two voices in the world have the power to fill my heart with joy, and one of them just said hello.

"Hey, Sweetheart. It's great to hear your voice."

"Thanks."

She sounds unenthused about talking to me, but I'll take what I can get. "How are you?"

"Fine."

"Glad to hear it. I've got some exciting news to share with you, but I don't wanna ignore the elephant in the room, either."

"Oh?"

"I heard your disappointment about how I treated Celeste. I don't blame you. You're right, and I'm sorry for being such a shitty role model of what you should be able to expect in a relationship."

"Thanks."

"I sense there's another reason you stopped talking to me, though, and I don't know what it is."

A derisive laugh comes through the line, sucking the wind out of me.

I sag onto the deck, letting my legs dangle off the side. "Satya, honey, I love you. I'm pretty sure I fucked up, but I honestly don't know how."

"Ugh." She sounds disgusted with me. Great.

"If I can make up for it, I will. If I learned one thing last week, it's the power of a sincere, well-planned apology. Your grandmother gave me that before she died, and it meant everything."

"That's nice."

"Come on, girl! God, I wish Celeste was here to help."

"She really did smooth things over between us, didn't she?"

"Oh. I said that out loud?"

Satya laughs.

"Hey, I made you laugh. There's progress."

"Not in a good way."

My kid's getting her thousand cuts in, that's for sure. "Satya, what can I do? I know I fucked up. Unfortunately, I will again, but there's no one in this world who means more to me than you. I would literally do anything for you. You get that, right?"

"Come off it, Dad. What have you ever done to show me you'd do anything for me?"

Shit. I take a deep breath, stalling for time while try to imagine how Celeste would handle this. "I thought I was showing you that every day. Guess I missed the mark by a mile."

"Guess so."

"Can you tell me about your experience with me?"

"Your friends suck."

"Satya," I protest.

"Yet you chose them over me."

"No, I didn't."

"You asked for my experience. Do you wanna hear it or not?"

"Sorry. Go ahead."

"I flew across the country alone to spend time with you. Alone. Just us, but we always had to meet up with Terry or Brent or that super fake yoga teacher."

"They love you."

"Please! They love themselves and you love them. It felt like I was interrupting your life."

"Oh, Satya. When you came out, you were my life. I am truly sorry that I ever made you think otherwise. I thought including you in my social life and bringing you to the lab was good parenting."

"The lab visits were fun."

I sigh, relieved. "Glad I did something right. I thought it was important for you to see who I was and for my friends to know you. I wanted them to love you like I do."

"That backfired. Did you see how Terry and Brent acted toward me at the memorial?"

"I picked up a weird vibe. What happened?"

"They gave me the evil eye, like I didn't belong there. Like they resented my presence."

"Oh, Rainbow, I'm so sorry."

"Neither one offered me condolences at my grandmother's memorial."

"Jesus."

"Right?"

"I had no idea my friends made you feel unwelcome that day."

"That day?" She scoffs. "They've made me feel unwelcome ever since I was a kid."

"What?" This makes no sense to me. "How? Didn't you enjoy playing with Terry's daughter?"

"Dad, I told you she was mean."

"That's how kids are. I thought you'd work it out," I mumble, as the reality of my child's words starts to hit me.

"I was always so sad when I came home. Mom would ask why. I tried to hide it because I didn't want you to get in trouble."

My kombucha curdles in my stomach. My child was protecting me. Meanwhile, I was oblivious to the pain I was causing her. "Your mom figured it out, I bet."

"Yup. I think I was around seven when she pried it out of me."

Which explains why Lynn went from cold to arctic. I wish she had said something. Did she? Did I dismiss her because of the tension between us? "Satya, I'm amazed you hung on for as long as you did. I can't excuse my behavior. Honestly, I don't know what the hell I was thinking or how I could have been so fucking clueless."

"I assumed you didn't care."

"Remember what Celeste said to you when we were cleaning out Grammy's house?"

"She said a lot of things."

"That you are now and always have been the most important person in my life. It's true. One reason I love Celeste is she's the only woman I've been with who recognizes that and supports it."

"Oh."

"I'm gonna have to unpack this with my therapist, sweetie, because I honestly don't know how I could have been so blind. Only thing I can think is I was reacting to my dad's behavior. When I visited, he hired babysitters, so I barely spent any time with him at all."

"Sounds painful."

"Yup. I was trying to do better, and it seems I actually did worse. Fuck. I'm so, so sorry, Satya."

I thought I could call my daughter and share an important moment in my life. I thought I could show her I can still be a good role model in some ways. Now, hearing she felt everything was about me and my needs and not about her, I realize this isn't a good time to share my news.

"I've gotta go, Dad. It's late."

"Okay, Rainbow. I love you. Thank you for opening up to me tonight. It means a lot. And I want you to know I'm doing everything I can to be worthy of your trust and of Celeste's trust. She may never take me back, but for the first time I really understand her perspective and I see a way forward, out of shame and into love, and I'm doing everything I can, Satya."

"That's good, Dad."

"Can we talk again sometime?"

She's silent a little too long. I'm about to give up, when she says, "Um... yeah. I'll call you. Okay? In a while."

The tension in my chest releases. "Great! Goodnight."

I stare at the dark phone screen for a while, imagining her smiling at me. If Celeste were here, that would've gone better.

Shifting my gaze to the sky, I drop my hands to the deck, the smooth teak grounding me. The biggest moment in my career and instead of sharing it with the women who matter most to me, all I can do is speak into the black night. At least the sky is clear tonight. I scan the constellations until I find the Pleiades. "Well, girls, it looks like the Albright lab has found a way to prevent wildfires. We'll know more after we test it in the field, but so far..." I go into way too much detail, considering I'm talking to a collection of gaseous bodies light years away.

Why am I talking to stars, when I know two people who will celebrate with me? I text Amira and Lila. They send congratulatory texts, then a video call. "We want details, Uncle Josh," Lila says, her New Orleans accent seeming especially strong tonight.

I oblige, and while the story seems to energize my niece, my sister's eyes are crossing. "Awesome, bro! We are so proud of you, right Lila?"

"Makes me wanna do my earth science homework." She blows a kiss and disappears.

Amira smirks. "Can you call every night?"

"Sure."

"This is huge. Why do you seem sad?"

I tell her about my chat with Satya and what she said about my friends.

"Wow," Amira says. "Talk about emotionally immature adults."

"They probably don't understand. Terry's the only other parent in the group."

"Derek doesn't have kids of his own yet, but—"

"Yet?"

Amira's face lights up, but she puts her finger to her lips. "Shh."

My hurting heart floods with joy. "Congrats! When?"

"We'll find out this week."

"That's wonderful. Keep me updated."

"I will. Anyway, he has always gone out of his way to let Lila know she is my priority, not him."

"Celeste tells Satya the same thing."

"Of course because, like Derek, Celeste has emotional maturity."

"And you're saying my friends don't."

She sighs. "I'm not saying they're bad people, but can you grow with them?"

"I have been for twenty years, Amira."

"Growing and hanging aren't synonymous. How are they supporting you through the fast?"

"They say it's ridiculous."

She gives me that know-it-all look, especially annoying coming from someone whose diaper I changed. True, it was just the one time, and I made such a mess Tanya would never let me do it again, but that's not the point. My baby sister is still talking.

"...guys in the program," Amira says. "I know you're more social than me. I prefer a few ride-or-dies over a crew of party people."

"I can count on these people for anything."

"For emotional support? Seems like you can count on them for a good time. That's what they tried to give you when they felt uncomfortable at Ellen's memorial."

"Doesn't the fact that they showed up say something?"

"Totally. They want to be supportive, but their idea of support is to pull you away from the things that help you grow, like grieving. First, they took you away physically, dragging you outside with them. Then they tried to take you away emotionally, offering you pot, so that you wouldn't have to feel the pain."

As usual, she makes sense, and I hate it.

"But that pain is how you honor your mother and the complex relationship you shared. And I was so proud of you for choosing to feel. That's crucial for your mental health."

Praise from Little Miss Bossy Pants. It feels remarkably good.

"The female fast is another growth opportunity," Amira says. "One you chose, so you can become a man who can handle and enjoy the deep intimate relationship your heart craves."

"True."

"Which must scare the shit out of your friends because when you get closer to Celeste," Amira flinches, "or find someone new, they risk losing you."

I stare at the constellations. "You're saying my friends are sabotaging me?"

"Maybe."

"Why would they do that?"

"Maybe they're afraid of deep emotional work? Incapable of it? I used to think you were incapable."

I groan. "Thanks, sis."

"But you're showing all of us you wanna be real and emotionally intimate with someone. And what does it take?"

"A fuck load of work."

"Exactly. Not everyone is up for that, but you are."

When we end the call, my body feels lighter. I lay back, eyes wide open, replaying both conversations in my head, noticing the feelings each thought triggers. As if the emotions were elements on the periodic table, or strands of DNA, they wash through my cells in waves one after another. Relief. Joy. Sorrow. Loneliness. Regret. Hope. Love. Each has its own signature. Each lights a different part of me. Which is the greatest of these when each has such profound teachings?

17

Celeste

BRIGHT SUNLIGHT CARESSES MY FACE AND WARMS ME despite the winter chill. It's significantly warmer than it was back east. Still, I pull my shearling jacket tight around me, and let the cafe door close behind me. I sip my lavender matcha latte and brace myself to face my colleagues in the co-working space. It's been months since I've been here, and they're bound to have questions. Questions I do not want to answer.

I don't want to talk about how Josh is, or what happened, and are we still together, and why not, and but I went to the memorial service and helped him and... Chances are, his well-connected friends have already been gossiping about all of it.

Note to self: never again date someone who has a reputation for breaking hearts. Never again believe that you might be the special one who can make them want to be faithful. As cruel as the saying is, it bears truth: I am not a special snowflake.

Okay, Celeste, here you go. Hand on the door handle. Feel the metal. Ground yourself. Feet on the pavement. Pull. And walk in, smile politely, pass everyone as you go directly to the office that you rent. Excellent! Slide the glass door open and shut. You have made it to your safe space. Hallelujah.

Light the incense in the corner. Take a moment. Close your eyes. Breathe. Count to nine, eighteen, fifty-four, one hundred eight. It feels weird to be here. Before my client arrives, I set the intention to be fully present, to provide a safe space for her to work through the blocks keeping her from the loving, committed relationship she wants with her boyfriend. I am a nonjudgemental container. I take another sip of my latte, feel the creamy burst of lavender on my tongue. Yes. I can do this.

By the time my client arrives twenty minutes later, I am ready. I greet her with open arms, invite her to sit and get comfy. Everyone loves the chairs in this room, so cozy, like a hug. So plush. Who doesn't like quality velvet? Oh, but she's talking and I'm thinking about upholstery fabric. Not a good start.

I take a deep breath, meet her eyes. "Shannon, let's begin again, shall we? Start with a nice deep breath in."

She inhales with me and exhales slowly as I lower my hand, indicating the beginning and end of the breath. We repeat several times, looking into each other's eyes, getting connected.

"Good. Now, tell me again, Shannon. How are you?"

"I'm better now," she says with a gentle laugh. "I forget how sometimes I storm into a room and just start talking. As we took that minute or so to connect, to just breathe and look in each other's eyes, I realized how helpful that would be with Kyan."

I nod, affirming her newfound awareness. "An important insight. Did anything else come up for you?"

"It's so rare that he and I connect like that, and I can see how if we're just getting together and I burst into the room," she shoves her hands forward, illustrating, "talking a mile a minute, not even taking a breath to connect with this man who I love so much…" She pauses, shaking her head in disappointment. "I can see how he might feel unloved. He might feel like I'm attacking him."

"Attack. That's a very strong word. Where does that come from?"

"That's how he describes me, and then I usually say, 'then why are you with me?'" Shannon's voice rises and she bobs her head, getting worked up again. I take a slow, deep inhale, lifting my hand to get her to breathe with me. She does, closing her eyes on the exhale. "Then we have this big argument and yell and storm out."

"And we know the results of that," I say quietly.

"I'm in a relationship where I seem to be the only one who wants commitment."

"Is the story you're telling yourself."

"With good reason, because right now he's avoiding commitment, and I can't say I blame him. Now that I'm seeing this pattern of mine and how it must feel." She slumps forward, resting her elbows on her knees and her chin in her hands. Her posture and gaze tell me she's discouraged when she has every right to feel proud of herself for the boost in self-awareness.

To highlight her achievement, I say, "You're already envisioning a different way. What if we take that to the next level? With the caveat that your vision may play out differently than you hope or plan. Can you see how coming in with a more joyful story might help you to turn your desire into reality?"

"Definitely."

"So, let's create that together. You walk in. Where are you?"

"I'm arriving at his house."

"What time of day is it?"

"It's the end of the day. We've both just finished work. We're exhausted."

"Okay, and what happens?"

"I take a deep breath before I even enter the room and exhale and smile because I'm about to see the man I love." Her face relaxes, indicating the fantasy feels real to her.

"Beautiful. Then what happens?"

"I say, hi, softly, and I wait for his reply."

"Ooh, and how does he respond?"

"He says, hi." She smiles.

"And?"

"I ask: 'how are you?' And I wait for his reply."

I nod, not wanting to interrupt her flow with my words.

"And he looks at me, maybe a little confused, but I just smile and deepen my breath, look into his eyes, enjoying this moment to connect, and then he deepens his breath. I don't know if it's on purpose or if he can't help himself, like when I'm with you."

I nod again, to encourage her. She keeps going, and I'm right there, holding that safe space. Listening, gesturing for her to continue, letting her know I'm fully present. Until she says that thing about Kyan that reminds me of Josh.

Suddenly, I'm lost. This has never happened in a session before. I feel him blaming me, shaming me as if his cheating was my fault. I'm living in that memory instead of the here and now, held hostage. Shannon's mouth is moving, but all I hear is Josh. If you hadn't put so much pressure on me. Why couldn't you just relax? It was a mistake. Why can't you let it go? On and on. I've done everything wrong, and he did nothing beyond reproach. Tension is flooding my muscles, making me want to scream.

Luckily, Shannon's voice breaks through the noise in my head. She's agitated, as if she's picking up my feelings, infected by my trauma. Not that it's a trauma. Only a betrayal. It's only affected how I see myself and the world and what I believe to be true.

And now she's got it, too.

"Do you know what I mean?" she asks.

"I think so," I say, though I have no clue what she said or how long I spaced out. "Shannon, sometimes, we pick up on the emotions that other people are feeling. Has that ever happened to you?"

"I think I know what you mean," she says, eyes wide.

"Let's breathe again."

I am such a fraud. Here I'm trying to tell her how she can heal her relationship, whatever's causing her—*Okay, Celeste. Breathe. Inhale. Slowly, deeply release.* Judging myself will not help me help her. Instead, I suggest, "What if we do some breath work? We haven't tried that yet, have we?"

"No." Again, she looks like a deer in headlights, wide eyed, excited. Is it Botox or eyeshadow highlights?

"You're not pregnant?"

"Not yet." She smiles.

"Not on any medications?"

She shakes her head.

I instruct her in a breathing technique that has helped me and so many others. We spend the next ten minutes doing only that.

We finish and review her vision and her strategy. She takes notes, and I pray to God she got something out of the breath work because I can't imagine how anything I said helped her today. Yet she's beaming and thanking me effusively as she opens her calendar app to schedule our next visit. "We are so lucky to have found you, Celeste. You're our hero."

I can't do this.

18

Four Months Later

Josh

WHEN I WAS LITTLE, MY DAD WAS MY HERO, AND I followed him everywhere. This made it especially painful when he didn't show up for my first science fair or anything else after the divorce. But Mom drilled my hero worship out of me after Dad left. Tragic in some ways. Then again, if Mom hadn't been so relentless, I might've followed in Dad's footsteps, using science to make rich White men richer.

Now, I follow the men and women of CalFire San Luis Obispo through an empty field to the test plots we prepared with them six weeks ago. Julio's bouncing like he's itching to shadow-box with fire. I'm burning an internal flame so bright I swear it's flowing out of my pores. Guess we're both eager to conduct our final site tests on the hydrogel's efficacy. The data we'll collect at these highly controlled burns will (I hope) prove that our hydrogel can truly be of use.

As it happens, today also marks the end of my six-month female fast. If our tests are successful, I get to call Celeste and share the news. She'll appreciate it more than anyone I know. Of course, even if we succeed today, we still have months of soil tests to conduct, especially since we had to adjust the viscosity after our attempts last fall.

"Rolling, Josh," Julio says, switching on the body-cam attached to his forehead.

I need to keep my eyes on the ground, so I don't trip, but I glance into the lens briefly, addressing our hypothetical viewer. "Indigenous people have used controlled burning as a wildfire prevention tool for centuries. In the right location and circumstances, prescribed burning is an excellent tool. But the logistics are a bitch. Shit, can you cut that last line, Julio?"

He flashes a thumbs up, then moves his hands to indicate he's still recording and I should continue.

"But the logistics are challenging. California requires you to write a burn plan that maps out your process, plus a smoke management plan, then get air-quality permits and burn permits from Cal Fire. Only a certified Burn Boss can lead the endeavor. I'm a firm believer in prescribed burning as part of a bigger tool kit. So far this year, the Forest Service has intentionally burned 10,000 acres, a tiny fraction of California's 33,000,000 forested acres. That leaves 32,990,000 acres untreated. Of those acres, the state estimates 22,000,000 need management, with either prescribed burns or fuels removal because they're overgrown. In theory, they would apply our treatment to areas at risk of ignitions, which is only 5,000-10,000 acres. Today, we're with the good people from CalFire San Luis Obispo. My colleague Julio and I get to observe while they put our hydrogel to work."

Julio turns around in a circle. I guess he's getting everyone on camera. He moves in a bunch of weird ways when he's recording. I've learned not to question his methods. The videos always look good. Facing me again, Julio points, and I continue.

"If we succeed now, the state of California, homeowners, and communities everywhere could have a solution in time for this fire season."

As we approach the test plots, I explain what video viewers will see. "Six weeks ago, we separated this field into sixteen ten-foot-by-ten-foot quadrants and gathered soil samples. We prepared each quadrant by putting a bucket in the center to leave an untreated spot that will ignite. With the buckets in place, we sprayed our gel over eight squares. We sprayed the pink fire retardant over the other eight squares. After gathering soil samples from the treated quadrants, we simulated a half-inch of rainfall, gathered more soil samples, and left the area completely exposed to the elements. Today, we'll arrive at the moment of truth. We'll start here, gather our data, then go to our roadside test site in Wildcat Canyon."

Andreas, a hulking firefighter who looks like he stepped off the cover of a romance novel but has a shockingly high voice, calls our names and holds protective gear aloft. The gear we wear in the lab is flimsy compared to the heft of these neon overalls, coats, masks and boots. Maybe the fire department's heavy gear is overkill, but given how fire can leap and jump, even create its own weather systems when it spreads, I gladly slip into it. Why take chances?

Properly attired, and with the go-pro stowed out of harm's way, Julio sets up the video drone. I open my phone's voice memo app, stow the phone under the protective gear, and speak into my earbuds.

Andreas lights a fire in Trial Plot #1, which we treated with the standard-issue pink stuff. The grass in that plot burns to ash in less than a minute. I describe everything in the voice memo. My breath catches as Andreas moves to Trial Plot #2. He's about to test our hydrogel. I'm rooted to the uneven ground, watching him ignite the untreated bit in the middle. It burns rapidly until the flames reach the edge of the untreated area. Our gel extinguishes the fire, preventing flames from spreading. I release the breath I'd been holding. One down, seven to go. Andreas repeats the controlled burn on each of the other plots. We get the same results every time.

As the last fire goes out unassisted, the energy I was bottling up shoots through me and I leap into the air, screaming, "Yes!" The heavy gear pulls me to Earth with a thud.

Julio and I high five each other, Andreas, and the other firefighters. They laugh at my antics. This vivid moment forms a picture in my mind:

Burly men and one woman in neon gear, masks off, soot-tinged faces upturned in laughter.

Julio shadow boxing, exuding pride.

Hazy wisps of smoke spiraling around us.

Remnants of our success in this golden California field.

What I wouldn't give to capture this on film, hang a print on my wall, send copies to Celeste, Satya, Mom. Ouch. I gaze at the sky and silently ask Mom if she can see me, if she knows the good that I'm doing.

But I'm getting ahead of myself. We're not finished. I turn to Andreas and the crew. "Wildcat Canyon?"

"Change of plans." Andreas thumps my back. Striding toward his white fire department SUV, he opens the closures on his jacket and strips it off.

"What's up?" I ask, keeping pace with him as I unhook my fire jacket.

"Crew's not coming with us."

"Okay," I say slowly, confused. We already prepared the site. Why would they refuse to run the trials?

Andreas stops my internal questioning. "This, you need to see. Come on."

The guys and gal driving the fire trucks shake my hand, thank me, and head out. Julio and I finish removing our protective gear and hand it to Andreas. We get into my black Jeep and follow Andreas' vehicle to the canyon. At the test site, I spring from the driver's seat, eager to see what's up.

"Three nights ago, we received a call about an ignition," Andreas says. "Crew responded ASAP and found this."

We step over the low guard rail and follow Andreas to a partially burned tree rising from the hillside. Charred grass surrounds the tree and extends all the way to the sandy shoulder and downhill a few feet. Beyond that, the field looks much the same as when we treated it six weeks ago.

"By the time they arrived, there was nothing for them to do. The fire had already extinguished itself."

This news sends a shock wave of electricity coursing through me. I'm gonna need a strenuous workout to move all this energy. "What caused the fire?"

"No clue. A fire started here. That's crystal clear, but in the treated zone it just went out."

"It just went out," Julio repeats.

Andreas catches my gaze as he puts a hand on my shoulder and one on Julio's. "Josh, according to our fire modeling, that fire should have burned a full acre by the time the crew got here."

"Your fire modeling," I say, dazed.

"Based on the heat, wind, and humidity levels that evening, this fire should have spread."

"My God."

"You still need to run that test?"

I shake my head and kneel by the small area of charred land. I crumble grass stubble between my fingers, bring the debris to my nose. It smells like charcoal, clean charcoal, not the awful burning chemical smell that's been wafting through California air every fire season.

"This is convincing proof, my friends. Something caused an ignition, but instead of spreading, the fire extinguished itself." Andreas' voice sounds like it's coming from somewhere else, like this is a dream. "Those of us at CalFire who've seen the data, we're just waiting for our supply of... what are you calling it, anyway?"

"Don't know yet." I lay a hand on each side of the tree. One side appears dead and feels lifeless. The other side still has leaves and pulses with subtle energy. "This tree might survive," I murmur. "Julio, feel this."

Julio runs his palms over the bark on both sides of the tree. "Whoa." The awe in his voice mirrors my feelings.

We're materials scientists having a metaphysical encounter with a half-dead, half-alive tree. An experience we made possible through our research. I've been working toward this, planning for it, expecting these results. Still, I think I'm in shock. Until now, all of our experiments have been within our control. But nature took over this site, giving us data that we could never have planned. Nature proved definitively that we can prevent wildfires.

"Josh, Julio, please sell this shit ASAP. We need it yesterday. Other scientists are working on tech to sense fires when they ignite. That helps us respond faster. But you prevented a fire that could have turned into a massive blaze if anything kept our crew from getting there in time to stop it."

You prevented... I'm processing this information in my head throughout the drive back to the lab. Sell this shit ASAP. How?

Luckily, the university offers support to scientists who invent products that can be manufactured at scale. When I walk into my office, I have a new task list in my head that includes writing and submitting the report on our findings to peer-reviewed journals. *Nature* and *Science* top my list.

Before all that, Celeste. With luck, she'll come out tonight and celebrate with me. I call the florist and order two dozen red roses with a card that says, "Celeste, I have fantastic news I'm psyched to share with you. Now that the female fast is over, I can. More important, I've worked hard to become the man you need and can trust. Can we start over with dinner tonight at Chez Magnifique? All my love, Josh." I book reservations online, in case she says yes.

The next person I want to tell is Satya. Over these four months, we've taken baby steps toward each other, repairing our relationship bit by bit. Having her back in my life is the greatest gift. She's grown into a kind and remarkable young woman who makes me outrageously proud. I open the messaging app and re-read the text she sent this morning:

Good luck today, Dad!

Now I write back:

> **We did it! Hope we can celebrate together soon.**

She sends me a GIF of an animated tree doing a happy dance. Cute.

By the time I say goodbye to my team in the lab and walk to my Jeep, I'm fried. My phone alerts me, again, to a voicemail that came through two hours ago. I listen as I get into the driver's seat. The florist couldn't deliver the flowers. Celeste no longer lives at that address.

That can't be right.

I ponder my options as I make the fifteen-minute drive home. The home that isn't home without Celeste.

I slump into one of the teak chairs on my front porch and dial her number, envisioning her beautiful smile. Her voice comes through the line.

"Celeste, it's Josh."

"Oh. Um, hi."

"Hi. How are you?"

"Good." Caution in her voice. "What's up?"

"My female fast ended. And I have great news I'd love to share with you over dinner. I tried to send you flowers, but the florist said they were undeliverable. You moved?"

"Yup."

"Oh. Uh, would you like to meet at Chez Magnifique and tell me about your new—"

She cuts me off. "I can't."

"I understand it's last minute. Another night?"

"I moved to Connecticut."

"What? When?"

"Couple months ago. There's nothing left for me out there, and I'm happier here."

My heart drops. "Good for you."

"Thanks."

"I don't suppose you're coming back to Cali."

"Going back to Cali?" She laughs. "Ha! I don't think so."

I sigh. "Guess I can't blame you."

Is this it for us? I've worked so hard to become the man she deserves, and I haven't had the chance to show her all I can offer. But it's not my choice.

19

Celeste

How could I be anything but happier here? My BFF's wide-eyed, expressive three-month-old gurgles in my lap as Josh asks about my plans. I make the silly face Felicia loves, and she chortles. "Anyway," I say into the phone, "I can't chat. I'm on kid duty."

"Felicia? Sage sent pictures. What a cutie!"

"Yup." I shouldn't blame Felicia, especially since Sage is in the other room and could totally take her child. I'm here to help, so Sage can putter without an infant strapped to her chest. The truth is, emotions are coming up. Emotions I've spent the last few months working through. Right now, I prefer to avoid that dark place.

"Listen, Celeste, can I see you?" He sounds different, more peaceful.

My breath catches in my throat. How do I respond?

"I can fly out, combine it with a trip to visit Satya."

"Satya. Is she... are you..."

"We're rebuilding our connection. It's been incredible."

I'm stunned. When Satya took off after the memorial, refusing to say goodbye to her father, I doubted she'd ever let him into her heart again. That she did makes me wonder if it's safe for me to, also.

"My female fast helped me learn how to be the father she needs, even as an adult."

"That's wonderful, Josh."

"I also learned how to be the kind of partner you deserve, if you're open to it."

I gasp. Those words tug at a loose string, threaten to unravel something inside me. I can't unpack this now. Do I need to?

"Can I come see you?" he asks. "I could fly out this weekend if you're free."

"That's two days away, Josh. Flights will cost an arm and a leg."

"It's worth it. But if you're busy this weekend, I can come next weekend, or..."

His timing is incredible, reaching out when I was finally starting to move on. While Josh throws out dates, I look for answers in Felicia's chubby cheeks and bright blue eyes.

"I can't stop you from getting on a plane, but you won't be staying with me. And I may not have time to see you. If you still wanna come, and I'm free while you're here—"

"That's great, Celeste." The brightness in his voice sounds forced.

"I'm not promising anything, Josh."

"Understood. Your reticence makes sense."

My heart pounds. "It does?" I know it does, but the last thing I expected was for Josh to understand, never mind validate my feelings.

"After the pain I caused you, I can only imagine how hard it must be for you to consider seeing me. It makes me appreciate your honesty and openness more. Which weekend is best for you?"

I guess I have to tell him. I inhale deeply and let the words fall with my breath. "I have a date Friday night."

"A... date," he repeats.

"Saturday morning, I need to write. I may have free time Saturday afternoon."

"I'll book flights and a place to stay. Any recommendations?"

"There are a bunch of Air BnBs in my neighborhood." My mouth is betraying me by encouraging him. Sure, it's exciting, but I don't need this kind of excitement.

"Great, I'll find something and let you know my travel plans. I can't wait to see you, Celeste."

"Bye, Josh." I end the call, stunned by his words and my reactions, by what's about to happen in two days.

He sounds so different, so humble. Josh has every reason to be pompous; he's achieved a lot in his field. But I always found hubris his most challenging character trait. That is until infidelity reared its ugly head.

"Did I hear you talking to Josh?" Sage asks, striding into the living room, making a silly face at her baby.

The weight of this child in my lap is heaven, so I appreciate Sage letting me hold her a little longer. "Is it bad that she's my comfort object?"

"Not at all. Felicia is my comfort object, too, sometimes." She kneels by the couch to meet her baby at eye level and coos, "Though we know that's not your function. Mommy and Daddy are your comfort objects all the time."

Sage kisses Felicia's cheek until she laughs and waves her chubby little arms.

"He sounds different, Sage."

"Yeah." There's an all too familiar look in Sage's eye.

I've seen that look many times in the years since we roomed together in college. "You know something."

"Me?"

"Twenty-five-years later, you still suck at feigning innocence."

She laughs. "What can I say, Cece? I'm a hopeless romantic. I love you. I love Josh."

"You're avoiding the question."

"I'm happy he reached out to you. That was brave and you need that quality in a man."

"He's always been bold."

"Not in relationships. That's why he kept cheating his way out of them."

"Fair point."

"As for you, I'd hate to see you take all the risk, but I'm proud you're risking your pride a bit. You may get the closure you've needed or, perhaps, a fresh start."

I nod, considering Sage's words as she joins us on the couch. Felicia launches herself at her mother and Sage speaks as if reciting a nursery rhyme.

"Your relationship is a rose bush. It started with big beautiful blooms."

"A rose bush. Clever metaphor, given my near-obsession with roses."

"Near obsession?" Sage snorts, then resumes cooing the story at her infant. "The fragrance was amazing and intense, the color startling." She lifts Felicia above her head until the baby chortles. Another sound escapes, eliciting a groan from Sage. "FiFi, did you save that for Mommy?"

I follow her upstairs to the nursery as she continues. "Everyone wanted to be near that rose bush, to absorb a little of its gorgeous essence. But sometimes, when it needed the most care, the rosebush got neglected." Sage strips her child, drops the dirty clothes into the hamper and changes her diaper.

As much as I've wanted a child, this is one part of parenting I don't mind missing, at least not too much. Unfazed by the stink and the mess, Sage keeps spinning the allegory of my relationship with

Josh, describing how the roses on our bush withered and died. "Like every perennial plant, you and Josh had your hibernation period. Now, it's spring, and you're blooming again. Who knows what these blossoms will be? They could be even more breathtaking than before."

"You forgot about the part of the rose bush no one, not even me, likes."

Our eyes meet and we finish my thought together. "The thorns."

If I give Josh a second chance, can we do better this time?

"That was lovely and poetic, Sage. Josh and I probably lasted as long as we did because we wore thick gardening gloves, so we rarely got pricked. When a thorn did prick us, we rushed to fix the tiny hurt."

Sage hands me her freshly diapered child and continues her tale. "Then a thorn grew so big that it poked through Aunt Cece's and Uncle Josh's gloves and caused a deep wound."

I follow Sage into the bathroom, mimicking her storytelling voice while she washes her hands. "So Aunt Cece tried to cut the rose bush down and throw it into the wildfire that was already consuming her. That's why the best she can hope for this weekend is closure." Felicia's rapt attention makes me giggle. "Besides, I have a date Friday night."

Sage turns to me wide-eyed. "With whom?"

"Elijah."

"And I'm just hearing about this now? My two best friends are going on a date, and neither of you told me until now? That's it. You're both on my shit list."

I feign a sheepish look.

"Hmm," she says, drying her hands. "Cece and E. Pulling each other from the stronghold of grief. This could be beautiful."

20

Dear Celeste,

We just spoke on the phone. If I could create a formula to replicate how your voice makes me feel, I could sell that drug and be a wealthy man. Did I mention the success of the trial? I was so stunned to hear you moved to CT; I think I forgot. The reticence in your voice was clear. Your uncertainty about seeing me makes sense. So I'm especially grateful that you're willing to connect when I fly to New Haven this weekend.

Maybe then, I'll tell you our site tests went better than expected. I'm nervous and excited about the possibilities for the gel.

I feel the same about the possibilities for us.

Now that we're on speaking terms and my fast is over, I might bundle all these letters and mail them. Maybe I'll wait until after our visit. Should I include the first few? Reading them made me cringe.

All my love,

Josh

21

Josh

As soon as I get off the plane, I text Celeste. **Landed. Can't wait to see you!**

The airport in Hartford is so tiny, it only takes five minutes to get out of the building. At ten-fifteen PM, the ride share drops me off outside my AirBnB. I scan the sidewalk. This is Celeste's neighborhood. Is it crazy I can feel her presence? If she had replied to the texts I sent from the car, we might be having a drink or taking a stroll under the stars. Instead, I use the access code to get into my rental. It's cute, in a Martha Stewart kind of way. Now that I've got privacy, I call her. Straight to voicemail. Shit.

"Hey, my flight was delayed, but I'm in your neighborhood. Are you up for a nightcap?"

I'm still on west coast time, which probably explains the energy thrumming through me. Of course, knowing I'll see Celeste soon is having its own effect. I wish I could reach her. Ten-thirty PM on a Friday night in New Haven. Is she out?

That's right. She's on a date. Fuck. Celeste is probably having a nightcap with her new man. How long has she been seeing him? Do I have a chance of winning her back?

The AirBnB welcome book says, except for a couple of bars, everything in this neighborhood closes by ten PM. Even on the weekend. Damn. Plan B it is. Shower. Journal. Bed?

Not this early. Maybe I'll take a walk. She made her ambivalence about seeing me clear. Was coming here a mistake?

Celeste

ELIJAH AND I GAZE AT THE FULL MOON FROM THE PORCH SWING, holding hands. This moment has all the ingredients for romance, except one: chemistry.

He bought and renovated this home with Farah. Their children were born here. Her presence is everywhere. "It's getting late," I say. "I should go home."

"I've had a lovely time with you, Celeste." Elijah turns toward me and gazes into my eyes. In his, I see the truth of what Sage told me at her wedding reception: part of Elijah is in the grave with his wife.

"Me too. Hanging out with you and seeing the girls was so fun."

"We communicate real easy," he says, his Oklahoma drawl and casual phrasing belying his Ivy League education.

"Like no time has passed since college."

"I'll walk you home."

"You don't have to leave the girls. I can walk alone."

"They're snug in bed. The house is locked, and I won't be long."

"True, but—"

"I'll feel better knowing you're safe. Alright?"

"I'm not used to anyone protecting me. It's nice."

"I'll just text Ellie to look after her sisters." He pulls his phone out and messages his daughter.

We stand. I'm not short, but Elijah towers over me, tall and muscular from cycling and construction work. He definitely makes me feel protected. I lean into him, enjoying his clean male energy.

We hold hands as we walk through the quiet, dark streets, talking about how our neighbors have decorated their homes. Nervous anticipation rises in me as we mount the steps to my porch. At the door, Elijah turns me to face him, tucks my hair behind my ear. I look up into his warm, open face; into those dark big, dark eyes with lashes that make every woman jealous.

"May I kiss you good night?" he asks.

"Yes."

He pulls me close. Through his button-down, I feel firm muscles and body heat. Elijah bridges the gap between us, his breath warm on my mouth. I want to kiss him, but my body has other ideas. My head shakes against my will and I step back. "I'm sorry," I say, surprised at my relief.

"Are you alright?"

"Yeah."

He bends down to catch my gaze and takes my hands. "That didn't quite feel right, did it?"

I shake my head. "It seems like it should. We're super compatible. I know if I can trust anyone, it's you."

He smiles. "Maybe we're both still grieving. Maybe the timing is wrong."

"You think?"

He chuckles. "Nah. I've always liked you, Celeste. You're beautiful and kind, brilliant as fuck. Funny. We're perfect on paper. And I love holding your hand, touching you, but—"

"No chemistry."

"None. I hope we can hang out more, though."

"Me, too, Elijah. Friends?"

"Definitely."

He bounces down the steps with more energy than he's had all night.

LIGHT FROM THE FULL MOON BEAMS THROUGH MY WINDOW and wakes me at an ungodly hour. Five AM on a Saturday. Ugh. Trying and failing to fall back to sleep, I get out of bed, set water to boil for tea and scroll through my phone. Four text messages from Josh. One voicemail. He's here. For me. Maybe it wasn't the moon that woke me but my body's response to Josh's arrival. I text: Good morning. Call when you wake.

By eleven AM, I've practiced yoga, meditated, started some laundry, cleaned the bathroom, written a chapter in the new relationship book, and met with a client online, all while trying to ignore the nervous energy coursing through me. Now, as I stroll down West Rock Road and gaze at the kids playing basketball in the park across the street, a knocking sound grabs my attention.

Behind the cafe's plate glass windows, Josh waves animatedly, a beautiful smile on his full lips.

Gorgeous as ever.

He's let his hair grow out a little, so that dark red really pops.

I'm a nervous wreck. Josh is here for me. Smiling like he's never seen anything more wonderful than me. What do I do with that? I try to keep Sage's words in mind. It's brunch, not a life commitment. By the time I reach the table, he's standing, pulling out a chair for me, opening his arms.

"May I hug you?"

Okay. Wow. Already, he's different. I walk into his embrace. He pulls me close, whispers into the top of my head. "It is so good to see you, Celeste."

I'm afraid to tell him just how good it feels to hold him because... well, because I'm afraid to trust him.

"Thanks for coming," is what I settle on. It feels inadequate, even insulting. Ugh.

We both order coffee with almond milk, something I never drink at home.

Without preamble, Josh tells me all about the successful trials of his fire prevention gel. He's always focused on his work. What's weird is that his words carry no trace of hubris. Hearing about the tests, I can't help affirming him. "Josh, that's amazing. I am so impressed by you."

His eyes light up. "That means a lot."

He holds my gaze, and all the old feelings return. Comfort. Safety. Love. Danger. I flash a quick smile and pick up the menu. "What are you in the mood for? The moros y cristianos is yummy."

"Not sure. But I need to tell you, Celeste, this was the biggest moment in my career so far. It could do some real good for people."

"All of your work has done good for people."

"This could be bigger, and I had a hard time celebrating the achievement."

I brave a glance at him, arching my brow in question.

"It didn't mean as much to me because I couldn't share it with you."

My eyes flood. "Josh." I swallow, overwhelmed.

"Is it okay that I'm sharing how I feel?"

I nod, biting my upper lip, trying to hold myself together.

"Can't tell you how good it feels to share this with you."

We both order vegetarian Cuban brunch. What blows me away is how, except when he's ordering the food, Josh focuses on me. His phone rests face down on the table, vibrating, ringing, dinging, and he keeps his attention on me. Who is this man? The Josh that I know is hyperaware of his responsibilities all the time, super focused on the importance of his work.

The conversation continues effortlessly through brunch, through the walk to West Rock Park, through our hike up the steep rocky path to the top of the hill. Josh gives me his full attention the entire time, offering his hand to help me over fallen trees, moving branches out of my way. If I'm not careful, I could get attached to this feeling of being the center of someone's attention.

At the top of West Rock, we sit on adjacent boulders to catch our breath. I'm enjoying the view of the neighborhood and the distant hills when a baby's giggle fills the air.

Josh looks around, confused. "Did you hear a baby?"

"It's Sage's text tone," I explain. "I made it from a recording of Felicia. Do you mind?" I ask, pulling out my phone.

"Go ahead."

I scan the message. "Sage and Wesley are inviting us to dinner tonight. Wanna join them?"

"I'd love to see them and meet Felicia, but I'm here for you. What would you like to do?"

I laugh.

"What's funny?"

"Who are you?"

"Come on."

"Old Josh would decide for us without asking what I wanted."

He winces.

Shoot. I wasn't trying to make him feel bad. I'm tempted to say something to soothe him, but snippets of Sage's rosebush story repeat in my mind.

I explain, "We kept watering our rosebush, fertilizing it, but we never treated the disease in the soil."

"Huh?"

"That's why it died."

"The rosebushes are alive and well in the backyard. I've been tending them for you, hoping you'd come back." That earnest and confused look in his eyes makes me want to take his hand.

"It's a metaphor. But thanks for tending the rosebushes. Not that I'm going back. I'm happy here." Happy enough anyway. I hoped moving would erase all the hurt. Like a change in scenery and lifestyle was all I needed. I forgot the most important thing to change in the healing process is me. God, it's hard work.

"Oh." Josh's face falls. "I thought we were talking about dinner with Sage and Wesley. Then you said I decided things without considering how you felt. I'm missing the metaphor."

"You chose what worked for you and I went along because I avoid decisions and wanted peace. A lot of our relationship was like that."

"Like what?"

"Soothing little hurts while ignoring bigger issues," I explain. "But you know what I've learned?"

"What?"

"I appreciate being asked."

"Good. I learned I enjoy asking, taking you into account. And I hear you're happy here. Now, I have to take that into account."

I meet his gaze. "Thank you." I take a swig from my water bottle, offer it to Josh.

"Thanks." He accepts the water. Wow. I forgot how much I enjoy watching him drink, the way his lips curl around the water bottle. I close my eyes. This is not a helpful train of thought right now, not when we're getting closure.

And that's all this is. I cannot reunite with Josh. This sweetness is endearing, but I don't know how to trust him. I don't know how to trust my judgment. I'm still trying to figure out how to forgive myself for trusting him the first time.

Josh returns my water bottle and helps me stand. "I learned a lot in this fast, Celeste. A lot about what I was doing wrong and how to do better. You already know I did the program with you in mind. But if all the changes I've made in my MO don't bring us back together, I'm glad I learned how to be a better man for all the women in my life, my colleagues, my sister, my niece, and especially for Satya. I feel comfortable in my skin. You know? Never realized I didn't before, but self-acceptance, self-compassion, self-love... that's some powerful shit."

"Truth. Are you seeing Satya this weekend?"

"That girl is super busy. I'll visit her in two weeks. Love to see you then, too, if you have room in your schedule for me."

"I'll check my calendar." I already know whatever's on my calendar, I'll make time to see him, and that scares me.

SAGE AND WESLEY WHIPPED UP AN AMAZING VEGAN MEAL THAT we're enjoying in the backyard. Josh has been nursing the same glass of wine all evening, setting it aside often to charm Felicia. She seems as much in love with Josh as he is with her. Josh also developed a fast bromance with Wesley.

Now, Josh mentions water pollution caused by wildfire ash, and he and Wes are off and running. Apparently, they've read the same toxicology reports from Colorado State University. Josh holds Wesley in sway as he talks about his experiments at the Albright Lab.

I understand Wesley's excitement. Josh's work is amazing. But the way Wesley's practically vibrating his enthusiasm strikes me funny. I bite my lip to keep from giggling, as he says, "Your hydrogel sounds promising. How often are you measuring soil chemistry?"

"After each rainfall. From fall, through winter and spring of last year, the treatments produced no alteration on soil chemistry or plant health."

I catch Sage's eye across the table, and we have a silent conversation. ***Looks like we lost them***, Sage says with a grin and an eye-roll.

I arch a brow and dip my chin to say, *Yup. They're in their own world now.*

Wesley whistles. "When will you release the product?"

"CalFire San Luis Obispo is chomping at the bit. It may take time for other counties to adopt."

"What about releasing it nationally? Globally?" Wesley asks.

"Once we get through U.S. Forest Service red tape…"

I'm about to jerk my head toward the door, to suggest Sage and I go inside to get dessert when Josh touches my arm. He catches my gaze. "We've been ignoring you. Forgive me." Now, he's caught my breath, too. Apologizing for diverting his attention from me? At a dinner party?

"Clearly we need to have a man-date," Wesley says.

Josh beams. "Agreed."

Two hours later, I park in front of his AirBnB. Josh asks if he can hug me goodnight. I step out of the car and he comes around to my side. When we embrace, I expect him to do that thing where he pulls back, catches my gaze, then leans in for a kiss.

Instead, he tucks a tendril behind my ear. "I had a wonderful time with you today. Would you like to meet for tea or breakfast tomorrow? My flight leaves at noon."

"Come over at eight. I'll make something," I say, stunned. Disappointed. Excited. Damn it. Confused.

"See you then," he says and goes inside. Josh never even reached for my hand, and he loves holding hands. Josh's affectionate nature is one thing I've always loved about him.

After today, I'm craving more than a goodnight embrace. Yet as I get ready for bed, I realize I'm relieved Josh didn't make a move on me. To my surprise, I feel more respected by Josh not making his typical romantic gestures than if he had. Instead of declaring his love or acting romantic, Josh showed me how he feels simply by paying attention to me. The caring in his eyes, his focused attention, the deep listening and vulnerability he expressed… I never knew I needed these things in a partner. Weird because I definitely promote them in my books and sessions with clients. Why did I think I didn't need or deserve the same level of care that I tell everyone else to request?

I always loved Josh's expressions of affection, but now I see that on some level they were also performative, like "Look, I'm being a good boyfriend." Today, his presence felt real, not like a show. Was it? And can it last?

22

Celeste

WORDS ARE FLOWING IN THIS CHAPTER ON EXERCISES that promote compassion in a variety of relationship types. The unexpected benefit of writing this book is how it's helped me heal. True, I had to skip the chapter on forgiveness. I'll write that chapter later.

The doorbell rings, breaking my flow. I open the door to find a man with a bouquet.

"You again?" I tease.

He grins. "I know we should stop meeting like this, but what can I do? Someone seems smitten with you. Can't say I blame him."

"Aw, thanks! Have a great day, Jim."

He returns to his delivery van. I close the door and place the blooms on the mantle next to the other bouquets Josh sent in the week since his visit. Daffodils and eggplant tulips with white striations and frilly-edged petals. The tulips might be my favorite.

I hate to admit that I love this. I love this. I love that Josh is sending flowers and calling me every night, texting every morning. Our conversations have been more real than ever. He's being more open, expressing his feelings and his vulnerability.

Newly uplifted, I return to my writing and knock out a thousand words in an hour. A new high for me.

Then it's off to the meeting space I rent at the co-working studio. My first session of the day is with a pro-bono client. Thanks to all the great press I've gotten for my work, I command high fees. Generally, people are happy to pay my hourly rate. Every once in a while, someone reaches out to me who wants help but doesn't have the funds. I'm so grateful to have reached this point where I can work with them for free or a reduced rate.

Since moving to New Haven, my sessions have been strong. Now, I remember why my clients like me. I can feel and see that I'm truly helping them. And I've discovered that what I offer isn't despite my failed relationships but because of them. I have lived many ways a relationship can fall apart. I know heartbreak from the inside. And I now see how some of my tendencies have played into my relationship breakdowns.

So, I'm gratified and not surprised when Natalia books a second and third session and leaves my office with a huge smile on her face. Although some of my work feels like therapy, there are distinct differences between how I work as a coach and how a therapist works. One biggie is that I have each client make commitments to themselves at the end of every session. Then I email them, reminding both of us about the commitments they made during our meeting.

Natalia declared that over the next two weeks she will meditate for five minutes every day and journal about her feelings. Plus, when someone she's close to—usually her mother, but sometimes her children or her husband—is getting on her nerves, Natalia will call a twenty-minute time-out and take a walk to burn off the anger rising inside her. Then she'll ask herself a series of questions: *Why is it bothering me so much? What need are they trying to express? Is it a need I can meet? What do I need in this situation? Do I feel comfortable asking for it? Why or why not?* These tactics help build self-awareness and compassion for the other person.

I'm excited for Natalia that she took on so much. At the end of the email, I remind her that following through on any one of these commitments will help her. The last thing I want is for my client to berate herself if she forgets to meditate or journal, or doesn't take a time-out during a conflict.

Part of my work with clients is helping them discover when they're asking too much from themselves versus when they're not challenging themselves enough. I think Natalia might be overreaching. This kind of enthusiasm is not unusual for new clients, and it's totally okay. If she is overreaching, then in our next session we'll get to talk about self-compassion, and how not meeting our expectations can lead to insights about what's realistic based on the situation, our personal challenges, etc.

Right now, though, I send the email praising her for making the commitments along with the recording of the session. When clients listen to the recordings, they usually find it powerful.

My next session starts in fifteen minutes. I meditate for ten, take three to review notes from this client's last session, then welcome Zander. He enters my office with a huge smile on his face. He reports feeling like a different person, enjoying his relationship with his girlfriend and her seven-year-old daughter more than ever. We dive into the work.

Ninety minutes later, I send Zander a follow-up email, pack my devices and notebook, and walk home. In the mail, I find a postcard from Josh with a beautiful botanical print of a California Wild Rose.

That's the closest he's come to saying "I love you" since we reconnected. Why do I feel angry? Maybe I should ask myself the same questions I sent Natalia. What a pain in the ass.

JOSH AND I HAVE ANOTHER BEAUTIFUL VIDEO CALL AS I'M getting ready for a bath. For some reason, I start crying.

"What's going on?" Josh asks, concern in his voice.

Good question. My stomach tightens. "I don't know. I guess it's just all so unexpected."

"Is it okay that I'm calling and sending you things?"

"I love it." I wish I hadn't said that. "I mean, it's a lot after so long with no communication."

"I'm making up for lost time, but I don't wanna overwhelm you, Celeste."

I sniffle, smiling my appreciation through my tears.

"You know, I'm visiting Satya this weekend. You could come join us, or I could get up early Sunday morning and drive down to you before my flight."

"That's a lot of driving, especially for a guy who hates to drive. One-and-a-half hours from Amherst to New Haven, then another hour back to Hartford?"

"It's worth it to me."

My heart flutters even as the tightness in my stomach intensifies.

"And judging by your expression, I'm guessing you feel conflicted about seeing me."

How do I respond? I don't want to hurt his feelings when he's being so kind.

"If you want to meet up in Mass, I'm sure Satya would love to see you."

I inhale deeply, trying to understand my reaction. "Can we talk about it later in the week? It would be wonderful to see her, but I don't want to interrupt your really important father-daughter visit."

"Thank you."

The tub is full. In another situation, I'd undress and sink into the bath while we chat, but I can't do that now. "My bath is ready. I'll talk to you later, okay?"

He emits a little groan, which makes me giggle.

"Sorry." He looks down, like he's done something wrong.

"It's nice to know I still have that kind of effect on you."

Josh lifts an eyebrow, opens his mouth, closes it, purses his lips in that sexy way he used to when we were moving toward physical intimacy. His eyes sparkle and I can tell he's dying to say something smutty. I kind of wish he would. Maybe it would get me out of this weird emotional state. Instead, he takes a deep breath and says, "Good night, Celeste. Enjoy your bath."

I slip into the water, fantasies about Josh rising. I cannot let these images take hold. Yes, we've shared many delightful baths, but I'm here alone for a reason. Why would I think I can trust him again? I don't even know if I can trust myself.

Sage always has helpful advice. I text her about the situation, share how scared I feel. She doesn't respond. She's probably asleep with her devoted husband and adorable baby. She and Wesley are living the life I thought I would have with Josh. Another fantasy about our relationship that had no hope of coming true.

I killed the chance to have a baby by ignoring my pain and my needs. Why? Because I was afraid to be needy. Because if I didn't have needs, then I couldn't get angry about unmet needs. And I wouldn't say things that make a person leave.

I take a deep breath and submerge myself under the bathwater, then lift my face up so I can breathe. Staring at the ceiling, I see my pattern play out before me. In one relationship after another, I have put loved ones first, taking pleasure in their pleasure. My Nana, my friends, they all reciprocated. They even tried to get me to put my needs first. The men in my life did not. They took and took. Including Josh. No wonder I feel angry. What would I tell a client in this situation? *Don't fight your emotions. Feel them.*

Screw that.

WEDNESDAY, SAGE TEXTS ME.

OMG, Cece. Sorry. Overwhelmed. Not ignoring you. Coffee next week?

Definitely. LMK if you want a sitter. I'm free tomorrow night and Friday.

> Thanks. Babysitters aplenty. Mom here
> all week.

That explains everything. Sage and her mom have never been on spectacular terms. The love is there, but sometimes it's hard to see. **Hang in there.**

Friday night, Josh texts me a photo of him and Satya. They look so happy together; it uplifts me.

> Satya and I are hiking up Mount
> Norwottuck tomorrow. Wanna meet us
> for dinner in NoHo after?

> Is she okay with that?

> She suggested it.

Now he sends a two-second video of his daughter saying, "Please come, Celeste."

> Aww. How can I resist that request?

Saturday night, we meet at what is probably the best Indian restaurant on the East Coast. A superb choice for many reasons, one being that chatting about the food helps us avoid other, more emotional, topics. Being with Josh and Satya like this—happy—feels kind of like it used to, like we're a family again.

When Josh and I were together, I always thought we'd round out that family with a child of our own. There's a train of thought that leads nowhere good. I must be telegraphing my distress because Josh reaches across the table to put his hand next to mine. "You okay?"

I force a smile. "Just tired. This is the best baingan bharta ever, though. The ginger and chiles are perfectly balanced with the garlic. And the texture..."

"Good?" Satya asks.

"Perfect. Not too oily. Seriously, you guys, try it."

Josh takes a spoonful of the smoky eggplant dish, moans his delight, and artfully changes the subject, bragging about his daughter. Her face lights up.

After dinner, we stroll downtown Northampton, chatting easily about Satya's life and how much she loves living in the area. "I can't see myself ever moving. Like you, Dad. You always said you'll stay in Wildbranch 'til the end."

"I used to feel that way. Lately, I've been reconsidering that."

That shocks me. "But your lab, and—"

"I know it seems a little crazy. I'll tell you more later."

"Okay." Why the mystery, Josh?

"I've been reconsidering a lot of things in my life lately, you know? Right now, I'm really enjoying being with both of you. Honestly, it's the best moment of my week."

My heart melts, and I catch Satya's gaze. It looks like she's feeling mushy, too. "By the way, Celeste, Dad and I got you something." She hands me a little paper box tied with raffia ribbon.

"Thank you." The hope in Josh and Satya's expressions is so sweet. I untie the bow, remove the lid, and find a tiny gold rosebud on a gold chain. "It's lovely. Help me put it on?" I extend the pendant to Satya.

"Turn around," she says.

I do, meeting Josh's loving gaze while Satya slips the chain over my head and fastens the clasp.

Josh smiles. "It suits you."

They walk me to my car, and Satya and I exchange numbers and invitations. I hug them both goodbye, and wave as I pull away from the curb. About ten minutes into my drive home, I start shaking. I think I'm in shock.

23

Celeste

A WEEK LATER, I'M FEELING SPOILED BY ANOTHER SIX bouquets, three cards, daily phone calls and texts exchanged with Josh. Felicia reaches for the gold rosebud pendant. I hold it up for her to see and touch. "That's a flower."

Sage leans in to see. "Pretty. Where'd you get it?"

"Josh and Satya bought it for me in Northampton last week." I tuck it into my shirt and make a silly face at the baby.

"Ahh." Sage's voice squeaks through a range of notes.

"Yes." I don't hide my annoyance with her matchmaking tone.

"Fill me in," she says, sliding a stack of shirts across the coffee table, then reaching into the laundry basket for more.

I give her the broad strokes while trying to entertain Felicia with a range of toys. All the baby wants is the pendant. All her mother wants is details, so I take a deep breath and dive into the nitty gritty, icky, confusing mess. In the time I take to tell her everything, she folds all the laundry in the basket.

"You sound angry, Cece."

"No. Maybe. I don't know. I keep thinking, why couldn't he have done this before?"

"Probably because he wasn't ready."

Of course, she's right. Annoying. Also annoying is what she left unsaid—that Josh is rare in his willingness to see where he needs to grow and then make the effort. Felicia fusses in my lap, rejecting the colorful rattle and reaching again for my pendant.

"Fifi, Aunt Cece doesn't want you to play with her necklace. How about the bouncy seat?"

"I'm the relationship coach. Why are you better at this stuff than me?" I ask, putting Felicia into the seat suspended from the doorjamb.

"I couldn't coach anyone to save my life. But I know you really well, and I know how much pain you cause yourself by meeting other people's needs while ignoring your own." She crouches by the seat and coos at Felicia. The trust, adoration, and exuberance in that child's face as she watches her mama—heartwarming. Heartbreaking. How long will I grieve that loss?

"My therapist says the same thing," I admit. "Because I ignored my needs and let myself be invisible, I will never have the experience I wanted most: to be a mother. That's why I'm angry with Josh. I held on believing we would have a family together."

"You gave Josh everything you knew how to give. He still betrayed you. What the fuck is up with that? Right?"

"Exactly."

"I'd be pissed, too."

She sees me. It's in her gaze, her words, and the way she moves to sit beside me on the couch. This connection is one reason I can't imagine my life without Sage. She adds, "Also, Josh has worked super hard over the last six, seven months now to change. I see it. Amira and Derek see it. It sounds like Satya does, too."

"Yeah, Satya mentioned how different he is now."

"Right? So, he's been doing the work to be the man you need, and the father that Satya needs. But you didn't get to witness this. Neither did I because I'm one of those females he had to ignore, other than when he sent a baby gift. But Amira had a front-row seat."

"I can't ask Amira about her brother."

"True, and one reason we love you is you keep clear boundaries with friends. Not so much with boyfriends, though. But Cece, Derek has been working with Josh closely. He can't open up about specifics, but he says Josh isn't that guy who cheated on you anymore."

"He could become that guy again."

"If he wanted to. But he doesn't. So what do you gain from holding onto anger and hurt?"

"I can't help it."

She squeaks. "But you kinda can."

"It doesn't feel safe to trust him."

Sage puts an arm around my shoulders. "I understand. Maybe the answer is to try a fresh approach. What if you treat the emotion like a challenging yoga pose? You don't resist Garudasana."

"True. I breathe through the intense sensations Eagle Pose creates in my thighs."

"Imagine the anger is a pose. Breathe, then ease out of it, like you release a tough asana."

"You think it's that simple?"

"You'll have to repeat the process. With practice, over time, it'll get easier, just like strength-building yoga poses."

"I guess it's worth a try."

"It helps me deal with my mom. She can't help having narcissistic personality disorder. There's no hope of her changing. So I work through my frustration about that in yoga."

"Maybe I'll make an angry yoga playlist."

"Oh, my God, yes. And please share it with me."

THE SUN RISES OVER THE ROOFTOPS. I STEP TO THE FRONT OF my mat, ready. Kendrick Lamar, Kanye West, and the Beastie Boys express how I'm feeling. As I move, I let primal screams of pent up rage rip through me. My neighbors probably think someone's dying over here, but I don't care. I'm sustaining Goddess Pose, breathing into and through another wave of fury. Yeah, it was sabotage, just like the Beastie Boys sing. I feel powerful moving from Goddess into a challenging Vinyasa flow. I breathe intentionally, using full inhales and exhales to propel me from forward fold into plank, Chaturanga, upward dog, downward dog, forward fold, mountain, repeating the sequence over and again as Kendrick assures me we'll be alright.

But will we? Now the part of the playlist that brings up all the feelings begins. The release, the crying. Thank God I'm doing this alone. I'd freak someone else out.

By the time I'm done, I'm sweaty, snotty, cried out, and my muscles are wrung out. I feel cleansed, energized, forceful. I think I'll write a chapter in the book about this, but right now, I need to journal about it. I pour a glass of fresh green juice and take my journal onto the patio. As I write about my angry yoga practice, I realize part of the problem was that Josh could never handle my difficult emotions. If we argued and I felt angry, he withdrew, which made me even more angry. That has to be why he couldn't accept I wanted a child. So now, the feelings are out. He doesn't know about them, but that's okay. I need to work on myself first.

24

A BEAUTIFUL BOX ARRIVED TODAY. INSIDE, I FOUND A stack of letters bound with silk ribbon, from Josh. He tied a single wild California rosebud on top. Between each leaf of paper was a pressed flower, mostly roses, but also lavender, pansies, hibiscus, and some flowers I couldn't identify. The fragrance is wonderful.

Along with the letters, he included recipes, culinary grade rose petals, and three cupcakes, each a dairy-free, gluten-free variation of Persian Love Cake:

Chocolate with cashew rosewater cream

Hibiscus with hibiscus rosewater syrup

Saffron cardamom with orange blossom rosewater syrup.

Josh spent hours searching for recipes, then experimenting to create the perfect cake for me. It's not a reason to take him back. But his letters...

I've spent the last three hours consuming each note as slowly and tenderly as I did each bite of cake. The progression of his mindset within them gives me hope.

All these months, I thought I was foolish to cling to the idea that we could reunite. I moved across the country, threw myself into work, healing, and friends—anything to build a new life alone because I was sure the one I wanted was impossible.

Now, as I swallow the last bite of the saffron Celestial Love Cake, my favorite of the samples he sent, and lick the syrup from my fingers, I think perhaps it's safe to hope after all. Time will tell.

A tear splashes onto the last page. I dab at it quickly, not wanting to smudge a single mark.

Dear Josh,

This simple Thank You note seems inadequate compared to the beautiful gift you sent with the collection of letters and pressed flowers, and those outrageously delectable cakes. Truly, though, reading your letters and journal entries helped me see your dedication to growth. I almost felt I was going through it with you. Thank you for your vulnerability and for the way you love me.

xo Celeste

25

Josh

OU'D THINK AFTER BEING COMPLETELY CUT OFF FROM Celeste for four months, I'd be able to handle a two-week separation. But these last two weeks since our dinner in Northampton have felt excruciating. How could I not miss this woman who's telling me about her angry yoga playlist as we stroll through her quiet neighborhood after dinner? The light of the setting sun highlights the contours of her face, the high cheekbones and straight nose, the arches of her brows.

"What?" She laughs. "You have the funniest expression on your face."

"Just appreciating you. This moment. The day we've shared."

She smiles. "I've been enjoying your visits."

If my body was a cartoon, you'd see little hearts flying out of my chest right now. "Did I mention my AirBnB has a hot tub?"

She gasps. "You know I love hot tubs."

"Mm-hmm. So I'll think of you while I'm enjoying it all by myself tonight."

She side bumps me. "Jerk."

I grin. "Oh, did you want to join me?"

"You know I do. Mind if we swing by my place first so I can get my bikini?"

"Not at all." My heart drops a little. When I think everything's going great, then I'm reminded: not quite. Celeste never wears a bathing suit in the hot tub, unless it's a public tub and we're around strangers. She's not shy about her body, and that confidence is one thing I love about her. Do I say something?

No. Whatever her reason, whether she's feeling less confident than she used to or she's afraid of what might happen between us, that's hers. During the fast, I came to recognize how rarely Celeste speaks up about her needs, and how often I used to shut her down when she tried. That she's speaking up, even casually, now shows she's been working on herself, too, and I'm proud of her. Thanks to the program, I now know when Celeste states a need, and it's within my ability to support her, it's my job and my privilege to do so. Luckily, I brought my swimsuit, too.

Twenty minutes later, the bubbles rise around us, soothing my aching muscles. "Man, flying takes a toll on the body."

"You've been doing so much of it lately. It's probably getting old. Huh?"

"Yeah, but the rewards are far too great to stop."

"You mean those frequent flyer miles?" she teases.

"Oh, yeah. That's what I'm talking about," I joke.

She looks into the water, then at me, then back at the water. Something's up.

She takes a deep breath and meets my gaze. "So, Josh, since your female fast ended, have you been seeing anyone? It must be a relief to—"

I interrupt. "Celeste, no. I'm waiting for you. Or waiting for you to tell me there's no hope and I should give up."

A hint of a smile lights her eyes.

"You had a date a couple weeks ago," I say, trying to ignore how the words turn my stomach.

"Yeah."

"How was it?"

"Lovely."

"Oh."

"An old friend from college. Super hot. The guy everyone crushed on."

"Great," I say, my heart sinking.

"But we're going to stay friends."

Relief floods me like a drug.

She giggles. "Sorry for laughing at you, but..."

"Wow. You're not even trying to pretend you're laughing with me."

She smirks. "How can I? You're not laughing and I've never seen you look so relieved."

I play it up, fanning myself. "Whew! Hallelujah."

She giggles.

I throw my arms in the air. "They're just friends," I yell into the night.

"Josh," she laughs, nudging my shoulder. God, what her touch does to me. I meet her gaze. It's playful at first, then turns serious.

"What'll you do if I tell you to give up hope?" she asks.

I let out a puff of air. "Tough question. Probably grieve a while then see what happens."

"With whom?"

I hold my hands out. "I can only see myself with you. That's been true since our first date. I know I hurt you deeply, Celeste. Whatever happens between us, I'll probably regret that for the rest of my life. But I would like to leave the past behind and see what we can create together. We had real promise before I fucked everything up, and—"

"It wasn't just you. I pressured you nonstop to do something that you said from the beginning you didn't want."

"You mean having a baby?"

"Yeah."

"I should've been more open. In fact, I want you to know I am." She's shaking her head like she doesn't believe me.

"I know being a mother is important to you, and—"

"Josh."

"How could I ever think it was okay to keep you from the joy—"

"Josh, no." She shakes her head.

"...the joy that I've had as a father? It was selfish of me, and—"

"Josh, really. Stop."

I look at her, confused. "I want you to know I'm willing. You don't have to sacrifice that."

"Actually, I do." Her voice shakes.

Shit. "What?"

"I found out last November. I can't get pregnant."

"Why?"

"Years of untreated endometriosis. Years of thinking I needed to take care of my Gram and work and clients and boyfriends while ignoring the pain I was having with every menstrual cycle. I thought it was normal, that I could ride it out. Grit my teeth, get through it."

"God, Celeste. I'm so sorry. Being a mother was important to you." My heart breaks for her.

"Yeah." Her voice is flat, resigned. "I appreciate that you came around, though."

"I'm not kidding. I'm serious about you." I want to reach for her hand, to hold her, but now's not the time. Instead, I inhale slowly and focus on her eyes, hoping she can see the sincerity in mine. "Celeste, I love you."

She smiles. "That's the first time you've said that since…" She lets her voice trail off and a mix of emotions crosses her face.

"I thought you needed to see it and feel it before I said it."

"You were right. I believe you now."

"Thank you. That makes me feel seen. Can I say more?"

She nods.

"I love that you are the kind of woman who gets pissed off and makes an angry yoga playlist. I love how you treat your friends, the way you are with my daughter. I love seeing you succeed and hearing how much your clients benefit from working with you or reading your book. I love that you are so multifaceted and so intelligent. I can talk to you about my nerdy science things, and you're right there with me, geeking out over polymers. On top of all that, you're stunning. I have never felt so attracted to anyone as I have to you."

"Truly?"

"Truly. Can I keep going, or should I stop?"

"You can keep going." Her demeanor is shy and sweet.

"Celeste, if I'm celebrating an accomplishment, I wanna bring that celebration deep inside you, to amplify it and spread it to every cell in my body and fill you with it, too. If I need comfort, I want you. I don't need to be in an altered state to find you attractive. You draw me in whether you've got dragon breath or layers of dirt and sweat coating that smooth skin. There's never a moment you don't turn me on. You've seen that. Right?"

"In the past, but—"

"I have literally never found you unattractive."

"But… that woman."

"I was drunk off my ass. And hurting. If I'd been sober, it never would have happened. If you'd been home, it never would've happened. Not to blame you. I'm the asshole who walked into a trap of my own making. But I need you to know it had nothing to do with your attractiveness, nor hers. She's nothing next to you. You understand?"

She nods.

"Is it okay to share this?"

"Yeah."

"Celeste, right now, after everything, honestly I would be so grateful if you would kiss me or let me kiss you."

"Could you stop there?"

"If that's what you want."

"What if I want you to kiss me? What if I need proof that you really do find me attractive?"

"May I?"

She bites her lip.

I slide across the hot tub seat, drop my voice, murmur in her ear, "Are you asking me to kiss you?"

"Yes."

"Come here, baby." I pull her close, breathe her in. This feels like the first time. There will be no going back after this. Where we'll end up is anybody's guess. I'm eager to find out, though. I tuck a long, wavy tendril behind her ear, call her by that special name I've only ever said when we're alone. I feel her cheek rise against the side of my face and I slide my lips across her high cheekbone down to her mouth. Her lips are parted. "Are you sure?" I ask, sending the words into her mouth.

"Yes."

I brush my lips across hers, a featherlight touch. She responds, caressing my lips with hers. We explore each other tentatively, moving slowly toward closeness. Her breath tastes delicious. I've been waiting so long and I've missed her so much. I'm taking my time, savoring this gentle reconnection, hoping she is, too. "Is this alright, Angel?"

"Mm-hmm."

Emotions well up and spill onto my cheeks.

"Josh, are you crying?"

"Yeah."

She pulls back and touches my face. "You never cry. Are you okay?"

"It's gratitude. I've missed you so much."

She kisses me harder, her tenderness turning to passion. Her hands slide around the base of my skull, making sure I don't leave her mouth. We consume each other.

Celeste's hands slide down my back, up my sides, back down into my hip crease, along my thighs, leaving a trail of fire.

I told her I would stop at a kiss. I'm receiving signals she wants me to keep going. Now more than ever, I must be sure I'm reading her right. I need to hear her consent. "Should we stop, or do you want more?"

"I want that fantasy," she says, "the one where you celebrate every good thing inside me."

"Now?" I ask, hoping to God she says yes because I have been trying to ignore the tension and heat rising with my cock.

"Now," she says.

"May I take you to bed?"

"Yes."

I take her hand, guide her out of the hot tub, dry her, then myself, and glance around. It's pretty private back here, but maybe not private enough to undress. I make sure the bottoms of my feet are dry enough I won't slip. She's trembling. "Are you cold?"

"No."

Oh, God. I scoop her up, and relish her weight in my arms and the tingling in my skin where her arms wrap around my shoulders, her breath on my neck. I carry her through the open French doors, across the small bedroom, lay her on the bed, slide her wet bikini bottom off while she removes her top. She is glorious. "I want to be inside you so badly," I say, dropping my swim trunks to the floor. "And I want to take this slowly, to savor it. Does that work for you?" I stand by the bed, drinking in her beauty, reveling in the feel of her gaze on my body.

"Whatever you want," she says.

But I know this trick of hers, so I say, "No, Angel. Tell me how to please you."

Celeste

He wants to know how to please me. I can't think. My insides are aflame. The only thing that will quench me is his luscious… Mmm. Everything I've fantasized about but couldn't admit I needed is happening. Josh stands at the foot of the bed, face wet with tears, firm muscles glowing in the moonlight coming through the skylight.

Emotions flow through me in waves. What do I want? "You want it slowly."

"Yes. I want to savor you. But what do you want?" His voice has that sexy gruffness it only gets when we're making love.

"You inside me." My gaze travels from his face down to his sexy thighs, back up to his ready staff.

He drops his knees onto the bed, crawls above me.

"Wait. No. Sorry."

"It's alright. Take your time."

I close my eyes. All those nights alone, I imagined him proving I'm the only one for him. He said it tonight, but now I know what I need. "Touch me everywhere. Show me you want me. I need to feel you desire every part of my body."

"Yes, love," he growls, eyes sparking with pleasure, hunger, playfulness. He caresses my toes, then rubs, and finally sucks on each one, sending me into an ecstatic trance. Now he moves his tongue to the inside of my ankle, encircles it, nibbles the inside of my calf, runs his thumb firmly up my shin. When he reaches the hip crease, he slides his hands under my hips. "I'm ravenous."

"Let me feed you."

"Show me what to eat." He kisses below my navel and my hips rise on their own. "Here?"

"Mm."

He kisses my hipbone. "Here?"

"Maybe."

Nibbles my ribs, making me giggle. "Here?"

"Hmm."

He licks my underarm. I squeal.

Bites my shoulder. "What about this?"

"That's nice."

He nuzzles my earlobe, whispers, "Angel," runs his tongue along the helix. "More?"

"My lips."

"Yes, love." He kisses my mouth thoroughly, grazes my cheeks, my eyelids, forehead, chin, back to my mouth.

"Mm. Lovely, but I meant the other ones."

"Oh." He laughs, as if he didn't know what I meant the first time. "You mean, you want me to eat this." He's caressing my entrance now, lightly, like I love it.

"Uh, huh," I pant. "Savor it."

"That's my favorite."

"Really?"

"Along with all the other parts."

He pushes my legs apart, kisses down my body, opens my entrance with his fingers, brings his face there and inhales like it's the most delightful bouquet. Josh groans and blows a gentle puff of air across the opening, making me shiver. He licks each lip gently.

I gasp.

"I love pleasing you, Celeste."

"You know where to go next."

"Tell me though."

"My rose."

"Yes, ma'am." He takes my clit into his mouth, sucks oh so perfectly, bringing me close to the edge.

Waves of ecstasy rise and ebb, each rise taking me higher, making me gasp. "Come."

He obeys, plunging his fingers deep, taking me over the crest. I scream.

He moans, "Angel," and tells me how much he loves it when I release into his mouth. He drinks and licks and sucks until I can't take any more.

I'm fisting the duvet, pounding on the bed, "Please. Please, Josh. I need you inside me."

"Yes, love."

"Are you ready?" I ask because sometimes he needs a little extra, a lick, a tug, a stroke.

But he says, "Feel me."

I slide my hand down his six-pack until I reach the mons. I'm beside myself, feeling Josh's body under my fingertips, sliding my palm between his legs, first to the hard stones and then to his cock. All these months I dreamed about wrapping my hand around him, sometimes shamed myself for fantasizing, but now I know it's right.

"Do you feel how much I want you, Celeste?"

"Yes."

"How attractive I find you?"

"Yes."

"Do you feel how I can only resist if you need me to? And I can, I really can, but I don't want to. I want you. Now. Always."

"Take me now."

As Josh slides his body over mine, hovers above me, feathers my mouth with his, deepens the kiss so I can't mistake his hunger, his hard length pulses against my entrance. Torture. Pleasure. Torture.

"Now?" he asks. "Please?"

"Yes."

He brings his tip to my entrance, lets it rest there just long enough to drive me wild. I scream for him to fill me and he does, splitting me open. And it is amazing. I have missed this so much. It's exactly what I need. This connection. And his attraction to me is unmistakable.

Wait.

Oh, God. No. Her face. I see her. Suddenly, she—

No. Please, no. Oh my God.

He's on me and it feels so good except—

I'm not me.

I feel that woman.

She's inside me.

This body is hers. She's the one feeling everything.

What's happening?

"Celeste, what's wrong?" Josh asks.

Where am I? Why is she here?

No. Oh my God.

Josh stops moving inside me. "What's wrong?" He's begging, still inside me. "Tell me, honey. Please tell me what's wrong."

I'm sobbing. My body is wrecked because I am wrecked. I'm going crazy.

"What, Angel? What? Tell me." He's soft inside me now.

This body is sobbing. "All I wanted was to be close to you, Josh. All I wanted was to be close to you. All I wanted was to please you. All I wanted was to feel..." I break down.

Emotions wash through me and over me. Sobbing, the only sound filling the room.

"Let it out, baby," Josh's voice is rough. "I'm here." He pulls me tight, but now—

"Please. Please stop."

"You want me to get off you?"

I nod and he slides off me. "Would you like me to hold you?"

I roll onto my side, facing the wall. I watch his arms wrap around me and tighten as the sobs rip through me.

What's wrong with me? I must've said it out loud, or maybe he's reading my mind because he says, "Nothing. Nothing's wrong with you, Angel. You're perfect. It was me, and I'm sorry. Please forgive me."

We lay in silence. There's a spot under the windowsill the painter missed. These walls used to be eggshell blue. Now, they're neutral ecru. The word ecru echoes in my mind as I stare blankly at the wall.

He apologizes again. Asks my forgiveness. Apologizes for asking my forgiveness.

"Josh, I forgave you a long time ago. The person I'm having trouble forgiving is myself."

"Beloved, please, if nothing else comes of this, please forgive yourself. It was my error, not yours."

"I hoped."

"We need hope. That's good."

"Everybody leaves me."

"No, angel. I'm right here. I'm holding you. Can you feel my arms around you?"

I'm not sure, but I think I shake my head. "I make them leave."

"That's not true. I'm right here. Do you feel me holding your body tight?"

"I don't feel my body at all."

"Why?"

"Because when you were inside me, she came inside me, too."

He stumbles for words. "Like... you were... having sex with... her?"

"Like I was her. Celeste was gone. Lucinda was this body being intimate with you."

"Oh, baby." He takes a deep breath and lets it out slowly. "What do you need to feel better?"

"I don't know. I'm numb. I probably need to go home."

"May I walk you?"

"No."

"Will you let me know you got home safe?"

"Okay."

"May I call you in the morning?"

"Okay."

"Can you look at me?"

I roll over to face him. There's love in his eyes, concern creasing his forehead. We gaze into each other's eyes for a while, breathing, until I have the strength to leave.

26

Josh

SHE'S GONE. IS SHE OKAY? WHAT THE HELL JUST HAPPENED? Is this a thing women go through? Who would know? Who could I ask? My mother, but she's not here. Amira. So, I'll call her right up and say, "Hey, sis, curious if while having sex with your ex-husband you ever felt inhabited by one of the numerous women he cheated on you with." Yeah, no.

Tanya. She's been like a second mother to me, and I know what my dad put her through. We Albright men can really fuck things up. Okay, I'm not gonna go there. I'm not diving into shame and self-pity. Thank you for visiting. Let's check on Celeste. She should be home by now.

I text:

Angel, Are you home safe?

Yes. Sorry. Forgot to text. Getting into
bed.

> Thank you for letting me know. I love
> you. Sleep well.

What do I do for Celeste? How can I help her? I need ideas,
guidance. I send Derek a video chat request.

His face says he knows something's wrong. "Hey. You're in New
Haven. Right?"

"Yup."

"Why are you calling me at 9:30 on a Saturday night from New
Haven?"

I cringe. "Sorry. Did I interrupt something?"

"Quiet evening in, as much as that's possible with a gaggle of
twelve-year-old girls having a sleepover. So..." He points his whiskey
on the rocks at me.

"Things were going great, until they weren't, and I don't know
what to do."

"Should we get the guys in on this?"

"Probably."

"One sec." Derek taps his phone, then Rory pops up on the
screen. Towheaded and blue eyed, a freaking life-sized Ken doll
with a Southern California drawl.

"Josh, my man. I hear you're in New Haven wooing your lady
friend. Why you calling us this time of night?"

"It's an SOS."

"What's the story?"

"I don't wanna betray Celeste's confidence, but things got
heated between us—"

"Heated how?" Derek asks.

"In a good way, but something happened that really affected
her. I don't know how to help her."

"When you say it affected her, what do you mean?" Rory asks.

"If I tell you it'll betray her trust."

"Respect." Derek nods.

Ned's grizzled face appears onscreen. I wave. He nods, but keeps himself muted, encouraging me to continue.

"This… bizarre experience… upset Celeste so much that she went home. Honestly, I can't blame her."

"Did you do something?" Ned asks in his raspy voice.

"No. She had a weird, unexpected emotional reaction, like a delayed response to the infidelity that happened last year."

"So, she's still processing," Rory says.

"I guess. But how do I help her?"

Derek takes a sip of his drink. "First, Josh, kudos for focusing more on how this is affecting Celeste than on yourself. Whatever happened, it obviously shook you, too."

"And you need your own processing time," Rory says.

"But you're right to focus on Celeste now. Seems she's in crisis."

"She's worked on herself these past months. She's asking for what she needs. I see it in other ways—"

"If I may," Ned says. "You two are reconnecting after months apart. We can only do so much healing in isolation."

Ned's insights always blow me away. "Right. This thing could only have happened with a man, maybe only with me."

Derek says, "I know it's different for men than for women, but when I learned my ex-wife was cheating on me, it blew me apart. Shot up my self-esteem, my sense of safety in relationships, made it hard to trust anyone new, made me question reality."

I blow out a puff of air and we're all silent for a moment. "Sounds like a vulnerable place to live from."

Derek nods. "It was. Of course, we don't know what Celeste is experiencing."

"She told me what was happening, but it confused her."

"You seeing her tomorrow?"

"If she'll let me. This is tough, guys. I know she's forgiven me, but I was hoping we could start building our future now. I want what Celeste and I had."

"No, Josh. What you want is what you believe you can have." Derek says. "If you wanted what you had, you never would've cheated on her."

Rory steps back from the camera so his body comes into view. "If you want what you always believed was possible, you gotta stay present. Look at me." He spreads his legs. "You got one foot in the past, one foot in the future," he says, squatting down, gesturing, "and you're pissing all over the present."

I shake my head. "There's something I'll never be able to unsee."

"That's the point, my friend," Rory says. "Keep it in your mind. Remember. Stay present. Be with Celeste where she is now. She's in pain for good reason, and you can help her."

"I was thinking maybe I should call Tanya."

"Who's Tanya?" Rory asks.

"My future mother-in-law," Derek says, alarmed. "Why in hell would you call her?"

"She knows firsthand the damage an Albright man can cause."

"One: you're not your dad. Two: what can you possibly gain from asking Tanya?"

"Tanya's irrelevant," Rory says. "What good does it do you to know about her experience?"

"It'd help to know whether what happened to Celeste is unique to Celeste. It was pretty crazy."

"So you're worried Celeste is going crazy?"

"Not exactly."

"Josh, focus on the woman you want," Derek says.

"Alright."

"You got this, Man. You really do. Sounds like you handled it well so far, and it was smart of you to send out that SOS and make sure you don't screw things up worse."

27

Celeste

I CAME HOME. I MEDITATED. I'M UTTERLY EXHAUSTED. STILL, racing thoughts are keeping me awake. I should be mad at Josh right now, thinking about him and what happened in bed. Instead, his mom keeps popping into my mind. My words had nothing to do with her death. And although I said horrible things to my mother, I didn't cause her death, either. It's ridiculous to think so.

Except, what kind of child says such horrible things to their parent? Google will tell me. I type three different versions of my question into the search bar. None of these so-called answers help.

Amira will know.

> **Mimi, what does it mean when a child says cruel things?**

Why do you ask?

Oh, God. Sorry! I didn't mean to wake you.

Lila is having a sleepover. Any idea how loud twelve-year-old girls are when they're wired on soda, snacks, and adrenaline? I'm hoping to sleep

tomorrow.

Yikes.

What's up? Sounds like you need to talk.

I'm fine.

The phone rings. Amira's name flashes on the screen. I answer. "Hi."

"Obviously, you are not fine."

"How do you know?"

"One, you don't text random questions about children in the middle of the night. Two, I heard Derek on the phone with Josh. I don't know what happened, but I know Josh is worried."

"Oh."

"Wanna talk about it?"

I sigh. "He's been amazing. We had a beautiful night until I fell apart."

"How?"

"I'll spare you the details. But I came home and can't sleep. It's bringing up guilt over Ellen, and my mom, and so much anger about this damn endometriosis situation. I keep thinking what I said to my mom made her... leave... and that's why I've been so neurotic about ignoring my needs while making sure everyone else's needs got met, which is how I ignored excruciating pain every month. And because I did that, I'll never get to be a mom. Like I set myself up for all of this when I was a kid."

Amira sighs. "Cece, that's a lot of crap. Why are you telling yourself lies?"

"I said horrible words."

"When you were angry."

"I shouldn't—"

"You're human. We say things in anger."

I groan.

"As I recall, your angry words helped Ellen heal."

My stomach cramps. "I've never shared this. But what I said to my mom—"

"Did not make her abandon you."

"It was bad, Amira."

"What did you say?"

"I told her 'I hate you.'"

"Okay," she says slowly, sounding confused. "What else?"

"I yelled it at her."

"You were ten."

I close my eyes in shame. "Horrible."

"Normal. Practically a rite of passage."

"What?"

"By age ten, kids understand they have unique needs and desires. They still expect their heroes, mom and dad, to meet those needs. When mom or dad lets them down and the ten-year-old learns their hero can't always perform, the kid has no clue how to handle it emotionally."

"So?"

"They lash out."

"But I could see Mom was fragile. I should've been more sensitive."

"Cece, you were a child having a tantrum. Your mom had bigger things weighing her down. Trust me."

I ponder that. On the line I hear Amira breathing, slow and steady. In the background, girls squeal and giggle. I try to remember myself at that age. Instead, I recall Mom's note in my hands. Roses spread across the top of the stationery. Blue ink, which was faded the last time I looked at it. Mom's handwriting:

"Dear Celeste,

I'm sorry. I love you. I've been fighting for a long time. I can't fight anymore."

The last line…

Pop music blasts through the phone.

"Girls, that's too loud," Amira yells. The music lowers. "Sorry. It's gonna be a long night."

A horn comes through the line.

"For crying out loud," she says. "Now, Derek is revving them up, stomping around playing hip-hop on the trombone."

Picturing serious Doctor Derek parading around for Lila and her friends makes me giggle. "Sleepover, NOLA style?"

"It's cute, actually. They're all dancing." Amira sighs and giggles.

"I'll let you go so you can take a video."

"No! This is important, Cece. You need to talk. I'm here."

The comfort those words bring is immeasurable, like the coziest hug. "I was recalling the note she left. The last thing she wrote before signing 'love Mom' was, 'It's not your fault.'"

"It's not your fault. Why would you think it is?"

"I don't know."

"I have an idea. Wanna hear it?"

"Sure."

"I think you needed a sense of control in a situation over which you had none. It felt better to believe you could make her go away than to accept that you had zero power over what she chose."

"Wow."

"Think there's some truth in that?"

"I do."

"It's normal for kids to come to conclusions that are oceans from the truth. With limited information and references, they're trying to make sense of the world."

"I know."

"Maybe you could write another story for yourself. One that's more truthful."

"I'll try that."

We end the call. I pull the journal from my nightstand and write until I fall asleep.

28

Josh

As soon as I turn off my alarm, I dial Celeste. She sounds rough. That concerns me, but she says she's doing better. When I ask if I can take her to breakfast, if we can talk, she invites me over. She wants to avoid people right now. I get that. I throw on my Sunday morning casual gear and walk to that cafe she likes across from the park. Without a car or any knowledge about where to buy flowers in this city on a Sunday morning, I'm hoping her favorite fresh green juice will cheer her up. I tried to reschedule my flight last night to give us more time together, but the cost was prohibitive. That gives us about three hours to unpack what happened, and I'm a nervous wreck.

She couldn't feel my arms around her last night. What was that? Rory's delightful illustration springs to mind. That, Josh, was the past. And what'll happen when you see Celeste this morning is the future. Get your mind in the present.

Right. Be present. I can start right now by paying attention to my physical sensations and my surroundings. Green clover and violets poking up through the broken cement on the sidewalk. The slight incline in the hill that changes the sensations in my calves as I walk. The air temperature. The way the sunlight warms my face and the shift in temperature every time a cloud passes in front of the sun. I'm paying closer attention to the architecture in this neighborhood than I have during my recent visits. House styles shift from street to street and block to block. Throughout the neighborhood, people decorate with bright colors. Like Wildbranch, a lot of homes sport rainbow flags and Tibetan peace flags. There are the standard green lawns but also a lot of wildflower gardens. Every so often, I pass a rundown house. Mostly, though, people here seem to have both pride of ownership and resources to take care of their properties.

My breathing is easier as I stride up to the Victorian duplex with the turret, where Celeste rents the first floor apartment. I call through the screen door. "Celeste?"

When she comes to the door, freshly showered, long hair flowing over her shoulder and down her chest, my heart skips a beat. Yeah, I'm that guy who says his heart skips a beat. So what?

"Good morning." I present her with the juices. "Didn't know where to get flowers so…"

Her eyes light up. "Aww, Josh. Thank you." She hugs me quickly and leads me inside. "I hope you don't mind staying in for breakfast."

"You know how much I've missed your cooking?" *And the sight of your hips swaying in a pretty skirt?*

"Really?"

"That tofu scramble."

"This morning I was thinking pancakes."

I let my eyes roll back in my head. "Heaven."

I leave my shoes at the door and follow Celeste down the hall past the parlor, and through the dining room. This place feels like her, with the floral prints and family photos in silver frames gracing the neutral walls and white-painted bookshelves. She lined the hardwood floors with woven rugs in soft colors. "This apartment come furnished?"

She flashes a smile over her shoulder. "I went shopping."

"Aha," I say, with a teasing tone. "Looks like the work of a pro decorator."

"Thanks. Connecticut has great antique stores. And people are always leaving cool stuff on the curb."

"It's cozy." Like my home was when you lived there.

"How'd you sleep?" she asks, as we enter the large, white and yellow kitchen.

"Pretty well. You?"

"Alright." Which means she probably didn't sleep at all.

I want to dive into the important conversation, and I never want to bring it up. I want her to know I care, because I do very much. I'm worried about her. But if I bring it up, will it upset her? "What can I do to help?"

"Nothing." She goes to the stove. "I made the batter already. I thought we'd eat on the patio."

"You have a back yard?" I glance out the window. Picnic table. Grass. Sky. Trees. I only half see the space. My mind is inside with Celeste. I cross the room to stand beside her.

"I can give you a tour later, if you want. At the moment, I need food."

"I'm hungry, too."

She lights the burner, adjusting it until the flame is just right, sets the skillet on top, and drops a spoonful of coconut oil into it. The oil melts. She tilts the pan to cover the surface evenly.

Should I bring it up now?

Celeste pours two streams of batter into the skillet. They form perfect circles, close yet not touching.

Here goes. "I think this is the second or third time you've mentioned not sleeping well. Is that new? You're usually a pretty sound sleeper."

"Oh." Celeste takes a couple deep breaths.

"Honey, we don't have to talk, if you don't want, but I'm here to listen. How you feel matters to me, and I think last night scared you."

"Yeah. Would you like one of the green juices?"

"Sure."

She hands me one, unwraps a straw and pokes it into the top of my green juice. My sweet girl.

"Thank you. That's very thoughtful."

"Sorry. Guess I'm being a mom again." She winces on the word mom.

"Babe, I love how nurturing you are."

"You used to tease me about it."

"I used to be more of a jerk."

She laughs nervously. "I didn't say that."

"No. I did. I used to be more of a jerk, and I'm sorry. You deserved better treatment than I offered, and that was before the betrayal."

She flinches on the word betrayal, which gives me pause. Should I continue? I caress her arm, hoping my words will ease her pain. "I wish it had occurred to me to do this before. Last night after you left, I stayed up and did some research about what happens to people after they've lived through infidelity. I read that insomnia is really common."

"I haven't slept well since October 5th," she admits.

A knife to my chest. "I'm sorry."

"Thanks."

"Would you like to tell me more? If you're not sleeping, I imagine that's having ripple effects."

"I've always been pretty sensitive, but now it seems I cry at anything. I'm afraid to tell you this."

"Tell me what?"

"Any of it." She opens a cabinet and drawer and pulls out plates, glasses, silverware sets them on the counter.

I reach for the dinnerware, but she takes it, goes to the glass-paned door and presses the handle down with her elbow. It doesn't work. *Oh, Celeste.* I shake my head, get the door for her.

"If you had known what would happen to you last night, would you have expected me to respond like I did?"

She half-laughs. "Not at all. The old Josh would have gotten defensive or freaked out or somehow..." she lets her voice trail off.

Made it about me. I don't say that because I'm not the one who needs to be talking right now. Unfortunately, she says it for me. "Made it about him."

Fuck. "Does recognizing things didn't go that way help you feel a little safer with me?"

"Now that you mention it, yes."

Relief. As long as she feels safe with me, we can work through this. We keep talking while Celeste nervously putters between the kitchen and patio, refusing to let me do anything. At last, the pancakes are on the table. She serves me, nurturer that she is. Eagerly, I lift a bite of pancake dripping with syrup to my mouth. "Mm. Incredible."

She smiles. "You're just saying that."

I quirk a brow. She knows I'm not. "No exaggeration. You know I can cook, too."

"Those Persian love cupcakes you sent were scrumptious."

"I have my specialties, but I've never been able to make pancakes like yours."

After breakfast, we stand side-by-side at the sink like we used to. She washes the dishes and hands them to me, and I rub them dry. Afraid to freak her out, I lay my fingertips on her upper back, tentative. She leans into my touch, so I run my hands along her muscles, feeling the strength and... Alarm bells go off inside me. "Baby, have you lost weight?" How did I not notice this last night? She's skin and bones.

"I've had trouble eating since October. But I get a green juice every day for nutrition."

Feeling sick, I look toward the heavens and let out a puff of air.

"Sorry, I shouldn't have told you."

"I'm glad you did. It hurts to know my actions had that effect on you." I slide my hand across her shoulders, and when she turns toward me I pull her close. "I'm so sorry, love." Feeling her cheek against my shoulder, even with the pain she's radiating, this is home.

I tilt my head toward her. She looks up at me with those big, beautiful brown eyes. Vulnerable and kind. There's a tiny drop of maple syrup on her bottom lip. So adorable. So Celeste. Softly, slowly, we come together. Her mouth is sweet. Things heat up really fast. She unbuttons my jeans. I slide my hand up her shirt. No bra. Hard nipples. Instant erection. She slides her hand into the back of my boxers. I run my thumb over the mound of her breast. She gasps and freezes in my arms.

"What, Angel?"

"I don't. I... last night."

"Is it happening again?"

"No."

"But you're afraid it might?"

"Yes."

"You want to stop?"

"No. Yes."

Instantly, we disentangle and step apart. I brush a tendril off her face. She meets my gaze. The fear in her eyes slays me. "Josh, what if this lasts a while? You have needs."

"I'm waiting for you, forever if I have to."

"What if I can never make love with you again? What if every time we try it triggers me?"

"Then I guess we'll explore other ways to be intimate."

Her heart, mind, and body are waging a war inside and it's playing out on her face. She wants to trust me, I think, but won't until she forgives herself. But for what? If I knew maybe I could help. Or maybe this is something she needs to work out on her own.

29

Celeste

HAVE BEEN AVOIDING THIS CHAPTER FOR A WHILE, MAINLY because I had no clue how to write it. Now, as I stroll briskly along the strand overlooking West Haven beach, I feel ready. It's chilly and drizzling, so I have the place to myself. I open my Voice Memos and record:

"Forgiving is one of the most complicated things a person does. Yet it's crucial for healthy relationships. I'm a relationship coach, praised for my insights into what makes relationships thrive and what destroys them. Yet I had to endure new levels of personal turmoil to be able to write this chapter. I believe writing it is the final step in forgiving myself and the people closest to me who have hurt me. The people we allow into our hearts can create the deepest wounds."

I like that. I pause to enjoy the view, then keep going.

"Recovering from those wounds requires forgiving our loved ones and ourselves. Here are the strategies I've used to forgive myself and the people who hurt me:

"1. Accept your feelings: I've mentioned this in other chapters, but I find accepting my feelings is essential as I strive to forgive. Feeling hurt and angry isn't wrong. It's when we try to suppress our feelings that they usually rise up in unhealthy ways.

"2. Find a healthy outlet to express the feelings: art, yoga, dance. Breaking things. Smash cafes are becoming popular for a reason. I haven't gone to one yet, but I see the appeal. There are no limits here. The key is to release the grief or anger in a safe way and a safe place. My outlet was yoga. I created an angry yoga playlist and let myself scream and cry during my practice. It brought great relief.

"3. Research: learning which parts of my experience were unique to me and which parts are common helped me feel less isolated."

Should I go into detail here? No. This book isn't about me but about processes. Besides, being that vulnerable to anyone who may read this book makes me uncomfortable.

What happened in bed with Josh made me think I was crazy at first, but through research, I learned I'm not alone. Other women trying to reunite with unfaithful partners have experienced that strange sense of being inhabited by the betrayal partner, too. I was afraid to tell my therapist about it, but she'd heard similar stories. Knowing that has helped me open up more to Josh. He really seems to have changed. He was always pretty devoted to me, but he's taking his commitment to a whole new level.

Until that horrible moment in bed, it felt amazing to be intimate with him again. Now, I can't stop thinking about his touch. Even as I take in the salty air, feel the delicious cool mist on my skin, I imagine Josh beside me, holding my hand, stopping me mid-stride, pulling me close so I can feel how much he wants me...

He wants me. That's what I've had trouble getting through my head since the betrayal. Josh didn't cheat because he stopped desiring me. I, Celeste, still turn him on. I replay my therapist's words in my mind: Josh is demonstrating his desire. It seems like Josh is more attracted to me than he ever has been to anyone.

That's why Dr. Rosen suggested I reclaim my power and be more assertive sexually. These last couple weeks, I've explored my bold side. I hated feeling disempowered in our relationship. Yet I accepted it. Dominating is not for me, but feeling like a doormat sucks.

Somewhere between walking on the beach and fantasizing about Josh, I forgot I was recording, even as I drove back to New Haven. Now, I'm home and I feel uplifted. I'll finish the chapter after I shower. I want to catch Josh as he wakes. I text him as I stride into the bathroom.

Good morning.

Hi Angel. Hard getting up today.

Oh? How hard?

Like a redwood.

Did I ever tell you how much I love climbing trees?

Tell me.

Wrapping myself around a tree trunk.

Enveloping it?

Yeah. And feeling its girth and hardness between my legs.

I can't believe I'm doing this, but I'm having fun.

Sometime I'll tell you more about it. Have to shower. All sweaty from yoga.

My phone rings. Josh, of course. His morning voice is gruff. "Can we talk while you shower?"

"Sure. I'll put you on speaker while I strip off these tight, damp yoga pants."

"God, I love your scent when you're all worked up."

"I'll be washing it away soon. Can you still hear me?" I ask, stepping into the shower.

"Yes, love. Are you in the shower now?"

"Just getting under the shower head." I let out an exaggerated sigh, both to release the tension from my body and for Josh's benefit. "It's huge, so the water surrounds me. God, it feels good."

"Tell me."

"Like standing naked in a rainstorm, letting it soak my hair and face. I love feeling the water pouring over the top of my head and running down my spine." I truly love this, and he knows it. We've had so many fun times in the shower. "Where are you?"

"In bed. Wishing you were here."

"That would be nice."

"Or that I was with you, washing your face."

"I'm doing that now."

"You always do, as soon as your hair is wet."

"It's very wet now. Dripping."

He growls. "I'm thinking about watching you climb that tree."

"That tree? Interestingly specific. What tree do you wanna see me climb?"

"Mine."

"It's especially fun when the tree is all wet, and…"

He groans.

"The trunk is all slippery. I can move up and down it so easily."

"I love watching you move your hands up and down my wood."

"I love how it's solid under my fingertips and between my legs."

"Tell me."

"Squeezing it with my thighs… You okay? Your breathing seems a little heavy."

"Hearing your voice, it's hard to breathe. I wanna be… Mmmm."

"Where are your hands?"

"Under the sheets. Where are your hands?"

"I'm putting shower gel on my razor."

"You're shaving?" He gasps. Yes. I've still got it.

"Mm-hmmm. I'm holding my calf with one hand and gliding the razor up my shin, up each side, starting at the bottom and sliding all the way to the top of the bone."

"I love watching you shave."

"Sometimes, I pretend you're helping me." His moan emboldens me, making me want to play more. "You stand behind me, arms holding me steady. All your hard... muscles press into my back and..." Another groan from his end. "And now you take the razor and run it up my thigh."

"Yes." Josh pants. "But I need to be careful, so I turn you and set you up against the shower wall, kneel in front of you, lean my face against your mons."

"Why do you do that?"

"So I don't slip and so I can breathe you in."

"Mmm. I like that, Josh."

He pants. "I glide the razor up the top of your thigh, and the bottom of your thigh, and the outside."

"Yes. I love how you make me feel Josh. You finish my thigh, going up the inside. I know you want to do the other leg, but first I need you to check that you made this one perfectly smooth."

"How do I do that?" He whimpers, getting closer.

"Run your palms and fingertips up and down my thigh, up and down, gripping it tight enough to feel everything."

"Yeah?"

"But that's not enough."

"What next? Tell me what to do."

"Use your tongue."

He moans again. "Yes, Love. Tell me."

"Run your tongue along every inch of my thigh until you know it's perfectly smooth."

"Yes, Angel. Now what?"

"Put down the razor. Sit back on your heels and look at me."

"You're beautiful."

"Are you leaning toward me, trying to get close to me?"

"Yes."

"Stop that."

"Why?"

"I want to see your long, hard wood while I wash myself. Lean back so I can see."

"Like this?"

I imagine him leaning back, looking at me, his hazel eyes so eager to please. "So good, Josh."

"You like my pole?"

"I love your pole. It's so thick and hard and perfect. I want it inside me."

He whimpers. "Are you washing between your legs?"

"I am." And I feel beautiful, touching myself and playing this game with him. "Are you getting close, lover?"

"So close. I wanna be inside you. I wanna please you."

"You're a good boy."

"I was bad, but I wanna show you I'm good now."

"I see you're good. Come back to me."

"I'm here."

"Stroke my thighs. Hold my hips."

"I'm close."

"Me, too, and I wanna squirt on you. Put my thighs on your shoulders." He's making all the sounds now. We've got seconds. "Wanna come together?"

"Yes, baby."

"Feel my thighs on your shoulders. Keep one hand under my ass and put the other hand on your gorgeous cock."

"Yes."

"Say please."

"Please, baby."

"Ready to come with me?" I pant.

"I'm ready. I'm licking your clit and breathing you in. Oh, Cece. Oh, God."

"Yes, Josh."

"Angel."

The wave is rising through me. "Open your mouth. Ready?"

He moans.

Reaching my peak, feeling amazing and empowered. "Come with me, Josh." I pant. "Now."

"Coming." His ragged breath and moans give me strength as I crest.

Until I release. With the peak comes the valley. Sobs rip through me, unwanted, unexpected waves of grief. I slide to the shower floor, gasping for breath.

Josh

That. Was. So. Fucking. Hot. Celeste rarely takes command. This morning she did, and following her lead, I felt safe. But now she's crying. And I hear the shower running. Damn it. I wish I was there to hold her.

"Cece?"

Sobbing.

"Baby, what happened?"

She sniffles. "I don't know."

"Did that thing happen again?"

"No."

Thank. God.

She takes a deep breath. "I guess the release brought up other stuff, too. I felt so good and now..." more crying.

"Are you okay in the shower? Do you need help?"

"I'm fine."

"I can call Sage."

"I'm fine, Josh. Just emotional. I'm sorry. I ruined—"

"You didn't ruin anything. It was beautiful. I loved it. Did you?"

"Yeah. It was fun."

"I loved hearing you take command."

Sniffling. "But then, I..." sobbing. My heart breaks for her.

"You honor me with your vulnerability, Angel. I only wish I was there to hold you, so you'd feel as loved and safe as I do now."

The water's still running on her end. I stay on the phone with her while she turns it off, gets out of the shower, and dries herself. For a while, neither one of us says anything. Strange as it seems, I'm enjoying her morning preparation sounds. Listening lets me pretend we're starting our day side-by-side. When she goes into the kitchen to turn on the teakettle, I do the same, brewing a cup of the yerba maté she got me addicted to, and settling on the couch in front of the fireplace facing the spot where she used to sit.

When her voice sounds calm, I ask if she'll visit me. She agrees, but she'll get a hotel because she won't sleep in the bed where I betrayed her. After what happened during our last visit, I do not question her feelings on the topic.

If she needs a new bed, a new bedroom, a new house, so be it. "It makes sense to me that you'd find the bed triggering. If I get a new bed, do you think you'd be okay in that room?"

"I don't know." She draws out the words, like she's weighing each one on a scale.

"What would it take for you to feel comfortable here?" I ask.

"I'm not sure."

"Okay. I understand. If something comes to mind, tell me, okay?"

We end the call, and I order a new bed, then set about moving furniture. The second bedroom used to be Satya's. Then it was the guest room. It's smaller, and the bathroom is smaller, but so what?

30

Josh

THE TUBE AUGUR SLIDES OUT OF THE DAMP GROUND easily. Just as I'm dropping the last of eight soil samples into the pail and mixing them, my phone rings and Siri announces a call from a 978 area code. Something tells me to answer, despite the shitty timing. I tap my earbud and greet the caller.

"Hi. My name is Dustin Reynaldo. I'm with the Harvard Forest in Petersham, Massachusetts. Is this Josh?"

Shit. A fundraising call. "Speaking." How did they get my number?

"I recently learned of your work in wildfire prevention solutions. We're seeking someone with your unique grounding in chemistry and materials science and a passion for ecology. We have a tenure track position opening up and I'd love to talk to you about the possibility of working together."

"Seriously?" If my hands weren't full, I'd do a victory dance right here on the edge of the mountain pass.

"The University is seeking to increase its work in this area. We haven't yet felt much threat of wildfire in the Northeast, but I'm sure I don't have to tell you it's a distinct and growing possibility as climate disruption worsens. We've seen bizarre weather patterns here in the last fifteen years. Tornadoes, and..."

"A tornado skipped right past my mother's house in Wendell in 2006."

"Wendell's near us. Have you been to the Harvard Forest?"

"Not since our seventh-grade Earth Science field trip. All I remember are dioramas."

He laughs. "The dioramas are still here, but the research is more advanced. We're quite proud of what we've been achieving, and we'd like to grow that, as I mentioned. Does that interest you?"

"Definitely. In fact, I was collecting soil samples when you called." Samples I need to be mixing.

"Intriguing. Can you say more?"

"This is the seventh batch. After we tested our new gel technology in the lab and saw its potential efficacy, I knew we needed to test its ability to prevent wildfires and its environmental safety. So I selected a few random locations around campus and in my backyard. We also tested on potting soil in the lab."

"Interesting approach."

About a hundred feet from me, a family of black-tailed deer lope across the field, ears twitching. I follow their progress as I describe our work, "Potting soil comes in clean packages from garden centers and remains uncontaminated by outside factors, like ash falling from nearby wildfires."

"Ahh."

"Earlier this year, when we conducted the tests with CalFire, we took soil samples at those sites. Now we're on the seventh group of samples from the random places and the sixth samples from the CalFire sites."

"When do you collect the samples?"

"After rainfall. Our gel works by clinging to the plant and holding the fire retardant in place until it's needed. However, with each rainfall, a trace amount of our hydrogel washes into the soil, so we suspect it will require an annual reapplication."

Dustin makes a sound like he's contemplating my words.

The deer stop at the edge of the field where the tall grasses meet the evergreens and wild blackberry shrubs spread. Watching the creatures feed on the wild blackberry leaves makes me glad we didn't apply the hydrogel to those plants. Although we've seen zero indication that the gel is toxic to any animal or plant species. Wild blackberry is rather tolerant of fire, anyway.

"What sampling pattern are you using?" Dustin asks.

"A grid pattern here on the side of the highway. Since we created a grid when we conducted the tests here with CalFire, it made sense to follow that pattern. At the other sites, we're taking field composites."

"Based on your findings, is that trace amount of gel affecting the soil chemistry?

"So far, it looks like we have an environmentally safe substance."

"Excellent."

"With a silica-based gel, I'm not surprised, but it's great to have confirmation."

"Sounds like you have a long-awaited solution."

"One that saves lives and property, and according to my friends in epidemiology at Yale and environmental toxicology at CU Fort Collins, human health. The toxicological effects of wildfire on soil health and water are astounding."

"I haven't seen these studies. Can you send links?" Dustin asks.

"Absolutely. The upshot is every time there's a wildfire, it's more than wood smoke in the air and wood ash falling into our lakes, rivers, streams, and fields."

The field darkens. Light, fluffy clouds block the sun now, but an ominous storm front is rolling across the sky, headed this way. Shit. I need to finish here and bounce. Walking toward the jeep, I match the cadence of my voice to my brisk stride. "It's industrial chemicals, vinyl siding, automotive paints, and rubber tires that are burning, landing in the soil and water, and presenting environmental hazards and risks for human health. It's quite a mess."

"Indeed. Yet thrilling to know that if we can prevent wild-fires, we may save lives from fire and from many diseases caused by contaminated water, air and soil."

"Exactly."

"It seems you've hit on a trifecta."

"Truly. And I'm excited to talk about how I can take this work further, but at the moment, I've got a bucket of soil cores from different spots at this site that I need to mix and divvy up into sample containers for testing before it rains."

"How about I email you the job description? Give you a couple days to think about it and get back to me?"

"Fantastic."

We end the call. Did he say tenure track position? God, I've been … how many years at this university with no offer of tenure? Now that I have interest from another institution and a product under patent review, will I get an offer from my university? If I got two offers, which would I take?

Working at the Harvard Forest would bring me closer to the two people I need more of in my life. My relationship with each one is still on shaky ground. Would being nearby make things better or worse? With Satya, probably better, as long as I don't hound her to spend more time with me. Celeste, though? How can I ask without pressuring her to make more of a commitment than she's ready for?

The question springs to mind again hours later, as my boss flashes her most persuasive smile and leaves my office, closing the door behind her. Wow. When the stars align, they really align. Three discussions about tenure in one week. Stanford, Harvard, and Yale. It's like my twenty-year-old self's wet dream. Hell. I had a wet dream about this last night. It's like I've entered a multiverse.

I'm excited to tell Celeste about these opportunities when I see her this weekend. If the visit goes well.

31

Celeste

MY FLIGHT ARRIVED EARLY, SO I TAKE A FEW EXTRA minutes at the bathroom mirror to fluff my hair, brush my teeth, and spritz my face with rosewater. Outside, the smell of jet fuel and car exhaust overpowers me as I scan the line of cars approaching the curb. I'm anxious about returning to Wildbranch, even for a weekend. Being away from that community, I see how unhealthy it was for me. I'm sure if I had stuck around, I would have met different people. But it's hard when your whole social life involves your partner and then your partnership falls apart.

Moving back to New Haven helped me heal. I may not stay in the city forever; in fact, I often fantasize about living somewhere quieter. But landing in New Haven gave me the time and space to decompress and… anyway, here's Josh pulling up to the curb. A thrill zips through me and when he stops the jeep, leaps out, and sweeps me into his arms, I release my excitement with a loud squeal.

Two hours later, we're strolling through downtown Wildbranch, and I realize I was as freaked out about being with Josh here as I was about being back in town. He's been all attentive and chivalrous on my turf, but this is his turf. (Even though I'm the California native and he's a transplant.) Will he revert to his old patterns with me here? We find a seat at our favorite sidewalk cafe, and the same bozos who showed up at Ellen's memorial service stride over to us. As if that isn't bad enough, Mina is with them. Drop the last letter from her name and you have a perfect description of her personality: mean. They hover around us like a pack of hyenas.

"Celeste, didn't expect to see you back in town." Terry's affected surfer-dude voice doesn't hide his disdain.

"Truly, I'm stunned." Mina looks me up and down, then settles her gaze so she's looking down her very long nose at me. She bares her fangs in what apparently passes for a smile in her world.

Brent nods in my direction and croons, "Celeste. Will you be joining Josh at our annual cacao ceremony tonight?"

"Hmm, I don't think so. Josh?" I ask, trying to sound light, willing the three amigos to leave.

Josh glances in their direction, "Was that tonight?" He quickly returns his eyes to mine. "We can join them if you like, but I was hoping for more time alone with you."

"You'd miss the highlight of the summer?" Mina asks. "Brent's famous raw cacao with plant medicines, and Terry's band and the drum circle…"

"The highlight of my summer is sitting across from me," Josh says.

"Oh," Mina gasps.

Terry covers a laugh with a cough.

"Our Josh has changed," Brent says, adopting his hypnotic voice.

"I'm so lucky." Josh slips his hand under mine, taps the inside of my wrist three times, our secret way of saying I love you. He glances back at his friends. "Nice to see you guys out and about. Enjoy your weekend."

They stand there a beat too long, but Josh doesn't seem to notice. That makes me smile. Josh is a remade man. It's funny; I always thought that I was happy with him, but the joy we've shared lately shows me how unhappy I was much of the time. Maybe that's why his friends... No, I refuse to blame myself for their rudeness toward me. They're assholes.

What's certain is that whatever Josh did in that female fast, it transformed his entire approach to me, to us, probably to relation-ships. If things don't work out between us, I could see him finding someone and being loving and faithful for the rest of his life.

Well. That's a thought I dislike immensely. I'm the one who went through all that shit with him, and I want to be the one to benefit from it. Not because the idea of him spending his life with someone else makes me jealous. Sure, it does. But what Josh is offering me now is what I wanted all along. I want this, him, us. I shiver.

"Are you cold, baby?" Josh asks, concerned.

I shake my head, loving that he noticed. "I'm fine, just a chill."

"Do you have room for three more?" Terry asks.

They've been standing here all this time?

Josh looks at them as if he's emerging from a dream. He laughs. "My bad, guys. I am so focused on this woman right now, I honestly didn't realize you were still here. Forgive me. We don't get enough time together and..." He shrugs. "I want her all to myself. Catch you later, okay?"

All three mouths drop open.

I flash a smile at them. "Bye, guys. Enjoy the cacao ceremony."

They walk away.

I resist the urge to squeal as I refocus on Josh. "Do you know how good I felt hearing you say those words? Watching you draw a boundary that said this relationship is sacred?"

"Our relationship is sacred to me." He chuckles as he intertwines our fingers. "You know, it felt great saying those words, which is wild because I resisted setting boundaries like that for seven years. I was too afraid of upsetting my friends."

"That program really affected you."

"The program. Therapy. Your love and patience. Thank you for being patient with me and for giving me another chance." He leans over the table.

I meet him halfway and we kiss. Zing. Sparks. We giggle, deepen the kiss. I'm tingling in all the right places. Too bad we're in the wrong place for that to happen. "If we keep this up, we'll need to get takeout," I murmur.

"Whatever you want, babe."

We stay at the restaurant, and dinner is wonderful. The food, the service, the building heat between me and Josh as we savor our meal and our time together, feeding each other, tempting each other, flirting. We're flirting again. God I've missed this.

THE SUN IS SETTING WHEN WE ARRIVE AT HIS PLACE, ITS LAST rays illuminating Josh's fine physique as he carries my bag up the stairs. Why am I trembling? The last time I was here, I was moving out.

Josh throws the door open, holds it for me, and closes it behind me. "The house looks great," I say, and inhale deeply. It smells fresh, like lavender, roses and mint. "Have you been using my homemade cleaning supplies?"

"I'm grateful you forgot them here. The scent reminds me of you."

"Aww, Joshy."

The living room and kitchen look the same as I left them, minus the beheaded roses and the angry notecard. I cringe, thinking about how badly I wanted to hurt him then. Hurt people hurt people. We've both healed since last fall. We're stronger, kinder, more forgiving. Empty nails line the hallway. I'm not sure how to feel about the fact that in all these months, Josh never replaced the photos and art I took.

But as he leads me to the guest room, confusion mixes with upset. He lowers my bag onto the chair in the corner and turns to me, smiling and holding his arms out. Until he sees my face. His smile drops. "What's wrong?"

"The guest room?"

"I want you to be comfortable."

"Alone?"

"What? No. I thought..." Josh mumbles and moves his hands like he does when he's piecing thoughts together. I wait, trying to give him the benefit of the doubt. He comes to me and takes my hands. "Cece, please look at me."

I meet his gaze.

"You said you wouldn't sleep in the bed where... you know."

"I remember."

"You said you didn't know if you could sleep in that room."

"But..." He's right. I said that. Why do I feel like I've been banished?

"I heard your need for a space without all that old energy, all those memories. So I got a new bed, new pillows, new linens, and I made this my bedroom."

"You did?"

"I haven't slept in that room for weeks. I slept in the guest bed until the new one arrived, then I moved the guest bed into the other bedroom."

"Oh." I still feel upset. "What did you do with the old mattress and stuff?"

"Donated everything to a women's shelter in Oakland." He caresses my cheek. "Come here, let me show you." Josh leads me to the perfectly made bed and runs his hand along the duvet. I do the same. "Soft, right?" he asks.

I nod.

"Organic linen duvet cover, and the duvet is filled with natural alpaca fiber."

I gasp. "No way. That must have cost—"

"Yup." He pulls back the duvet and strokes the sheets. "Mulberry silk, so it won't dry your skin or hair."

"I always wanted silk sheets," I say, running my fingers along the fabric. It's as luxurious as I imagined.

"Mm-hmm. Now check this." He pulls the fitted sheet back to reveal the new mattress. "GOTS-certified organic cotton, organic wool, Forest Steward Council certified latex. And zero PFAS, zero polyurethane, zero any of the other toxic crap you find in most mattresses."

"Oh, my God." I press my hands into it. Plush, yet firm. Tempting. I step back.

"Hand tufted in Los Angeles."

"How much did you spend?"

"Enough so I hope you'll be comfortable," he says, putting the sheets back in place.

He did all this for me. I'm turning into a puddle inside, but I still have questions. "And if I'm not? If this doesn't work out between us?"

He purses his lips. "Then I'll keep enjoying this fine setup alone. But I don't think that's gonna happen."

"You don't?"

"I think you're gonna love this."

"You're awfully confident in yourself."

"I'm confident in love. Our love, to be precise."

A squeak escapes me.

"And in the damn good craftsmanship I invested in."

"Craftsmanship." I giggle.

"Nothing like a man who's good with his hands, right?" He holds his hands up, reminding me how good I feel when they're on my body.

"Mm," I say, feeling flirtatious again. "Or a woman who's good with her hands." I hold my hands in front of his.

"That's a fact." He gazes at my hands, then lets his eyes caress my body.

My body warming under his attention, I let myself savor the sight of him, too, wondering if my gaze has the same effect on him. Now, I see it does. I tap his hands. "How're you feeling?"

"Excited you're here. Eager to know whether you'll be comfortable."

I smile. "Let's find out." I drop on the bed. "Mmm. Perfect firmness."

He grins. "I know you like it firm, and I aim to please."

I laugh. "Ooh, show me your nice, firm mattress and I'll let you put your face in my soft, sweet pillow."

Josh groans but continues the goofy punning with me while we undress each other. Tonight, we take it slow and the way he touches me so gently has me beside myself with arousal. I want to be with him, to feel him inside me, but there's this enormous elephant in the room. In Josh-Celeste 1.0, I would have shared my feelings but had trouble telling him my needs, and he would have leapt to defend himself from an imaginary accusation. But this is Josh-Celeste 2.0, so I stroke his arm and scan his eyes and tell him I'm afraid. "What if it happens again? I need to know I'll be safe no matter what."

"Maybe we can stop it."

"How?"

"If you feel it starting, can you say 'help'?" He caresses my cheek, soothing.

"Then what?"

"I remind you who you are, say your name. See if that works. If it doesn't, we stop. I pull out of you. What do you think?"

"That could work."

"Worth a shot?"

"Yeah."

But he doesn't need to pull out. Josh pins me to the bed and fills me with his big, luscious manhood and I'm in heaven. He's riding me, repeating my name, like it's the most beautiful word in the universe. I'm writhing and arching up and he's teasing my nipples with his tongue, rocking his hips, until he brings me right to the edge. I'm so close I'm shaking. I hold his gaze, "Come with me?"

"Not yet, baby. Your turn."

"Josh—"

"Can I watch?"

I nod, closer.

"Thank you, Angel."

"Josh." I moan, about to tip.

"I'm yours, Cece. Use me like you want, Angel."

I squeeze him and tip my hips into his, as I crest. I scream his name as he rides me through the first wave.

"Take control, Angel?"

I agree. He hooks his leg under me and rolls me on top of him. I grind into him, feeling his already solid dick grow, reaching beneath him, finding his beautiful rocks and squeezing them. He groans in pleasure, growls, and bites my neck. Heaven. Now he's sucking my neck as I ride him.

"Honey, you're gonna have to go lower. It's not turtleneck season."

He lowers his mouth to a secret spot and sucks so hard, I can feel the mark forming. Ecstasy.

"Celeste."

"Yes." I rock into him.

"Will you claim me?"

"Claim you?"

"Tell me I'm yours and no one else's. Would you like to say that?"

"You are mine, Josh Albright." I murmur in his ear.

"I have always been yours." His hot breath tickles my ear.

"You have always been mine." I nibble his earlobe.

"I will never be another's."

"You will never be another's."

"I am yours."

"You are mine." When I say the word mine, a wave pulses up my spine, so I lift off him, open to let him enter me again, grind into him as I sit astride him like a cowgirl. Vibrations rise from his cock through my center, up my spine. His energy is splitting me open as it rises. I deepen my breath. He deepens his, too, and every time we exhale, the energy rises higher. "Feel that, Josh?"

"Yes, Celeste." He growls.

The slow-moving wave of energy gains momentum as we rock our hips in unison. I'm in an erotic trance, held by his gaze, his scent, and his movements under me, and now the energy transforms from a gentle wave to a raucous thing that makes me moan and writhe back and forth on him. And he's growling, "Yes," and "So hot," and "Sexy," and "Goddess."

And I'm screaming now with the ecstasy of this-him-me-us together, coming so hard, energy shooting out the top of my head so fast I have to throw my hands in the air to let it out, as I press deeper into him. "Yes," we scream together, and when I finally finish, I collapse on top of him.

"Amazing," he whispers.

"Did you come, too?"

"I was waiting for you. So close. Can I now? Can I, goddess?"

"Yes. Take me as you want me," I say, offering a gift, not subservience, but service.

He rolls back onto me, presses himself into me, over and over again, slow and deep and hard and then faster and faster and he's crying he's gonna come, and now he's coming, his seed spills into me, filling my everything. And he collapses onto me, slides his arms under me and melts into me as he squeezes me tight. "Baby," he whimpers. "Baby."

"Yes, love?" He wants to say more, but he's holding back. "I'm right here, Joshy. Tell me what you need."

"I need you," he whispers into my neck. "I need you, Celeste."

"I'm right here."

He brings his mouth to mine, and we kiss. He sucks my tongue then speaks into my open mouth. "I need you always."

"Good."

We lay here, holding each other. He's nuzzling me, making sweet little sounds.

"Are you alright, Joshy?"

"Missed you. Missed this. Need you."

"I'm here."

"Was it beautiful?"

"Yes. Was it beautiful?"

"Beyond. Are you ready to sleep?"

"No."

"Wanna go lie in the hammock and look at the stars?"

"Yes."

Josh wraps me in a blanket and carries me outside to the hammock, then climbs in next to me. We lay in the gently swinging hammock looking into the night sky. "Celeste?"

"Yes?"

"I wasn't kidding when I said always. It wasn't just a word or sex talking. I've been thinking about it a lot."

"Really?"

"It's a fact."

"Scientific fact?"

"Irrefutable. Proven in nightly lab tests."

I giggle and snuggle deeper into him.

"I keep running equations in my mind. If we mix this element called Celeste and this element called Josh, what kind of substance does it form? A liquid? A gel? A solid? A gas?"

"What have you discovered?"

"It's a unique substance, never before seen in the universe."

"How so?"

"Like a liquid, it can flow around the most difficult obstacles. Like a hydrogel, it clings to form a protective boundary around anything and even deliver healing medicine on a time release. Like a solid, it can hold steady against wind and rain. If it's protected, it can even hold fast against fire."

"That is an amazing substance."

"That's not all."

"Oh?"

"Like a gas, it burns bright in the night sky, bringing hope to all who are fortunate enough to see it and make a wish upon it."

"That is powerful."

"So you can see why I'm serious."

"It makes sense."

"But one thing this substance can't do forever is have its elements separated at such a distance for such a long time."

"Oh." My stomach drops. He wants me to move back here.

"Now, before you get upset."

"I wasn't getting upset."

"I thought I heard a little tone in your voice. Anyway, I've been thinking the solution might be for the masculine element to move closer to the feminine element."

"How much closer?"

"I don't want to put pressure on you, but how would you feel if I moved back east?"

"I'd be fine with that."

"Just fine with it?"

"No, I mean." I take a second to check in with my body. "My heart's pounding and there are butterflies in my stomach. I'd love that. Is it a possibility?"

"Yeah."

"Wow. When?"

"I'm not ready to say more, but I promise to tell you when I know."

"Okay." I kiss his cheek and lay back against his bare chest. "I wanted us to feel close like this for so long. Now, it's happening, and it's even better than I ever dreamed. Since we reconnected, Josh, you've shown me over and over that I'm safe with you. The way you've treated me these last two months..." I sigh.

32

Josh

WAKING BESIDE CELESTE, MY BODY SINGS WITH gratitude for the second chance at true love. I bury my face in her hair, search out her warm, slender neck, and inhale her scent. Her natural fragrance is all I need. More than anything, I want to show Celeste I'm worth it. We are worth it.

I slide my palm from her hip to her stomach, recalling her stoicism when she shared her inability to get pregnant. It broke my heart. She was almost desperate to be a mother, and it would have been beautiful to raise a child with her.

Celeste stirs, mumbles something in her half-wakened state. I love this part of the morning when I get to gaze at her, feel the heat of her skin. She used to like it when I'd wake her with a massage, gently roll her onto her stomach and straddle her, knead my fingers into her muscles until she woke. Would she like that now?

I know her better than anyone else. Yet it seems like I'm just learning the basics. We've both grown and changed, and I want to avoid making assumptions based on how things used to be and what she used to like. I'll just cherish her and this moment as-is.

She rolls over, smiles at me, stretches in my arms. I pull her close until she giggles, the sweetest music. She says my name, and I melt.

"Ooh, I had too much garlic last night." She covers her mouth.

"Give me some of that dragon breath!"

She arches her eyebrow sexily, then blows a stream of morning breath into my face.

I try not to recoil, but can't help laughing. "Whoo! You weren't kidding, lady." I devour her mouth, like it's the best taste ever. She giggles and pushes me away until I relent. "How'd you sleep, Angel?"

"Better than I have in months. This bed is amazing, and falling asleep in your arms, waking with you." She sighs happily, a smile lighting her eyes.

"It's the first morning together in Celeste and Josh part two."

"Is that what we're calling this?"

"What do you think we should call it?"

"I don't care. I'm just happy here with you. Feeling your smooth skin and the rough hair on your legs and chest, and..." She purrs.

"I like you feeling me up. It's making my hairs stand on end."

"Mm-hmm. And other things." She bites my neck.

Oh, so we're going there on our first morning together. I'm up for that, literally and figuratively. "Have I told you how happy I am you're here? How grateful I am for this second chance?"

She murmurs. "I think I heard you whisper it in my sleep about a hundred times last night, and while we were lying in the hammock, and while we were making love, and during dinner." She kisses her way from my neck to my chest. Delightful.

"I'm getting redundant, huh?"

"I don't mind." She licks a circle around my navel, and all thoughts leave until she rests her chin on my stomach and gazes up at me. "I half expected you to wake me in the middle of the night and finish those thoughts with some hard proof."

"Proof was there. But one thing I've learned these last nine months is to make no assumptions. Since we're starting fresh, I wanna make sure you truly want what I always believed you wanted."

"Why do you say that?"

"You've always been eager to please me." I cringe. "Sometimes, I took your desire as a given, acted like you should try to please me, and I wasn't required to reciprocate."

"Wow."

"Was I wrong?"

"No. But I've always enjoyed waking in the middle of the night to the hard proof of your affection."

"Damn. Missed opportunity."

"No worries, some opportunities rise again." She winks. "I've learned, when an opportunity rises again, it's best to take it firmly in hand and explore it."

"Yes, I see where you're going with this. Depending on various factors, examine by feel. Other times, taking a mathematical approach is best."

"Correct." She shows me the sensing method of savoring the opportunity that has arisen between us. Clever woman has also positioned herself so I can demonstrate my understanding of the mathematical method, which I do. Oh, Lord, I do.

I begin by narrating my survey of the opportunity, then I slowly, gently, explore it with every tool and every sense available: sight, touch, scent, taste, even sound. For example, I'm testing a theory about chanting Om in what Celeste likes to call her sacred temple. The data I'm gathering suggests my hypothesis was correct: it brings the woman immense pleasure. She always said sex was a spiritual experience for her. Now, with her giggling and writhing, squeezing her thighs around my neck and sucking more urgently, I understand her meaning. Makes me wanna spend more time on my knees.

Like every good prayer, this one results in the kind of ecstasy only a loving God would create. We're panting, chanting, moaning, screaming his name, so it fills the room like we're filling each other. Until all we can do is lie spent and sated, stroking each other's legs.

Her touch has me so relaxed I could fall asleep again, but Celeste moans, "Caffeine," and I spring to attention.

"The usual? I made fresh almond milk for us yesterday."

"Yum. Yes, please." She rolls off the bed and dashes into the bathroom. The door lock clicks. In seven years together, five living in the same house, she never once let me see or hear her on the toilet. Now, she's singing to cover the sound. Cute, when you consider the sounds she makes in her sleep, and that they've never phased me in the slightest.

"I need to brush my teeth, too." I rap on the door.

"One minute."

Which means ten, so I dash into the kitchen and brew our pot of yerba maté. I hurry back, hoping to see Celeste brush her teeth. I tap the door and she lets me in.

"You brush your teeth already?" I ask.

Her eyebrows rise. "I'm getting to it. I thought you liked my dragon breath."

"I do, but all good things must end." I grin. "Besides, I wanna watch you brush your teeth."

She lifts a cheek in her famous lopsided smile, spreads toothpaste on her brush. "The in and out thing?"

"Nah. I just missed these little moments." Do I still get to have secrets if I'm being transparent? One of my secret pleasures is watching this sensual, sophisticated, brilliant woman get toothpaste all over her face. She has no idea how adorable it is, and I think if I told her, she'd find it annoying.

We discuss brunch options while brushing, rinsing, and spitting. Celeste wants to help prepare the meal, but I'm excited to take care of her this weekend. My father taught me little of value in the personal realm, but he is a damn fine cook. One of his ex-wives is from Mexico, and she taught us all these phenomenal recipes. She was pretty nice, too. A shame he drove her away. Marta was her name. When I tell Celeste I have all the ingredients to make Marta's huevos rancheros, she shimmies in excitement. Fucking adorable.

We hold hands and stride from the bathroom to the kitchen. Celeste settles onto a bar stool at the kitchen counter and lets me serve her tea, which she sips while watching me move around the kitchen. We chat easily as I crack the eggs into a bowl. Because of Marta, I never buy canned beans. I buy them dried or fresh, cook them, and then refry them with Marta's special blend of spices. The only difference is I replace lard with olive oil. Now, I empty half a jar of cooked pinto beans into the skillet with olive oil and spices, and start the slow mashing, stirring process. Standing at the stove means my back is to the kitchen island, so I'm surprised when Celeste arrives at my side, fully caffeinated, no longer content to sit and watch.

"I think I remember the tortilla recipe," she says. "It's just masa, salt, water and lime, right?"

"You got it, but I made dough already. It's in the fridge. Wanna roll them?"

"Fun!" She lays a sheet of wax paper on the counter next to me, gets the rolling pin and the dough, makes balls and flattens them into perfect... Hmmm... Looks like she's off her game.

"How's it going there, babe?"

"Great!"

"The circles are a little... uh..." Maybe I should just shut up. Who cares if the corn tortillas are lopsided?

"Aren't they cute? See? They're hearts."

My heart melts. "Aww, baby." I kiss her cheek. "Let's take a picture. It could be the cover of your next book."

"Heart-shaped tortillas?"

I reach for my phone. "Okay, no, but Satya will love this. Smile." Celeste strikes a goofy pose with her creation, and I snap the pic. "So fucking cute."

My phone dings. A text from Terry:
Mountain biking. 30 minutes. Meet by
the trailhead.

Celeste and I in our private heaven, RN.
Thanks, though.

Good luck with that.

Thanks! Have fun.

I flip the phone over and catch Celeste's questioning look.

"Terry invited me to go mountain biking in thirty minutes."

"Are you?"

"Silly. Why would I do that when I get to spend the day with you? Unless you want to?"

"Not particularly."

"What would you like to do today? Hike? Hang out in the hammock all day? Take a yoga class at the studio you like?"

"You don't like yoga classes."

"But if you want to—"

"Let's practice together on the deck after brunch?"

"Beautiful idea."

We take the huevos, fresh OJ, and more yerba maté outside, and relax at the table. The food is fucking awesome, if I say so myself. Celeste raves about my homemade tomatillo sauce, cashew-based sour cream and fresh guacamole. I compliment Celeste on her tortillas, which are as delicious as they are cute.

These visits are too short and I hate to think about her leaving. "No need to go home tomorrow, you know."

"That's when my flight is."

"You could change it. Stay a few days or a week?"

"I wish."

"Come on. Stay."

"I left my laptop at home, so I have no way to work. Plus, I've got appointments this week."

"Use my laptop. You see clients online, right?"

"I see some clients online, but these appointments are in person. Also, I'm meeting with my editor in New York, and I have a doctor's appointment."

"Everything okay?"

"Mm-hmm. It's a follow-up, but it took months to get the appointment. If I miss it, I'll probably have to wait another four months."

"Understood."

"But next time I come out, I can plan my appointments so I can stay for a week."

"Sweet. When do you wanna come?"

"Two weeks? You've been coming to me every two weeks for the last three months. I know it's been a lot for you, so I can do it."

I swallow. Two weeks is right before I fly back east to meet Dustin at the Harvard Forest. Then to UMass Amherst's Materials Engineering department, and finally I'll go down to Yale to check out their new Green Chemistry lab and talk about tenure positions there. Shit. I don't wanna get Celeste's hopes up before I have a solid offer. I planned to surprise her once I knew more.

"What's that look on your face, Josh?"

"Thinking about my obligations the following week." This could be fantastic, actually. I could book the same flight home as her, then tell her what's happening. She'll be psyched. She loves surprises. "That's perfect, honey."

"Yay. And I can stay the week. I'll plan all my client meetings on zoom, and… Okay, now you definitely look disconcerted."

"Well," I draw out the word to stall for time. What do I say? If I tell her about my interviews and don't get a job offer, it'll disappoint her. She might even think I was leading her on, playing games to get her back. If I make up an excuse, then I'll be lying. I've worked so hard to rebuild trust with her. The last thing I wanna do is say anything that's less than one hundred percent honest. Shit.

"Honey? What's wrong?"

"Uh..."

"I thought you'd be happy."

"I'm so happy, Celeste."

"Then why are you frowning?"

"Uh... I want to be really honest with you." Now she looks scared. "Don't worry. I'm just not ready to talk about... this... thing. How about I tell you in two weeks?"

Her face is saying Hell no. Her mouth is saying, "I guess, but I dislike you keeping things from me."

"That makes sense," I say quickly. "Especially with our history and the mistakes I made in the past. I totally understand why you feel bad about me keeping information from you. And..."

She sighs. Even the way she's eating has changed. She's chewing in that very specific way she only does when she's mad.

"I want to tell you."

"So tell me." Now, she's sounding snarky. Fuck.

"Angel, I know I broke your trust, but I've worked really hard since I entered the program last November to learn healthy skills. It's the end of July. That's nine months I've spent shining light in my darkness, so I could show you it's safe to trust me."

Emotions cross her face I hoped never to see again: hurt, anger, suspicion, frustration. Her walls are going up.

"I understand why you'd feel better if I share everything right now. Ultimately, though, I think you'll appreciate me waiting. Have I done anything since we've reconnected that made you question my honesty, sincerity, or openness?"

She takes a deep breath, lets it out, meets my gaze, looks at her eggs, then back at me. "You have not."

I drop my shoulders in relief. "Do you see I'm trustworthy now?"

"Yes. Still, it scares me when I don't know what's going on."

I nod. "I know."

"I know you know, but I need to say it."

"Okay."

"It scares me because I didn't question things before, and I missed some obvious signs. That makes me fear I'll miss signs again."

I take her hand. "You needed to be hypervigilant. What I did traumatized you. It turned your world upside down."

"Yeah."

"And you can't risk that happening again. It was too hard on you emotionally and physically." As evidenced by her insomnia and how thin she's gotten, but I don't need to tell her that.

"Exactly."

"If it's that important to you to know now, I'll tell you because I have your best interests at heart."

She nods.

"Should we take a deep breath together?"

She meets my gaze and holds it as we inhale slowly and exhale with a long sigh.

"Come sit with me?" I ask.

Celeste plants herself in my lap, and I hold her tight, kiss the side of her head. She buries her face against my shoulder. Her breath gets faster, more ragged, and now my shoulder is wet.

I stroke her hair. "I'm sorry, baby. I didn't mean to scare you. Tell me what you need."

"I wanna trust you," she whispers.

"What can we do to help you trust me? How can we work this out?"

"I wanna stay with you that week."

"I wish you could. Really, I do, but I have to travel on business."

"What if I come with you?"

"Sorry, Angel."

She growls in displeasure.

"I promise when I explain, you'll understand." I hope. I'm getting nervous. "You might even be pleased."

"Then why are you shaking?"

I sigh. "Please trust me. I promise it won't hurt this time."

33

Josh

GET CELESTE'S TRAVEL INFO SO I CAN BOOK THE SAME flight. While she goes home to New Haven, I'll meet with Dustin at the Harvard Forest, spend a couple days in Mass. Then I'll make my way back through New Haven to meet with Lyrion at the new Green Chemistry Initiative at Yale. Two unique positions in very different departments. In green chemistry, I'll get to collaborate with foresters at the School of The Environment and on toxicology projects with epidemiologists. Maybe even Wesley. That's the benefit of having my own lab in general research.

In the meantime, Stanford's business consultant is helping me set up our company. Hopefully, sooner rather than later, we'll be manufacturing our fire-retardant hydrogel at scale, meeting the flood of incoming requests from around the country sparked by our report in Science and Nature. The University is also helping me apply for approval from the US Forest Service to use our product on federal lands. God, my head is spinning so hard, I have no clue how I got home. What's today? Thursday. Celeste arrives tomorrow.

A familiar car is in my driveway. Is that Erin? As soon as I pull up, she gets out of the car and opens her arms for a hug. I throw an arm around her and pull back quickly. "Erin, my God. It's been forever. How've you been? I thought you were in Idaho."

"I was in Vancouver, then the Seattle area, then in Portland, and then I went down for Burning Man and I got on the whole eclipse circuit, like teaching yoga at all these festivals, and it was really beautiful, and then it just got a little bit too toxic for me, and like, um, you know, there was just a lot of energy, and you know, like a lot of people were being inhabited by other spirits and, I just, I needed to bounce. You know?" She pauses, at last, for a breath, tilting her head so her feather earrings dangle.

"Uh, sure. Okay. Wow. Well, it's good to see you. What brings you here? I mean, when was the last time we even spoke?"

"I don't know. I've just been like, so, so, intense, you know? I mean, of course, you know I think about you all the time, Josh, all the time, but I've been like just really needing my own... You know?"

"Uh, huh." I have no idea what she's talking about and she's not giving me time to ask. "So..."

"And, like, the thing is, I know you, like I, I really. Do you know what I mean?"

"Actually, no. I don't. I'm just getting home from work..."

"Can I come in to pee?"

"Um, sure."

Erin is a pretty good yoga teacher, but she always seems to have trouble getting her life together. Or speaking in coherent sentences, but that's another matter. I mount the steps onto the side porch and unlock the door. She follows me into the kitchen and disappears into the powder room around the corner.

She emerges a few minutes later and slumps onto a barstool at the kitchen counter. "Oh, Josh." She sighs. "I don't know what to do. You've always been so good at figuring things out. You and Celeste. I hear you guys are getting back together?"

"Where'd you hear that?"

"Oh, you know, we're all looking out for you."

"Okay." I don't think I want to know what that means, so I keep the focus on her. "What's going on? Are you moving back here?"

"I just need a little TLC, you know. I just. It's been. You know how hard it is when you're always putting other people first, right?"

"Mmmm. And so..."

"Actually, I just need a place to land for a little while. You know, like a few days, or maybe a week or two or three." The numbers seem to increase as her volume diminishes.

"What about... Sasha?"

Blank stare.

"Or Ariel?"

She looks at the floor.

"Mina. Aren't you two pretty tight?"

"I know." Erin drags out the word know and shifts her gaze to the ceiling. "We are, but like, she can be really difficult. You know? Like hard to live with? She's got like OCD or something."

"Huh." Funny, most of our friends describe Mina as slovenly.

"Anyway, I think she's mad at me."

"Sorry to hear that. I'm sure you'll work things—"

"I was hoping I could stay with you for a little while."

"Aha. Celeste is coming tomorrow for the weekend. You can stay tonight."

"Oh, I love Celeste. I mean, she wouldn't have a problem with my staying here. Would she?"

Celeste is the most open, loving, generous, nurturing person, and if anyone ever has a soft spot for someone in trouble, it's her.

"She probably wouldn't. But we're just reconnecting, and I'd like us to have some privacy."

"I will totally stay out of your way. You won't even know I'm here. I'll just like lock the door to the bedroom and disappear."

"Or, I could get you a hotel room for a couple days."

"Oh, Josh, I could never ask you for money. And this is so much easier. Right? I mean, besides, I can even. Like, I can even give you guys a free yoga class while she's here! And, you know and like for you, as long as I'm staying here, I'm happy to do that kind of exchange. I would love to offer that to you."

"Thank you." Shit. I don't like yoga classes. I like to practice by myself, get into a rhythm. Doesn't she know that about me? Maybe I never had the heart to tell her. "Okay, I guess this is... this is fine. Yeah."

"Oh, my God, Josh, you are the absolute bestest," she says, throwing her arms around me.

Interesting. After the female fast, I am not as comfortable with this kind of affection from someone I'm not sleeping with. Boy, there's a shift I had never expected. "Thanks, Erin." I gently pry her arms off me. "I've moved bedrooms, so you can take the one on the right at the end of the hall."

"Do you have anything to eat?"

"See if there's anything you want in the fridge. I'm just gonna—"

"Or we could order pizza."

"Yeah, I'm up for that. I'll spring for pizza."

"You're such a good friend, Josh. I totally appreciate you."

I smile and dial the pizza place. Something about this doesn't quite sit well with me, but I'm not sure what. It's probably because there's so much on my mind right now. Probably unrelated to Erin. When I meditate and clear my mind, I'll feel fine about this surprise.

34

Josh

ID I MESS UP BY LETTING ERIN STAY WITH ME? AS WE pull into the driveway and see Erin's car, and I explain what happened, Celeste's face falls. Suddenly, I remember some things Celeste has said about my friend over the years. Celeste is nurturing with me and my daughter, but less generous with my friends. It makes no sense to me. I thought hearing about the bind Erin's in would bring out my girlfriend's compassionate side. Instead, she scowls.

Celeste

"Was this the surprise?" I ask, staring at Erin's obnoxious purple sports car in Josh's driveway.

"Uh, no. Well, it is a surprise. She was here when I got home from work last night and needed a place to stay."

"How long is she here?"

"I don't know."

"How long will you let her stay?"

"I hadn't thought about it. I have so much else on my mind."

This does not sit right with me. I got a bad vibe from Erin the moment I met her, and over the years, I grew to trust her even less. She and Josh used to be super close, which never made sense to me because they have nothing in common. Is she trying to make a play for him now? Unlike most of the people who live in this town, Erin grew up here. Her family is here. I don't believe for a second that she has nowhere else to stay. "You and Erin never got romantic, did you?"

"No... actually, I have a vague memory of something maybe fifteen years ago. Being really drunk, her throwing herself at me the way she does."

"Oh?" Now's a good time to practice deep breathing. I slow my inhale and stare out the windshield at the sky while Josh explains.

"She's a physical person."

"I've noticed."

"Really? Funny, I never noticed until last night. I realized it's one of her personality traits. Since doing the fast, I feel less comfortable sharing physical affection with any woman outside my family, unless I want to be intimate with her. So, you know what that means."

"Tell me."

"It means the only woman I want throwing her arms around me is you."

I smile. "That was the right thing to say."

Josh blows out a puff of air. He's uncomfortable. "Anyway, she knows you're coming this weekend, and that you and I want time alone together. She promised we won't even notice she's here."

"Okay." Well, at least the woman has a clue about decorum.

Famous last thought. As soon as we open the door, it's clear Erin's promise to lay low was hollow. We're assaulted by strong-smelling incense. I have no problem with incense, but Josh hates it.

He coughs. "Erin, are you burning something?"

"Hi," she sings, as she rises from the couch. "I lit some Nag Champa. Is that a problem?"

"Josh is kind of allergic to incense. That's why he never has it in the house."

"Oh, my goodness." Erin strides across the enormous living room and grabs the incense burner from the mantle. "I am so sorry." Her super fake valley girl voice grates on my ears, but at least she's handling the situation, running into the powder room and dousing the incense stick. "I will never burn incense here again, okay?"

For someone who planned to disappear, she sure has taken over. Candles burn on every available surface in the living room and kitchen, some dripping wax onto the wood. Wow. Now, she approaches me like we're long-lost best friends. "Hi, Celeste! How are you?"

"Erin. How are you? I hear you're having a rough time." I let my voice drip with faux sympathy. If she's smart, she'll hear that I'm ready to defend my relationship with Josh.

He invited me here because he wants us to heal together. In our first go-round, I was unaware I needed to protect us, but now I see it with crystal clarity.

Case in point: despite her promises to disappear, Erin hangs out with us. The quiet romantic dinner we planned to share at home becomes a threesome. So, who could blame me for what comes out of my mouth when Erin offers us a "special private yoga class" on the deck tomorrow morning?

"Oh, bummer. If only Josh didn't hate yoga classes. Our favorite way to practice is alone together." I interlace our fingers, and he squeezes my hand. "We get into a super juicy flow. Right hon?"

He winks at me, which always gives me goosebumps.

Catty? Sure, but I'm speaking the only language I know Erin understands. The funny thing is, Josh seems completely unaware that Erin and I are going toe-to-toe. Such a man. Show me the guy who can sit in the middle of a swirling, aggressive bitch fight and notice it occurring, and I'll show you a unicorn. It's bizarre. Are they intentionally clueless, or do they feign innocence because they enjoy when women fight over them?

The weird thing is, even with her super-aggressive physical "affection," I'm sure she's not into him. There are literally zero sex vibes. He's definitely not interested in her. Every time she touches him, he backs away and shakes it off, like a dog shaking off mud. So what is Erin doing? I have no clue why she's here, especially on this weekend of all weekends, but this situation reeks like a fart in a yoga class.

His friends have always been weird. From the moment we met, I felt them protecting their turf. Josh gives a lot, hosts a lot of parties, helps friends in financial need. They're a band of misfit toys, so maybe they like having a Peter Pan. Well, jerks, Josh decided to grow up. You should try it because I'm done putting up with your bullshit.

When I recall how Satya described the way these idiots treated her, it makes me want to stand up for us more. Now I know I wasn't the problem: they were and still are. So, throughout the evening, I make my presence felt in every way I can.

When we finish dinner and get into his huge soaking tub and he seduces me, I open up and enjoy every moment. At first, I'm concerned that Josh might shush me so his friend doesn't hear, but I let myself go wild and take control. Damn, it feels good. I'm discovering the thrill of telling Josh what I want, and watching, or—even better—feeling him obey, like I'm a Queen or a Goddess. I used to keep quiet in bed, focus on pleasing him. Now, I let myself moan, scream, purr and growl. I'm discovering my power to please myself and my man at the same time, and he's totally into this. Someone may be in the next room, but we're alone in a paradise of our making.

Saturday morning, we wake bright and early and practice yoga on the deck before we even make our tea. When we walk into the kitchen, Erin sings, "Good morning, sleepyheads," and reminds us of her special offer.

"Thanks! We already practiced," I say, keeping my voice low, husky, powerful.

"Oh." Her voice goes up a notch. "How was it?"

"Beautiful," Josh says. "At first, it was rough getting past the lack of caffeine, but then we got into a flow state and—" He interrupts himself to brew the tea. "Practicing beside this woman first thing in the morning was heaven."

"You two are so cute." Sarcasm from Erin. There's a surprise.

Josh gives her a side-eye. Some Californians may miss the messages behind a sarcastic comment, but Josh is from Massachusetts. He knows sarcasm. "No matter what anyone else thinks, we're happy." He wraps his free arm around me and leans in for a kiss. I oblige, moaning in delight as I savor his taste and our first public display of affection. We might have to try PDA more often.

Erin clears her throat. She's still here?

I turn in Josh's arms and lean into him, smirking as the proof of his pleasure presses against my low back. "How long are you staying, Erin?"

"Just until I get on my feet."

"Wow. Sounds like it could be a while. You have a place here?"

She frowns. "Ever since the studio burned down, I haven't been able to find a place to land. All over the Pacific Northwest, people are struggling."

I nod. "Times are tough all around. Good thing you have a wide network of friends and relatives to turn to."

"Yeah, and Josh is the bestest."

"I agree." Though, I prefer to use big-girl words.

"So, listen, Erin," Josh says, handing me a steaming cup of yerba maté with fresh almond milk. "It was great catching up last night, and I know Celeste enjoyed it as much as I did."

I smile up at him. Smooth operator.

"But tonight," he continues, "we plan to have a private dinner here. The two of us. Alone. Cool?"

"Totes. I'll make myself scarce. You won't even know I'm here."

"Yeah, we'd appreciate having the entire house to ourselves."

"Understood. I'm sure I can find somewhere to hang out for a few hours."

"Or the night," Josh suggests, helpfully.

Erin makes an exaggerated nod. "Or the night."

"We're going hiking, and as long as we've got the house by like 5:30, that's perfect."

"Awesome," Erin says.

35

Celeste

Hiking this rugged trail is like visiting an old friend. One thing I always loved about living in the Sierra Nevada mountains was easy access to the wilderness. Before wildfires became an annual event, we had air unlike anywhere else. Fresh, crisp, clean. Almost ethereal.

The scent of sequoia trees brings me back to happy childhood moments, when Mom managed to climb out of her depression and be present with Nana and me. We'd pack a picnic and walk the trails along the base of the mountain near our home. Then depression killed her, and Nana and I moved to Vermont to live with her sister. Coming back here in my thirties brought up a lot of memories, and the chance to connect with my paternal roots. But watching this land smolder feels like losing my parents all over again.

Have you ever watched something or someone you love fall apart? You stand there, helpless, feeling it happen, but so blinded by the flames you can't see past them. You wish more than anything you could stop it. All you can do is stand very still, close your eyes, and wait for it to end. If you're lucky, you might find remnants of the life you loved in the ash.

Now, ash falls, leaving a light dusting of gray over everything. Yet it doesn't dull the fragrance completely. I inhale. "Sequoia scent brings up so many memories. I miss it living back east."

"I'll miss it, too, if I leave."

"What else will you miss if you leave?"

"These mountains. The wacky culture. My friends. I guess it depends where I end up."

"Where would you like to end up?" It's a risky question because the answer could leave me hurting.

"I'd like to end up with you."

"But where?"

"Somewhere we both love."

"That's a nice non-committal answer," I say, annoyed at the evasiveness.

"Hey, what do you want me to commit to: a place or our relationship?"

"Good point. You're right."

"Wait. I'm sorry. What? Could you repeat that?"

"I said, I can't argue with…"

"No, I mean the last two words."

"You're right?"

"Yeah, that! One more time, with feeling."

"Josh." I push him away playfully and he laughs.

"That's okay. I heard it. And I'll savor those words for the rest of my life."

"Oh, you are such a drama queen."

"Me? Come on." He grabs me around the waist and hoists me onto his shoulder. I screech in surprise.

Josh carries me up the trail like a sack of potatoes, and I'm laughing as I bounce on his shoulder, making sure my face doesn't bump into his backpack. After five or ten minutes, I protest. "I won't get any exercise like this!"

"You need to save your strength. I intend to put you through a workout later."

"Oh, really?"

He lowers me to the ground with a grunt. "Whoo. I need to save my strength."

"I coulda told you that, boy." I purr.

He growls in response, pulls me close and nuzzles my earlobe, then holds my hand the rest of the way up the trail, past the ponderosa pines and eucalyptus. Chipmunks scurry out of our way.

At the top of the mountain, clouds of smoke obscure the spectacular view across the canyon. Josh pulls a picnic blanket from his backpack, spreads it over the flat, rough ground, then lays out a feast, including his homemade tomatillo salsa, homemade tortilla chips, fresh guacamole, and veggies to dip. Plus my favorite non-dairy chocolate.

"When did you pack this?"

"While you were getting dressed."

"And you brought my favorite kombucha, too. Josh, that's so thoughtful!"

"I know this weekend hasn't gone exactly how either of us planned, but I hope this makes up for it a little."

"Life rarely goes as planned."

"True dat," he says. "My life has been in upheaval lately."

Now, I'm concerned. "I thought everything was going great with your fire retardant."

"It is. But it added a shitload of tasks to my list that I hadn't considered, like starting a company to manufacture it. You know, time is of the essence. Looks like fire season is starting early this year."

"I noticed." I gesture to the view.

"It was clear until Wednesday. A couple fires started up in the canyon Thursday morning. They seem contained, but I wanna move this forward. We're still doing soil testing. We've got data from spring and summer and we're moving into fall now. I need data from fall, and I wanna be closer to you. It's a lot to think about."

"You're saying if you hurry things forward, you'll be able to help people sooner."

"Right, but we need US Forest Service approval before we can sell this to state and federal fire departments, et cetera. We received our patent at last, we're getting income from homeowners and utilities companies using it, but evaluation of the product is slow, even though I requested a rush." He lets out a loud sigh. "I can only do so much."

"Oh, honey, I didn't realize you had so much pressure on you. I'm sorry I've been insensitive to that."

"Thanks." The softness in his eyes lets me know he appreciates I see the strain he's under.

We relax in silence, enjoying each other's company, the picnic, and this beautiful spot.

After about an hour, Josh looks at his watch. "Shall we go back the way we came, or take the circle route?"

"The circle route is longer, right?"

"A little. And the terrain is a little rougher. You up for that?"

"Definitely."

We pack the picnic items into his backpack. Each time our eyes meet or our fingertips graze, I feel a zing, even after seven-plus years and all we've been through. I'm so glad I gave him another chance.

He looks at his watch again, calculating. "We should be back by six and have the place to ourselves."

I hope he's right. I'm still suspicious of Erin, but we sent such clear signals, she'd be a fool to hang around.

Josh

WE HOLD HANDS MOST OF THE WAY DOWN THE TRAIL. I HAVE to remind myself to stay present and look at the ground because my mind is spinning off in all directions, planning various versions of my future with Celeste. I've gotta hand it to the female fast. That program made it possible for me to have a better relationship with myself and with the woman I love than I ever knew was possible. I never dreamed that I could feel this comfortable with someone, this supported, and want to give so much all the time. I catch myself thinking of ways to please her now.

More than anything, I hope I get a solid offer of tenure this week. It will probably mean being bicoastal for a while, as I get the company off the ground, tie up loose ends in the lab, and start working back east, but I want to move forward with Celeste. Live with her. Hell, I can't believe I'm thinking this, but I want to marry her. I want to marry Celeste Cairan. I've never wanted or believed in marriage before. Now, it's half my fantasy life. Putting that ring on her finger. Saying vows. Knowing we'll be there for each other 'til death do us part.

"What are you smiling about?" she asks, as we reach the parking lot and get into the car.

"You. Us. I feel like a new man."

"You seem like the man I always saw deep down inside but was becoming convinced I had imagined."

For the umpteenth time today, I send a silent prayer of thanks for this woman's patience and love. And I cannot wait to tell her the surprise. Tomorrow, I will take her to the airport and park the car, walk through security with her, and she'll ask, "What are you doing?" That's when I'll tell her. First, she'll say. "Really? Oh, my God, Josh, this is amazing!" Then she'll throw her arms around me. We'll both feel so amped, we might join the mile high club on the flight back east.

Then I'll crush my interviews and find the perfect match for what I want to do in my career, and I'll get a phenomenal offer from all three universities. Celeste and I will discuss options, and she'll help me figure out the best move because it's not only a move for me and my career; it's a move for us.

But first, dinner.

We pull into the driveway at six. "I told Erin we needed privacy tonight, right?"

"You did."

"Why are there two cars in the driveway?" I know the second car, but I forget who it belongs to.

"Maybe we'll go out?"

"Yeah." Disappointing. "Or maybe they're just getting ready to leave."

"Yeah."

"Maybe if we're lucky, it's a date and she won't come back tonight."

"That'd be nice."

"Right? Let's not get our hopes up, though."

"I see your point. Everything will be fine."

"Exactly."

Famous last words. I hate to sound trite, but what the hell else do you say when you walk into your house and you find your friend and the woman you cheated with? Fuck.

Celeste gasps and tenses. Words fail me. We're both silent a bit too long, apparently, because Lucinda says, "Hi, guys. it's great to see you!"

She beelines across the room and hugs me. I back away. She reaches for Celeste, and Celeste puts her hands up in defense. "Don't even. What the hell, Josh?"

"I don't know. Erin, we told you we wanted space."

"Why would you bring her here?" Celeste asks Erin, then glares at Lucinda. "Why would you come here?"

"Come on guys," Erin says. "We're all adults. So there was a little drama. Let it go."

Oh, shit. I have lived in Northern California for twenty years, but I never bought the new age "energy" idea until right now. The vibe coming off my girlfriend is murderous. She looks at me. "Is this the surprise you were telling me about?"

"Babe, come on. No!"

"Then why are they still here?"

I stare at her, then at them.

"I have to go." Celeste flings the door open and storms out, slamming it behind her.

I point at Erin, then at Lucinda. "This is not cool, Erin. And Lucinda, you should know better than to show up here."

"Josh, let's talk about this," Erin coos. "Don't you think Celeste is being unreasonable?"

"No, I don't." I leave my house to make things right with Celeste. She's pacing at the end of the driveway. "Angel? Are you okay?"

"I can't believe you."

"Me? What did I do?"

"It's what you didn't do. You didn't tell Erin to find somewhere else 'to land,' and you didn't tell her to get the fuck out of your house just now and take that piece of trash with her."

"This isn't you. You don't call people trash."

Celeste stops in her tracks and glares at me. "You're turning on me? After what your friends just pulled?"

"Lucinda is not my friend."

"Well she's in your house because your friend Erin invited her. If they're such good friends, Erin should stay at Lucinda's."

Celeste is right. I know this. I know this, and I don't know what to do first. She seems to think I'm okay with the situation.

"The thing is Josh, you told me I couldn't stay this week or travel to wherever you're going. Are you really going anywhere? Was Erin's arrival really a surprise? Or if she the reason you didn't want me to stay?"

"Can't you see I'm as upset about this as you?"

"I see you're upset. Maybe because your plans with that heinous bitch and her skanky friend got exposed while I was here."

"Celeste, that's not what happened."

"I thought you had changed. Obviously, once again, I'm the fool."

"Cece, please, you have to know..."

"What I know is, the man I trusted lied to me, and some people can't change. Apparently, my feelings and our relationship matter less to you than whether your friend is comfortable and has a place to stay."

"You don't wanna put her on the street. Do you? She'll be homeless."

"Please. She's an adult. She'll figure something out."

"Homelessness is real, Celeste. It happens to adults."

"Erin has family here. And if she's alienated them, she can stay with the skank she invited to your house. I'm calling a ride share." She pounds her fingers against her phone screen so hard it falls out of her hand. "Fuck! And I don't have my bags."

I hate seeing her like this. Worse, I hate knowing that I triggered this. I fucked up by letting Erin stay, and I can't fix this fast enough.

"Fuck. It's two minutes away. Please go get my bags because there's no frigging way I'm going back inside with those women."

I jog into the house, past Erin and Lucinda, into the bedroom and grab Celeste's stuff. I'm making the wrong choice, but what else can I do? Celeste is pissed. I can't blame her. I also can't ask her to come back in while they're here. Obviously, Erin has zero respect for my wishes or my relationship. Lucinda's presence is a mystery. I throw whatever I see into Celeste's backpack and purse and run outside. Without a word, she takes her things and gets into the ride share.

Ash falls around me as I watch my love leave. All my energy drains away.

36

Josh

I STARE MINDLESSLY AT THE EMPTY STREET. I'VE FUCKED up many times in my life, but this has to be the worst. All because I trusted a friend. How can I make things right? I text:

I love you and I'm sorry

I stare at the screen, awaiting her response. None comes. Not even those three little dots that let me know she's thinking. She probably deleted my message without reading it.

Celeste gave me another chance and I blew it. I canceled myself from the most important relationship in my life. What a fuckup. Why did I trust Erin? Because we've been friends forever and she's never let me down before now. What the hell was she thinking?

Who cares? The important thing is, Lucinda must go.

I stride into my home and brace myself for whatever onslaught these two will throw at me.

They're at the kitchen island, bent over their phones, speaking in low tones that make me suspicious. It feels shitty thinking of a friend that way.

"Lucinda," I say, using my stern voice.

Her head snaps up, eyes wide.

"You are not welcome here, ever. Get out of my house."

"Excuse you."

"I said, get out. Now."

"Could you be reasonable? Celeste was—"

"Do not speak her name. Get the fuck out of my house before I call the police and have you removed."

Lucinda huffs. "Erin, call me." She stomps out with an exaggerated sigh. Good fucking riddance.

Erin turns to me, a fawning look on her face. "Oh, Josh. I'm sorry."

"Thanks."

"I didn't know Celeste would be upset about me bringing Lucinda here."

"You serious?"

I think about how thin Celeste felt because she couldn't make herself eat, how she had insomnia for months.

Didn't know she'd be upset?

Even not knowing her struggles, how could anyone think she'd be cool seeing Lucinda in my fucking house?

And Erin, of all people, the oh, so compassionate yoga teacher. Did she play me? No clue why she would, but she's oozing insincerity as she says, "You guys seem so solid. I thought she was over it."

Anger shoots through me. "Bull. Shit." I glare at the counter, gripping it so hard my knuckles match the white tile.

"Come on, Josh. You know I love you. I totally support you, whatever you want."

"Right," I say, drawing out the word.

"Truth be told, Lucinda can get a little annoying. It's good you kicked her out because now we can talk this through and put it behind us."

This woman is a snake. How have I never noticed how easily she throws people under the bus? "I don't know what you are playing at, and I don't care."

"Nothing! Josh." She opens her eyes extra wide, like I've offended her.

"You showed up here asking for a safe place to land. I opened my home to you."

"And I offered you free yoga classes in return."

"I told you how important my time with Celeste is. You promised to make yourself scarce, then made sure to be in the way."

"In the way." She puts a hand on her hip, indignant. "I don't like this treatment. I'm your friend, and I put up with your ego, and your boring science talk, and now you come at me with all this negativity, and—"

I look into her eyes, a scary sight. For all her talk of love and seeing the light in everyone, there's nothing behind those eyes. They're as black as my mother's after her death.

Erin's still talking, but I'm done. I grab a kombucha from the fridge and walk around her, spitting one word as I exit the kitchen. "Leave."

"If you're not careful, I will. How long do you expect me to stand here and take this?"

"As long as you're in my house," I yell over my shoulder as I stride down the hall into the guest room. "You packing your shit, or am I?"

"You're not kicking me out, too."

"You have five minutes to leave my property. The clock starts now." I start the timer on my phone.

Her duffle bag lays crumpled in the corner along with a bunch of clothes. I grab anything and everything that looks like hers and throw it inside. The fucking incense sticks and holders, all the scented candles. So many fake scents. Her clothes spill over the edges of the dresser drawers. I rip those out and shove them into her bag.

"What are you doing?" She stands in the doorway, horrified.

"What's it look like? I want you out of my house and my life."

"Where am I supposed to stay?"

"You are not my problem. My only regret is thinking you were."

"Josh, you're gonna wake up tomorrow and realize you made a huge mistake. Celeste isn't right for you, and you're killing all your friendships because she threw a fit."

"Whatever friendship we had is over." I zip the duffle closed and shove it into her arms. "Time to go, Erin."

She takes the bag. I follow her down the hall to make sure she actually leaves, reading the timer's countdown aloud for her benefit.

She reaches the door with ten seconds to spare. "I'll call you tomorrow. You'll come to your senses."

"I'm blocking your number right now. See?" I shove my phone in her face so she can see I'm serious.

Erin lifts her chin in defiance and strides out to her car, throws her duffle into the backseat. Just when I think I'll have some peace, she gets her revenge, keying the length of my jeep before she gets into her car and drives away.

Great.

I slam the door. I need to run, cycle, do some yoga, something to burn off this anger, but that's out of the question. My flight leaves at eleven AM tomorrow, and I haven't packed a damn thing.

I hop in the shower and rinse away sweat and ash, as ideas tumble around my brain in no logical order. Probably low blood sugar, but food is out of the question. My stomach is one huge angry knot. Who am I mad at: myself? Erin? Lucinda? The universe? Damn it all.

I dry myself, grab a garment bag from the hook in my walk-in closet and stare at my suits. Which fucking one do I pack? I'm gone for a week, so two suits. Shirts. Ties. Can I get away with an open collar and no tie? We're scientists. I never wear a tie to work.

Brent calls. Relieved to hear from a friend I can count on, I feel my heart rate slow as I answer. "What's up?"

"I'm thinking dinner."

"If only. I've got a morning flight and need to pack."

Celeste helped me buy everything in my closet. I don't frigging know how to put these colors together.

"Pack in the morning."

"Staying near SFO tonight." Which wasn't the original plan, but since I need to find her...

If she doesn't take me back, I'm buying everything monochrome. Fuck this matching autumn, winter, warm, cool bullshit. Who has time?

"How about I come over with a six-pack and a bowl?"

"Man, I'd love to chill. You wouldn't believe what just went down here."

"Heard about it."

"Oh?"

Forget suits for now. Let's start with dress shoes. Black or brown? Black. I'll wear my hiking boots on the plane and bring my five-finger running shoes. Into the pockets of the garment bag they go. Done.

"Lucinda and Erin stopped by," Brent says.

"When did you get close to Lucinda?" And why didn't I know about it?

"Last year. They're both pretty upset, Josh."

Hiking shorts. Undershirts. Casual T-shirts. Boxers.

"Dude, what're you doing?" he asks.

"Packing." Laptop. Charging cords. I hurry into my office and grab the electronics and laptop bag, and return to my room.

"You kicked your friends out after how Celeste treated them?"

"Excuse me?"

"She yelled at them. What the fuck?"

"Come on."

"Dude, I don't know why you're with Celeste. Everyone celebrated when you two broke up."

"You serious?"

"You've gotta see how bad she is for you."

"Enlighten me."

"Josh, in what way did that relationship work? She was so intense all the time."

"She's passionate."

"And controlling. Once you got with her, you shut down."

"How so?"

"You couldn't do anything without taking her temperature. If Celeste wasn't up for it, you said no."

"I think it's called being considerate of your partner."

"So you lost the ability to decide for yourself? And honestly, dude, she's boring. I mean, I can see the sex appeal, but Jesus, the way she stares with those wide eyes—"

"Goodbye, Brent." I hang up.

Now, I'm hot. How dare he insult any woman like that, never mind the woman he knows I love? Were these people always so shallow? 6:42 PM. No clue where I'm staying tonight. Fuck. Okay. Deep breath in. Slow exhale. Packing is easy. Let's finish this.

The first thing Brent offered was alcohol and pot. Wow. I truly am a different person. A year ago, those would've been my go-to strategies for relaxing. Glad I have better tools now. He texts:

You hang up on me?

I leave my phone in the closet and get my shave kit and travel toiletries from the bathroom. Throw everything into the bag.

I'm trying to help you, man.

No need. I choose Celeste. You can support my relationship or delete my number because I'm not interested in games.

Dude.

It's a surprise to me, too, the way you're acting. Disrespectful. Crass. I thought you were different.

From what?

Thought you had some substance.

Fuck you.

Same.

For the second time in an evening, I block the number of a long-time friend. A year ago, I couldn't have done it. If my friends had put overt pressure on me to ditch Celeste a year ago, I might have caved. Even if I didn't, I would've bent over backwards trying to make things right with them. Sucks I had to lose the love of my life to see what fakes my friends are. But I can't think about that or I'll crumble.

Maybe Amira can help with these damn suits. I call and give her the lowdown about the interviews I lined up, and how, right before we walked into the house and saw my so-called friend and Lucinda, I was thinking about the surprise I had planned for Celeste tomorrow.

"I'm sorry, Josh. I know it hurts to let long term friendships go. But hallelujah! The assholes are gone."

"These people have been my found family for twenty years."

Amira's nostrils flare. I don't know what she's about to say, but I'm already planning defense. "Let me tell you about your so-called found family. When I went to see you and we hung out with your found family, they treated me—your sister—like an intruder."

I sag in defeat. "You, too, huh?"

"They were the most unpleasant, unwelcoming group of people I had ever met, and I couldn't believe you felt so close to them, but whatever. It's your life."

"I'm sorry, sis. I never realized. Frankly, I can't fathom their motives, but at the moment, I need your help choosing my suits, so I can finish packing and get on the road." I hold the three best ones in front of the phone for Amira.

"The dark blue and the charcoal."

"Shirts? Ties?"

"Gray and blue shirts. Ties? Ugh. Derek," she turns and yells. "Josh needs help with ties. He's good at this."

While we wait for Derek, Amira grills me. "What's your plan to fix things with Celeste?"

"She's done with me."

"Now is not the time to give up, Josh. Go find her."

"How, Miss Bossy Pants? How do I find Celeste? I assume she's at one of the eight hotels by the airport, but which one? I have no time to research. I need to pack, find a place to stay, drive there, and prep for my interviews."

"You need me to book your hotel?"

I sigh in relief. "Would you? I have points at the Hilton. If they're booked, find anything nearby."

"You got it. I'll call with your reservation number once I have it."

Derek's face pops onscreen. "Hey."

I greet him and hold the phone up to my suits and shirts. I'm reaching for ties when sirens blare. "Fuck."

"What's that?" Amira sounds panicked.

"Evacuation sirens. Gotta go."

"Hold up," Amira says. "If you can't find her, get your butt—"

"I'll call from the car. Thanks guys."

She's saying I love you as I end the call. I throw my suits, shirts and a couple of random ties into the garment bag. Did I pack jeans? I'll have to buy casual clothes on the road.

Zip the garment bag. Grab my laptop bag and the Go Bag in case I get stuck somewhere. Pull the smoke mask off its hook and slip it over my face. I need to take a piss, but that'll have to wait.

The lock clicks into place as I close the door behind me. The air is thick with smoke now. Not so thick I can't see, but thick enough, I'm glad to be wearing this mask. I get in my car and peel out of the driveway, wondering if my house will be here at the end of the week. If it is, that's going into the marketing materials. Fucking saved my house from a wildfire with my invention. That is, assuming the fire gets here. Just because the smoke is thick and they're evacuating, doesn't mean the fire will touch us. God, I hope it doesn't.

Maybe it'll peter out. If it gets out of control, slim chance rescue teams will stop it without herculean efforts and loss of life.

The line getting onto the freeway is long. I turn on the radio for news about the fire. Sounds like everyone near the university is in danger. Though I'm not much for praying, I send a silent prayer for Julio, Rachel, all my colleagues and friends, and the people I blocked today. I pray no wild animals and pets get trapped this time. I pray everyone who needs to evacuate gets to safety, including me. And I pray Celeste is already relaxing in her hotel room, wherever she is. She has a Hilton membership, too. God, let her be there.

Leaving when she did may have saved her life. Because wildfires are unpredictable, there's a chance my life will end on this highway.

If that happens, Celeste will spend the rest of her days believing I betrayed her again, and she'll tell herself that awful, stupid story about being unworthy of a man who stays. The idea makes me sick.

I have to get to her. She'll never take me back. Still, she needs to know I didn't betray her again. She's not someone people leave. Maybe once she knows that, she can find a man she'll feel safe trusting. I wish I could offer her more, wish I could be that man, but at least she'll have a chance at the love she deserves.

Finally, I enter the on-ramp. Traffic is bumper to bumper. It's gonna be a long drive. "Siri, call Amira."

All circuits are busy.

37

Celeste

So what if it's only seven-thirty? The way this day ended, I deserve to order room service, eat French fries and drink wine in bed, and go to sleep early. And that bed looks cozy, like Josh's new bed. The bed he bought to make me feel comfortable. Supposedly. Talk about disappointing. Understatement. Devastating is more like it. I thought we were healing together. My dreams were finally coming true. Now, this bullshit. My life is falling apart again.

No, it isn't. The old life couldn't be resurrected.

Fortunately, I recently built myself a new life in New Haven, where I'm happy and have loving, mature, intelligent friends. When I get home, I'll clear away the few reminders of him, especially that box of letters with all the pressed flowers and the stupid rose cake recipe. True, it was the most delicious cake ever, would've been a perfect wedding cake. Anger turns my stomach.

I gave Josh another try. I thought, "Maybe he really is my soulmate." Apparently, I was wrong. Who cares? Even if we are soulmates, I refuse to play house with a soulmate who's incapable of being faithful and holding my best interests in his heart.

I call Room Service and order my fries and wine. They say forty-five minutes.

I get in the shower. Washing away the day, feeling the water slide over my skin feels wonderful. For a hotel airport, this place has a really nice bathroom, and I adore this shower head. The downpour massages my head and neck, easing my tension. I envision it flowing out of my cells, through my pores, off my skin, right down the drain. It almost works. I'm sure the wine and fries will help, too.

I dry off in a super fluffy towel, take my time applying lotions and face creams. Now, I slip into the cozy silk and lace negligee and kimono I would have worn at Josh's if things hadn't gotten so steamy in the bath last night. But we went to sleep spent, wrapped in each other, skin on skin. I sigh. At least I have some happy memories.

Room Service arrives. I put the tray on the king-sized bed, sip my Sauvignon Blanc, swirl it around my mouth. Light, refreshing. A tinge of spice. Perfect with these hand-cut fries with mayo and mustard. I am savoring this treat, chewing and swallowing slowly, like a meditation. I take another sip of wine, dip a delicious fry into the mayonnaise and slowly, carefully bite it, as if I may never eat again. I'm feeling more relaxed by the minute, closer to laying my head on the pillow.

My phone dings with Amira's text tone.

> Hey. I've been trying to call you. Can we talk?

Oh, that's right. I heard the phone ring while I was in the shower, then forgot to look at it. I was thinking how rejuvenating it would be to have a night without staring at that tiny screen. But now I see Amira left three voicemails in six minutes. Something's up. I dial her number.

"Hey, sorry, I was in the—"

She interrupts. "Celeste, I don't know what to do. I can't reach Josh."

"Okay, well, um—"

"Listen, I know you guys had a misunderstanding, but we were on the phone and that siren went off and—" The panic in her voice is real and very unlike her. Suddenly, I'm wide awake.

"Shit. The evacuation siren?"

"Yes. He said he'd call from the car, but he didn't, and every time I call, I get 'all circuits are busy.' "

"Oh, my God." Poor Amira. My heart is pounding. I'm not just empathizing with her. I'm freaking out, too. He may be a lying, cheating asshole, but he's still the man I love and if Amira's right, he's in danger. "When was this?"

"Like an hour and a half ago."

"Okay, well, don't panic."

"Too late!"

"I know. I'm saying that more to myself."

"Celeste," she whines.

"Sorry. We'll... shit... let me find the news." I grab the TV remote and try to turn it on, but damn, these complicated hotel TV systems. Forget that. I open all my social media channels, looking for posts from the local news stations. They're pretty good about updating people. "Yeah, shit. Okay. It looks like the wildfires spread. Alright. I don't know. Um. Okay..."

"This isn't helping," Amira sings, her voice rising in pitch.

"I know. I can't think." I munch on a French fry. It turns sour in my stomach. I take a sip of wine. Not helpful. Now, I'm out of bed and pacing. "I don't. I don't. I don't know. I... we've never had to evacuate before. Shit. Let me try to reach him. Maybe the problem is you're calling from out of state."

"Yeah. Where are you?"

"I'm at the hotel by the airport. I honestly don't even know what it's called. Hilton? Hyatt? It starts with an H. I just had the ride share driver drop me off. I gave the person at the front desk my credit card and came up to my room. I wasn't paying attention. All I know is my flight leaves at eleven AM, and I wanted to be away from Josh and as close to the airport as possible."

Amira's voice is ragged with tears. "Right. Well, if he makes it out of there, he's coming to find you."

"I can't think about that right now, Amira."

"I get it."

"I know you do. Have you tried texting him?"

"Yeah."

"Okay. Let me try calling him. I'll be in touch as soon as I reach him."

We end the call, and I dial Josh. It rings. A good sign. Then, "All circuits are busy. Please try your call again later."

Fuck. ***Where are you, Josh?*** I open my messaging app. He texted me!

I love you and I'm sorry.

Wait, he sent that over an hour ago. That's right. I saw his name in the message alert and ignored it.

I text him:

Amira said you evacuated. Are you safe?

One good thing about Josh is he doesn't play games intentionally. Even if he's hurt by me leaving, he won't ignore my text. If he receives it. I stare at the screen, waiting for his response. Nothing.

Option two. There is no option two. I can't reach him. Amira can't reach him. All lines are down. He's probably on the road somewhere, hopefully far from the fire. I envision him driving with his smoke mask on, focused on the road, drumming the steering wheel in time to Led Zeppelin if he's freaking out, or maybe rocking back and forth to Bob Marley or the Grateful Dead if he's trying to calm down.

Our little community is a couple of hours from the city on a good day. If there's traffic… who knows?

Amira said he's coming to find me. He knows I have a flight and need to be near the airport. Maybe he's coming here. How would he know which hotel? How many airport hotels can there be? I eat a few more fries. Now, they're cold. Not satisfying. The wine helps, though, and pacing. Actually, pacing is making me dizzy and anxious. I grab my phone and my room key.

Too antsy to stand in an elevator, I take the stairs from the seventh floor all the way to the main floor and stride to the concierge desk. This guy's vibe is a blend of snooty and retro goth. Like he stepped out of a fantasy novel but is wearing the staid hotel uniform. Blue-black suit, red tie, white shirt. Not flattering. The problem is the white washes him out.

Let it go, Celeste. The concierge is giving me a strange look, but whatever. Maybe he's having a bad day. I'll try to keep that in mind. I take a deep, centering breath and make eye contact. "How are you?" I ask.

"I think I might be doing better than you, dear. How can I help you?"

"My… ex-boyfriend was apparently evacuated from our community a couple of hours from here, and his sister just let me know their call was cut off, and she's been unable to reach him, and he was supposed to call her, but she hasn't heard from him, so she asked me to try, and I keep getting the message that all circuits are busy and I—"

"Okay, wow! That was a lot of information, Mx..." He brings his palm down through the air in a calming motion.

"Ms. She, her, hers. Cairan."

"Ms. Cairan, I'm sorry. I understand that's stressful. Let's try and breathe and figure out how I can help you."

"I don't know if he's coming here, but she said he was looking for me, and if he makes it here, is there any way you could let me know? I wouldn't want you to give him my room number."

"We would never."

"I mean, he's a liar and a cheat, but I still love him. You know? I don't want him to die in a wildfire!"

"Of course not. You're a compassionate person."

"Yes. Thank you for seeing me. And if you'd be so kind as to let me know if he shows up, that would ease my mind tremendously."

"I understand knowing he's safe would make you feel better. Unfortunately, just as I can't give out your room number, if he is to check in, I can't inform you or anyone else that he's a guest here."

"Really? Why?"

He leans toward me, like he's telling a secret. "You and I know you're perfectly sane, but some of our guests..." He gives me a pointed look, then continues in low tones. "I'd hate you to worry. I simply can't risk the safety of our guests. Some of the people I've seen..." Another dramatic pause, this time with raised eyebrows. "They go through a hard time with an ex and... The fact is that when there's a breakup, sometimes one or both parties feel justified in seeking revenge."

"Oh." I cringe. "And I just told you he's my ex-boyfriend."

"Yes, you did. Not that I'm suggesting you would do that. It's simply our policy. We can't give out guest information under any circumstances."

"But this is an emergency."

"I understand. The wildfires are very distressing for everyone in the community. I'm feeling the stress myself."

"Of course you are! So you understand how important this is. It's worth making an exception, this one time. Right?"

"If anything is worth an exception, this situation is. You are. And I wish I could. Truly, I do. Unfortunately, it's not possible. If you'd like to go back to your room and rest."

"I'm too anxious to rest now."

"I could send you a little treat. We've got some soothing edibles: CBD, THC, a blend. Sativa is very—"

"Thank you. I've already had a glass of wine. I tried to eat the French fries. They were so good, but then she called and they got cold, and—"

"I understand, and I apologize. I know it's disappointing."

There's that word. Disappointing. The word of the day. I thank my new friend and walk toward the elevators.

No, I can't go back to my room now. My next best hope is to reach out to his friends, those whose contact info I didn't delete already. I stand in the middle of the hotel lobby and call and text Mina, Terry, and Brent. All lines are down. Deflated, I call Amira as I look for the hotel bar. "I'm sorry, honey. I've tried everything. I'm going to the bar to watch the news. The TV in my room—" I grumble.

Amira half-laughs, then sniffles. "Trust me. I get it. You need an advanced degree just to operate a television these days. I still need Lila or Derek's help to watch anything."

"And the last time I owned a TV was before the digital revolution. It's a miracle I can operate a smartphone."

"You truly are a luddite." It's a relief to hear Amira teasing me instead of crying, a relief to talk about something silly and stupid. "Anyway, thanks for trying, Cece."

"I'll let you know if I hear anything. Will you do the same?"

"Absolutely," she says. "Love you."

"I love you, too. And Amira, with everything that's happened between your brother and me, I'm so grateful you haven't let it affect our friendship."

"You're one of my ride-or-dies, Celeste. I'm not letting you go for anything."

I SETTLE ONTO A BAR STOOL AND ASK FOR A HOT TODDY. I WANT something soothing and warm. Am I giving off vibes, or does this hotel train its staff to approach all the guests with an air of superiority? This chick looks more comfortable in her uniform than the concierge, with good reason. The Gatsby-era vest and collarless button down are super cute, and she wears them well. She. I shouldn't make assumptions about gender, especially not in San Francisco. *They* are giving me the side-eye. But I slide my room key across the bar and tell them to charge it to my room and their demeanor changes. Thank goodness.

"I need to relax and watch the news in peace, and if you can bring some French fries with mayo and mustard, too, that would be great."

"Absolutely." They make a show of handing my key card back to me. "May I suggest you might be more comfortable in one of our cozy armchairs near the fire?"

"Ugh. Fire."

"Oh, I know. Sorry. It's actually a gas fireplace, for appearances and warmth only. And it's near our other television, where you'll be able to watch the news without being distracted by the busy bar."

I look around. There're only a couple of people here, so I'm not sure what busyness she's referring to. Still, a comfy arm chair sounds a lot more relaxing than a bar stool.

"Thanks." I follow her to the new spot and she hands me the remote. "Oh, God. Please. I have no idea how this works. Would you mind putting on the local news?"

"Happy to."

Words and images flash across the four-foot screen. Nothing's making sense to me. Wildcat Canyon is ablaze. The Santa Cruz mountains are up in smoke. I'm waiting for news of our town. There's a helicopter and a reporter talking about what CalFire thinks started this wildfire.

The bartender places a hot ginger tea mixed with rum and a plate of piping hand-cut fries on the side table next to me. Perfect. I'm still having trouble eating. Every potato I swallow seems to land in my stomach like a stone. But this hot boozy tea is soothing and leaves me pleasantly buzzed.

Honestly, who cares what started the blaze or where it started? I need to know if everyone got out of Wildbranch safely. Is Josh okay? The helicopter footage shows the I-84 and the I-5 freeways with bumper-to-bumper traffic, though all you can really see are headlights and taillights. It's hard to make out anything clearly in the dark. Everything is shadow and firelight, until the reporter gets on camera and of course they light her up with... who cares? I try calling Josh again, but lines are still down. Oh, God.

Does Satya know? Should I tell her? Amira is her aunt. If anyone tells Satya anything, it should be Amira, but maybe there's nothing to report. Maybe Josh...

Maybe I'll find something on social media. That way I can check all the news coverage. On television, they're showing a horrific map with doomsday graphics that make me wanna scream and throw things at the TV. I scan my phone, scrolling through one social media feed after another, finding nothing helpful. This drink tastes yummy, but it's making me woozy. And now I'm depressed. I sigh. Nine-fifteen PM. No news I can use. And I need to be up early for my flight.

I wave my thanks to the bartender as I leave, trying to keep steady on my feet. I'm not drunk, just tired and... it doesn't matter. In ten minutes, I'll be sound asleep.

Suddenly, my phone goes crazy with text messages and voice-mail alerts. Josh. I lean against the wall and read:

I'm safe.

Sorry, I was stunned and slow to respond. Told Lucinda she's never welcome in my house. Kicked Erin out. Ended the friendship.

Blocked her number.

Whoa.

You were right about my so-called friends. Turns out they were scheming to split us up. Blocked Brent's number, too.

I wish I could say I'm surprised. At least Josh is safe. I read his apology again, taking it in. Another text flashes on my screen:

I know you're done with us. I don't blame you. I betrayed you once. You gave me a second chance, and I let you down. I did NOT betray you this time, but I imagine it felt as bad.

Thank you.

Too tired to take the stairs, I walk to the bank of elevators and hit the UP button. Doors that had been closing slide open.

I know those hiking boots and the hairy legs with the well-defined cycling muscles. I had my hands on those hips at the top of a mountain mere hours ago. I know that dark t-shirt with the chemistry equation and the firm chest and abs underneath it. I know those arms that hoisted me over that strong shoulder and carried me like—

The doors slide toward each other, but Josh juts his hand out to stop them. "Celeste." His voice is breathy, like he's excited. His full lips curve into a half-smile. Our eyes meet, and I stop breathing. Or maybe I stopped breathing the moment I saw his boots.

38

Celeste

"JOSH," I SAY, STEPPING INTO THE ELEVATOR, TREMBLING.

"Thank God, you're alive."

"Got out just in time." His eyes are tired, but lit with joy.

My hands go to his face automatically. "You're covered in ash. Are you okay?" My thumb travels the ridge along his hairline left by the smoke mask still hanging around his neck.

He leans into my touch. "I am so sorry."

"I got your texts. Thanks."

"So happy to see you."

"What are you doing here?"

He swallows and takes a deep breath, visibly steeling himself. "I needed to find you to make sure you know the truth."

"What truth?"

Cradling my face in his palms and scanning my face he says, "You are not someone people leave."

"Josh—"

"Stop telling yourself that lie. I'm here. I fought for you, and I would've kept fighting for you 'til the day I die because you're worth fighting for." He puts his hand on my heart and stares into my eyes. "Please know you are worth fighting for, Celeste, and go find a man you feel safe trusting, so you can have the love you deserve."

I lay my hand on Josh's chest. His heart is pounding as wildly as mine. I want to say what I feel: I'm looking at that man. But can I trust him? I appreciate he finally got his jerky friends out of his life, but he never explained his secrecy.

"Why wouldn't you let me stay at your house this week?"

"Because I booked a seat on the flight next to you."

"How would you know where I'm sitting?"

"Silly, you always book seat 11C if it's available. I booked seat 11B."

I shake my head to clear the buzz of alcohol and exhaustion. Obviously, I misheard him.

"Yes, I did. I'll be sitting next to you on that flight."

"Why?"

"Monday, I'm meeting with the Director of the Harvard Forest in Petersham, Mass, to talk about a tenured position at Harvard. Wednesday, I'm meeting with the Dean of Materials Engineering at UMass to talk about a tenured position, and Thursday, I'm driving down to New Haven to meet with the Dean of Yale's Chemistry department to talk about a tenured position that would allow me to collaborate with research faculty in the School of the Environment, the School of Architecture, Yale Epidemiology, and people around the world."

"What?"

"Remember how I said if you could be patient and trust me, then you'd be happy about the surprise?"

I nod. "Why didn't you tell me all this before?"

"If it didn't pan out, then I'd be letting you down again. I hate disappointing you, Celeste, especially about something so big. I was afraid you'd think I'd said it to win you back."

"Which position will you take if you get all three?"

"I had hoped to discuss where you'd like to live and what you think of each opportunity. I know I don't deserve another chance, but the thought of going through life making big decisions alone, without you." He looks at his boots, then meets my gaze. "We had a sacred partnership. I wanted to plan with you."

I swallow hard. "That's the most beautiful thing you've ever said to me."

"I mean it."

"You have changed. Your whole mindset about relationships is we-based instead of me-based, but I let fear cloud my vision and prevent me from seeing your growth."

"I appreciate you recognizing that."

"I'm gonna kiss you now."

"Thank God."

I run my hands through his hair. Ash coats my fingers. I don't care. I wrap my arms around him, rise onto tiptoes, and bring our mouths together, biting that plush bottom lip and kissing Josh thoroughly. We ignore the elevator's ding and the sound of the doors sliding open. He pulls me closer, deepening our kiss. I think I hear people walk in, then leave. The doors close again. It seems like the elevator's going up, but it might be standing still. He speaks into my mouth, enhancing the spell. "Hey, baby?"

"Mmm?"

"Can I ask you something?"

"Sure."

"Why are you wearing your negligee in public?"

"What?"

"That skimpy silk and lace getup?"

I pull away and look down at myself. "Oh, my God!"

"I mean..." He scans me head to toe. "... you look hella sexy, but..."

Heat fills my cheeks as I recall the interactions I had downstairs. "Maybe that's why people were giving me strange looks and a wide berth."

Josh bursts out laughing. "What people?"

"The concierge, the bartender." I bite my lip. "The parents with small children." Now I'm giggling with him.

"Oh, baby. You know, I love you in silk and lace and that kimono is just fucking... well, you can see the effect it's having on me."

I follow his gaze down. "We make quite a pair. You with your ash covered muscles and the wet spot at the crotch of your pants."

"Mm-hmm, and you with the lingerie and hiking boots. Magical as fuck. Together, we probably look like something out of a zombie apocalypse, except you are very alive, with those pert little nips and flushed cheeks."

"This may be the most embarrassing thing I've done."

"I'm digging it, though."

"Yeah?" I ask.

"Makes me wanna take you right here."

"Remember the last time we were in an elevator together?"

"Right before Sage's wedding." He purses his lips.

"Uh huh."

"Were you thinking about our fantasy then?" he asks.

I nod. "And it pissed me off."

"I was, too. And you know I love it when you're pissed off. All fiery and aggressive. Like you're gonna take charge and boss me around."

I hit the stop button. Alarms blare. "Drop your pants," I command, as I press myself against the wall opposite him to watch him spring to freedom. Josh is big and ready for me. I lick my lips.

"Are you ready, Cece?"

"I started dripping the moment I saw you."

"Fuck."

"Exactly. Get over here."

In two steps, he's pressing his hips into mine, hands on either side of me. "Are you wearing panties?"

I take his hand and slip it under the hem of my negligee. "Find out for yourself."

He moans into my neck as he caresses the inside of my thigh, my hip crease, my golden triangle and finally, my entrance. "You're so hot."

"I am as hot inside as the fire you just escaped, Josh."

He growls. "How'd you get so hot?"

"You lit a fire in my temple."

"A fire," he pants.

"And only you can quench it." I grab his long, hard pole and rub the wet tip with my thumb as I pull him closer.

"Tell me what to do about it, Angel."

The bar spanning the wall is digging into my lower back, but not for long. I grab it, press my hands down hard so my hips lift, then wrap my legs around his waist and pull him flush against me. "Bring that big strong firehose into my temple and douse the flames."

"I'm here to rescue you, baby." He laughs as he grabs my ass and fills my flaming temple with his luscious firehose. Ecstasy.

We're kissing, moaning, sighing, panting. He's thrusting. I'm squeezing and releasing, again and again, faster and faster. The temperature's rising inside and out, and if only we had more time we'd climax right here and lie spent against the wall, but the alarm stops.

"Shit," Josh says, pulling out, grabbing his shorts and stepping into them. "Does that mean someone's here to save us?"

I hit several number buttons at once, to confuse the elevator and give us more time. Who knows if this will work? In all our fantasizing, we never researched the logistics of elevators. I smooth my negligee and close the kimono, hoping I look less like a sex worker in case the doors slide open and someone's waiting to save us.

"All set?" I look back at Josh.

He winks, pats his bulging fly. "Can't hide the feeling."

I giggle and face forward as the doors slide open. A family of five stands in front of the doors, sees us, and clears a path for us with lightning speed. "Thank you." I stride past them, turn and watch Josh as he follows me.

"Daddy, what's that?" A little voice asks.

"Sir, is that your gas mask on the floor?" the father asks.

Josh turns. "Thanks." He grabs the protective equipment.

The doors slide closed. We hear people running toward the elevator, but we stride casually down the hall and into my room, then tear each other's clothes off and get into the shower. It's as big as the elevator. Because of the drought, we can't linger under running water, so while he rinses the ash away, I lather my hands then turn off the tap.

"Hey," he complains.

"Shh. Stand still." I rub the suds into his hair, enjoying his appreciative moan, then open the tap and rinse him. I grab a washcloth and scrub his face, neck, shoulders, and those solid pectorals.

"Clean enough?" he asks.

"Shh. Not yet." I scrub his taut abs and waist, his strong back. Touching him makes me tingle and swell with need. I drop the washcloth and clean his sacrum, hips, and legs with my bare hands.

"You're panting, Cece."

"Am I?"

"It's turning me on."

"Good." I massage the palm of each hand with soap and water, then encircle each finger as I clean it. His cock bobs up each time I rub one of his fingers. I giggle. "Are you doing that on purpose?"

"Doing what?" He teases.

I take the hint and wash between his legs, loving the look in his eyes as he watches me stroke him. Fiery, strong, and vulnerable at once.

He turns off the water.

I gasp.

"Need you now." He cups the back of my head and captures my mouth as he backs me against the wall. My nipples harden against his chest. His cock presses against my mons. "Tell me what you want," he murmurs.

"Finish what you started in the elevator."

"Give me details."

I tell him exactly where and how to touch me. He obeys my every command, like I am a goddess and he exists to serve me. When I say it's time to worship, he enters the temple. Moving his hips with the rhythm of my desire, he brings me closer to the divine with each thrust. I'm losing my mind, rolling my head back and forth against the tile when he says, "Cece, look at me." He holds my gaze as he fills me with his life-saving essence, quenching the fire inside me.

"Yes, Josh, yes," I scream with my release, wrapping my legs around his waist and holding tight.

"I love you, Cece," he croons into my mouth. "Forever."

"Take me to bed."

"Not yet." He pulls my legs off him, making me stand. I whine, but he places a finger on my mouth. "Trust me," he says, and holding me upright, he sinks to his knees and pleasures me with his tongue until I'm pounding the tile. In ecstasy, I slide down the wall into his arms. He kisses and licks my shoulders and breasts, nuzzles my navel, then lays me down and feasts between my legs.

"Come... here, Josh."

He shakes his head, sucking my bud and probing for my g-spot. I feel incredible, but I want what I want. "Bad boy, I said come here."

He presses my legs further apart, and my eyes roll back as he licks and sucks and pulses his finger against my g-spot. I try to protest, but I'm powerless because now I'm writhing and screaming as my hips lift off the floor with another climax. Josh holds my ass, licking me outside, flicking my pearl with the tip of his tongue as I ride the next wave to completion.

"Yes, Angel," he croons, caressing my stomach as ecstatic aftershocks roll through me. "I'm sorry I disobeyed. Tell me what to do now."

"Come kiss me. I wanna taste us, too."

He does. The flavor of his essence and mine combined is salty and sweet and perfect because we belong together, and we always have. And nothing and no one can change that.

Epilogue

Two Years From Now ~ New Haven
Celeste

ADRENALINE FLOODS MY HALF-AWAKE BRAIN, PUSHING me into overdrive as I try to make sense of what's happening. Wildfire. In Connecticut. Since evacuation sirens woke us at 6:22, our phones have been buzzing with Emergency Alerts.

> 6:22 AM
> Hamden Firefighters working to contain fire detected at 6:20 this morning at East Rock Park's Davis Street entrance.
>
> Hamden residents advised to evacuate.

As the crow flies, a mile and a half from our house.

6:23 AM
**New Haven. Fire at East Rock Park
spread to Soldiers & Sailors Monument.**

I moved here to escape this. Josh has worked tirelessly for over a decade to prevent this. He sprayed our trees and yard with FireGuard just last week.

My heart pounds as I slip into my sundress. Xavier's playing on the floor. "Honey, go potty right now, please."

He whines, of course.

"There won't be a bathroom for a long time, honey."

Xavier grumbles and stomps into the master bathroom. So cute.

6:24 AM
**Air Quality Advisory for New Haven and
Fairfield Counties. Close windows. Use
respirators or n95 masks and goggles
outside. Avoid outdoor activities.**

6:25 AM
**Fire spreading rapidly at East Rock Park.
Residents of East Rock neighborhood
advised to evacuate.**

Evacuation sirens sound again, making me jump.

6:28 AM
**All New Haven residents advised to
evacuate.**

My phone dings with Sage's text tone:

Should we come to you?

Yes. Almost ready.

Cece, OMG. No time to dawdle!

I know. Still waiting for Satya, Max and
Tanya.

Hurry!

Stop texting me, so I can think.

Across town, Amira's mom is waiting for Satya and her boyfriend to pick her up. Josh sprayed their properties a month ago, and they're far enough away from East Rock Park that their homes and yards should only suffer a coating of ash. Unless the fire spreads throughout the city.

Focus, Celeste.

The back door slams and Josh's voice booms up the stairs, "Cece, Xavier, let's go. Now." He's trying to keep the panic out of his tone for Xavier's sake, but his voice trembles. "They're all here."

"Be right down," I yell, running into the master bath and discovering my child playing with bath toys, shorts around his ankles, no sense of urgency. Thank God. After losing his birth parents two years ago, the last thing we want is to make him aware of the danger he faces now. "Did you pee, Xavier?"

"Yup."

"Thank you." I pull his shorts over his hips and turn him in the direction of the sink. "Run down to Daddy. I'll follow in a minute."

"Can I take Solly and Mel?"

"Sure."

He obeys, thank goodness, then skips out, bath toys in hand, calling for Josh. Josh's footfalls sound on the stairs.

6:31 AM
**New Haven. Route 91 Willow Street
entrance and exit closed.**

The screen door bangs. I imagine that's Josh carrying Xavier to the car, strapping him into his booster seat. Josh knew exactly what the siren was and sprang to action, running to get Xavier from his room while giving me instructions, then calling our friends and family in the area.

If the city had listened, we wouldn't be in this mess, but the mayor deferred to the state. The state decided that Josh was an alarmist wanting to sell a product, so they refused to use FireGuard on state-owned properties, despite the drought.

"Celeste! Seconds matter!"

"Coming." I throw on my goggles and n95 mask, grab the bags, and run down the stairs and out the door into the thick smoke.

Our eyes meet as Josh takes the bags from me. Fear. Love. The same things I feel. With my gaze, I do my best to offer comfort. The crinkles at the corners of his eyes deepen a moment, then he gestures at the car. I lock the door to the house and get into the passenger seat while he stows the bags in the trunk and slams it closed. Now, he's beside me, squeezing my hand, and pulling out of the driveway.

"Did you see Willow Street's closed?" I ask.

"Shoot... State Street entrance?"

Think, think, think. "No. Go through Westville to Route 15. We'll skirt around Hamden and avoid the traffic jam close to the city."

"Good idea. Thanks, Angel."

Satya's car idles in front of our house, and she, her husband, and Tanya wave as we pass. Sage flashes the headlights of their bright orange ElecTrek. Wesley and their four-year-old Felicia wave from the passenger windows. I send a group text explaining our route. As we caravan away from home, I say a silent prayer for the community and breathe a sigh of relief. The hard part is over. Maybe.

Now, I text Amira:

> **Satya has your mom. We're driving to MA now.**

Amira replies with a heart emoji and a gratitude emoji, then writes:

> **Keep me updated. Safe travels.**

The streets are packed, but most people seem bound toward State Street. Josh turns onto Canner, drives up the hill, turns onto Prospect Street, and drives past his lab, turning right at the Whale, Yale's iconic hockey rink. Is traffic worse than usual for this time of day, or does it feel worse because panic fills the air?

"Daddy, will we get in trouble 'cause we didn't have breakfast first?"

"Huh?" Josh asks, then realizes what our child means. "Oh, no, honey. The breakfast rule says sometimes it's okay to eat in the car or to have a breakfast picnic."

Satisfied, Xavier goes back to playing.

Josh puts kid music on the stereo while I scan my social media feeds for news.

"Are you hungry right now, Xavi?" I ask over my shoulder, grounding myself in the sight of his little face protected by its dinosaur-patterned n95 mask and goggles.

"Not yet." He yawns. "I can wait for a picnic."

I squeeze Josh's thigh and he takes my hand. Safe, despite the news flashing across my phone screen. "You think it'll spread?" I ask Josh.

He bobs his head with the beat of the cheerful kid music, but his face and voice are solemn. "If it's not contained ASAP, it'll be on our street within ten minutes."

"What?"

"Spreading at 14.27 miles in an hour? We're less than two miles from the park." He grips the steering wheel tighter, making his knuckles go white as he yawns. "I'd give anything for a cup of yerba maté right now."

"Me, too. Or another two hours of sleep."

If Josh is right, most of our neighbors will lose their homes. We're escaping to our place in Western Mass. Where will everyone else go? Will they evacuate before it's too late?

Eight Years From Now

Amira

SHADE WOULD BE NICE. I'M PERSPIRING. SWEAT STAINS BLOOM under Derek's arms. Sage slips sunscreen from her pocket. "Felicia, honey, come get more sunscreen."

Felicia gives Sage a smart-aleck look, annoying, but appropriate for an eight-year-old.

"Wes, please?" Sage asks.

Glancing up from his conversation with Derek, Wes follows Sage's gesture from the tube in her hand to Felicia. He takes it and corrals their child, slathering her face and arms while she groans and declares he owes her ice cream now.

"Anyone else need sunscreen?" Wesley asks, as he applies the cream to his face, neck, and arms.

We all take some.

"I miss the days when this park had a tree canopy," Wes says.

"Same," I say. "It's shocking how much East Rock has changed since my first elementary school field trip here in 1993." Mainly because the East Rock fire made charcoal from every single tree in this 427-acre park and surrounding neighborhoods. Now, saplings rise where tall oaks, maples, and birches used to stand.

I'm not bragging about my brother. He'll forever be a pain in my behind. But thanks to Josh, all our loved ones still have homes, trees, and gardens. Connecticut had been in a drought for a year, so Josh went on TV, radio, and social media offering FireGuard free to all residents of New Haven. A few people accepted, including my mom. Most folks said Josh was exaggerating the threat of wildfire.

One of those positive thinking types actually posted a video saying, "Stop the negativity. It's New England. Wildfires don't happen here," and people listened to her. #NewEnglandWildfireHoax and #AlbrightConspiracy went viral. We even caught wind of it in New Orleans.

People claimed Josh was trying to build his business, even though he didn't charge anyone a dime. My brother made the front page of The New York Times. The article quoted him saying, "I want to protect my home and loved ones." When the reporter asked how many loved ones he had, like it was a joke, Josh replied, "New Haven is a tight community. I don't know all my neighbors personally, but I know we're connected. I want everyone safe."

Josh shared data about how FireGuard decreased wildfires all over the American West and Southwest. The Canadian government applied FireGuard on all public land in 2024 and their wildfires stopped. But people in my brother's own community dismissed him. I wonder how many of them died or ended up homeless.

These last four years, Connecticut Firefighters have been applying FireGuard everywhere, including curb strips, every six months. They only complained a little when Josh started charging them for the product this year.

"Careful, girls," Celeste warns our daughters as they skip along the dirt path.

"We know, Auntie Celeste," Felicia says, the snark in her voice making Sage bristle.

"Manners, Felicia," Sage warns, then grumbles under her breath, "Had I known what eight would be like…"

I giggle. "Almost makes you not want kids, right?"

"Don't say that, Aunt Mimi." Satya hunches over and kisses the bald head poking out of her baby sling. "River will always be perfect," she coos.

"Of course he will," I croon. "Eight is a special perfect, and every age has its joys and its challenges." I point at Lila, my twenty-one-year-old altruist, and seven-year-old Terra, an athlete with the mind of a surgeon, like her dad.

"I'll keep these guys in check, Auntie Sage." Lila corrals Terra, Felicia, and Xavier.

Xavier seems oblivious to his cousin shepherding him down the narrow path. He's engrossed in the rocks he found earlier. "This one is quartz," he announces to whomever might be listening.

We emerge from the rugged narrow trail onto the wide road, and the monument at the top of East Rock Park comes into view. Our progress is slow, which gives me time to mourn the landscape.

Ever the optimist, Lila shows us all the wildflowers springing up on the sides of the road. I point out a dogwood sapling, my mother's favorite. I wish Mom was with us, but she has less energy these days, and she's never enjoyed long hikes in the heat.

Sage looks confused. "Dogwood seem like such delicate trees, with their thin limbs and white and pink flowers, and these appear full-sized. Are they coming back faster than the sturdier trees?"

"Yeah. They're pyrophilic," Lila explains.

Sage taps at her phone screen, then says, "Ahh!"

I nudge her. "You had to look that up. Didn't you?"

"Shh," she teases. Pyrophilic. I know Lila's an adult, and it's not like using big scientific terms is new for her. Still, I vibrate with pride over that child.

Meanwhile, Felicia challenges my seven-year-old track star to a race. They dash up the wide path toward the monument at the top, and Xavier follows at a leisurely pace.

Sage snaps photos of the kids running, of Celeste and Josh, Satya and the infant strapped to her chest, and Derek and me. Sage turns her camera on my brother. "You know we just passed the fourth anniversary of the East Rock Fire?"

He blows out a puff of air, glances into the camera lens, then refocuses on the broken pavement in front of him. "What a mess. Huh? We were making the hydrogel at scale, had US Forest Service approval for use throughout the nation. Canada was using it. Australia was about to start. But in my own backyard, we were hobbled by mistrust and fear. And everyone paid the price."

"Except for those of us who accepted your help." Wesley claps Josh on the shoulder.

"Community suffered, though. I appreciated the roof over our heads, but so many families wound up homeless. Didn't you say heroin use skyrocketed afterward, Wes? Liquor stores were running out of stock."

"Yeah, that was rough. But as wildfire incidences dwindled, asthma rates went down globally. New incidences of cancer declined," Wesley says. "Data doesn't lie."

"No, it doesn't," my brother agrees.

"Unfortunately, after so many wildfires, we'll be cleaning toxins from the water for a while."

"Which is what I'll be doing as soon as I graduate next May," Lila sings.

That's my girl. Following her dreams and saving the planet, just like her uncle.

I elbow Josh and catch his eye. For a moment, I feel like my nine-year-old self, gazing in awe at my big brother. I like to give him shit, but I'll never let him forget that his work is changing lives.

Sage

THIS HIKE IS A LOVE-FEST. AFTER ALL THESE YEARS, WE'VE FORMED a family, with each of us playing an integral role in the development of the others and of the group.

Amira idolized her big brother until she discovered his relationship skills sucked and were causing Satya and Celeste pain. But thanks to Derek, Josh got involved with that program and turned his life around. Witnessing his transformation and the way it affected the women in his life has been beautiful.

Admiration flows between Josh and Amira now, and for a moment I see nine-year-old Mimi and her doting older brother.

I switch from photo to video mode to capture the full effect. How better to show that the person behind the science that saved us is human, with a life and a family outside the lab? I'm envisioning an installation with sound coming through canvases where I've augmented photos of Josh running experiments. I might project this video onto a microscope stage, transfer images of East Rock before and after the fire onto lab goggles, or maybe beakers.

Amira says Louisiana hasn't had a hurricane in two years and she's seeing positive shifts in her clients' emotional state and life choices. "Families used to be hypervigilant, living in chronic fight-or-flight mode. It's impossible to think clearly or plan a meaningful life from that mindset."

"Careful, Brat. It almost sounds like you're proud of me."

Amira makes a gagging noise but wraps her arm around his waist and leans into him. "Since we've had fewer hurricanes on the Gulf Coast, folks are less fearful that a storm will take away everything and everyone they love. To think my big brother had something to do with that?" She hums. "I feel a poem coming on."

Josh grins. Tonight, more friends will join us for his birthday dinner. These days, we all have reason to hope.

"Hey Josh, why do you do this?" I ask.

"Do what?"

"Work so hard to save humanity."

He hitches a shoulder. "Science has always made sense to me. Since I can make a difference, don't I owe it to myself to try?"

"So humble," Celeste says.

Josh shakes his head. "Nah. On the rare occasions I got to spend time with my dad, I watched him use science to benefit a few privileged individuals."

"You're not Dad, Josh." Amira shoots a warning look up at him.

"Exactly my point," he says. "I made a conscious choice to serve the greater good, and I'm glad I did, even if sometimes it seems like I can never do enough."

Literally everyone does a double take. Derek, always getting to the heart of things, asks, "How could you, of all people, ever believe you're not doing enough?"

"Because there's always more." Josh takes a long swig of water. "What leads anyone down the path they choose? Sage, why do you take photos?"

"Easy. When I'm making art or snapping photos, everything makes sense. The rest of the time I walk around confused."

"Only in your mind, Lovely." Wesley kisses my cheek. "To the world, you look like a woman who's got her shit together with or without a camera in hand."

"That's right," Amira agrees.

When we reach the summit, I'm overheated. From this vantage point, sunlight sparkles on the water. The panoramic view of the Long Island Sound and New Haven Harbor marked by Lighthouse Point looks much as it has since my freshman year in college thirty years ago. Scanning west, the neighborhoods once populated by giant elm and chestnut trees look barren, although they're finally coming back to life after the fire. Our community, like so many others worldwide, has been through hell and back, and I'm grateful to have my loved ones close.

"Daddy, who's that lady?" Xavier asks, pointing.

"What lady?" Josh follows his son's gesture to the statue topping the monument. In one hand, she holds a wreath. The other lifts an olive branch to the sky.

"That's Mommy."

Xavier gasps and looks at Celeste. "Really?"

Celeste rolls her eyes and giggles. "No. Daddy's playing. That's the angel of peace."

"Like I said," Josh says, taking her hand. "It's you."

A collective "aww" travels around our group as we all gaze at the angel statue.

Green from oxidation, the angel of peace stands tall, a reminder that through horrific storms, tornadoes, and wildfires, peace prevails if it's in our hearts. And where there is peace, there is hope.

June 21, 2033

Satya

BREAKING NEWS – New Haven, CT

The words "Climate Change Ends" flash across the television screen along with graphics that look like confetti. The camera zooms in on news anchor T'nahesi Dikoko, smiling broadly as he announces, "Some said it couldn't be done. Others claimed it didn't exist. Today, scientists declared Climate Change is officially over!"

More confetti fills the screen, followed by a montage of historic news footage. Dikoko narrates, his deep voice equal measures jubilant and reverent. "NASA scientist Jim Hansen sounded warning bells with the United States congress in 1988. Yet it took decades for the federal government to take action. Researchers fought an uphill battle, desperately seeking money to discover both how humans were contributing to climate change and how to fix it."

Archival footage and still shots of people marching in front of landmarks around the world flash across the screen in rapid succession. "While environmentalists across the globe worked to raise awareness and inspire laws to stop climate change before it was too late, climate deniers fought for what they considered their right to keep doing business as usual, regardless of the environmental impact or human cost."

Iconic images fade into one another:

Cows stranded in a flooded field as a factory belches black smoke in the background.

Horses abandoned in a paddock.

Forests ablaze.

Families wading through waist-deep flood waters, carrying belongings on their heads.

An elderly man climbing out the skylight of his flooded home, reaching for the helicopter hovering above.

A child standing alone in front of a shredded house, presumably destroyed by a tornado.

A close-up of a tornado with a lightning bolt.

"Hey, Sage took that photo." Dad leans forward. "At that farm where she and Wesley—"

Sage's tornado image fades and again we see the anchorman at his desk. "Today, nearly fifty years after Dr. Hansen's original testimony in congress, the nightmare is over. Our reporter Michelle Zimmerman has exclusive interviews with researchers in the Albright Lab at the Yale Green Chemistry Department who are celebrating this magnificent turn of events."

Now we see the reporter standing in front of Dad in our lab. Shocking, how the pound of makeup she was wearing this morning looks completely natural on TV. She turns dramatically, inviting the camera to follow her to Dad's side as she introduces him. My normally charming father looks stiff.

"Why do you look so uncomfortable, hon?" Celeste asks.

"See that little black mic on my collar? They clipped a battery pack to my waistband and ran the wire under the back of my shirt, so the mic would be less obvious. It tickled."

I lean over the back of the couch. "Guys, we're missing the story."

The reporter continues, "...in 2026 ended the scourge reducing forests and communities to toxic ash. Dr. Albright, we have you to thank for this moment in history, don't we?"

Dad blushes and gives the reporter an awkward half smile. "I'm one of many scientists who have worked tirelessly for decades to end climate change."

"Does this mean we can relax and go back to life as it was?" she asks.

"Not entirely. If you think about climate change as a broken heart—"

"A broken heart." Michelle quirks an eyebrow, skeptical.

"Correct. We humans have been in a toxic relationship with our planet for centuries. We've abused her, taken what we wanted, and demanded more, more, more."

"Toxic masculinity was a buzzword back in the early 2020s. Are you comparing that phenomenon to climate change?"

Dad shifts his weight, forcing a smile. "Patriarchy and toxic masculinity have distorted the best parts of every philosophy and economic system."

"But what does that have to do with science?"

"My relationship coach wife has helped me see the interdependence of all systems."

"Aw, honey!" Celeste squeezes him, keeping her eyes on the TV.

TV Dad continues, "When someone escapes an abusive relationship, it takes time, sometimes years, for them to heal. Earth also needs time to heal."

"You're saying although climate change is over, we're not out of the woods?"

"Correct."

"How long will it take before we can feel safe?"

"That depends on us. How willing are we to nurture this healing planet?"

"Help me understand this concept, Dr. Albright. Nurture the healing planet?"

"If we return to life as it was in the aughts, we'll quickly resume the toxic cycle of violent storms and worsening conditions here on Earth."

"But thanks to you, even violent thunderstorms that ignite little fires won't spin out of control. So, it can't get that bad."

Both TV Dad and real Dad sigh. "We're preventing wildfires now, but you may recall, climate change was created and worsened by many factors. Wildfire was only one."

"What's our next step, Dr. Albright?"

"We take this opportunity to practice a new, healthy way of life, to create cycles that benefit everyone."

"Such as?"

"Reducing global manufacturing of everything. Buying less for our homes and our offices. Those of us in the United States need to make sure congress passes the bill that would make producing petroleum-based plastic for commercial products illegal. Healthier alternative exist. Using less electricity instead of seeking new ways to generate more energy. Using fungi to clean rivers, streams and lakes had ripple effects on the ocean. We're still searching for a solution for soil pollution. To avoid recreating old problems, we must exercise mindfulness in—"

Dad turns off the TV.

"Hey, I was watching that," Celeste complains, reaching for the remote.

"Angel, you've heard my spiel a thousand times. Doesn't it get boring?"

"Not on the news."

"Jeez. I'm sick of hearing myself."

She strokes his cheek. "This is a once-in-a-lifetime moment. Let's savor it."

My father struggles to hide his smile, but truly, he blossoms under Celeste's attention and care, as she does his.

Dad switches the TV back on and buries his face in her neck. "I can't watch the television version of me drone on about how we still need to use FireGuard on the vulnerable areas, blah, blah, blah."

"You're talking about my work, now, Dad." Before I finish my sentence, the image cuts from Dad's interview to mine.

"Oh, look, there's she is." Celeste gazes over her shoulder at me. "Satya, sit down and enjoy this!"

"I've gotta get the kids. Max texted his meeting is running over."

Now Dad's riveted to the television. "Xavier," he bellows. "Come see this. Satya's on the news, talking about her experiments with biomimetic air scrubbers that mimic tree stomata!"

"What's up?" Xavier strides into the room, sweaty and smelling as only a thirteen-year-old boy can. He flips his bangs away from his face and points to the image of me on television. "Why are you on TV?"

"Your sister's brilliant invention could accelerate the healing I droned on about with Michelle What's-her-face."

"Huh?" Xavier asks.

Celeste answers, "Because your sister and father worked hard fighting climate change and now it's over."

Xavier says, "Cool," high fives me, and flops onto the handwoven rug in front of the couch.

Cool? Is it because Xavier grew up in this family, surrounded by people striving to end climate change, that he doesn't recognize the threat it posed humanity for half a century? People lived under the cloud of climate change. Farmers ended their own lives in droves, rather than face the uncertain world with its devastating weather patterns. Yet Xavier acts like it's no big deal.

"Cool?" I ask, annoyed by his nonchalance. "That's all you have to say?"

Does my kid brother not see how people like me and my dad devote ourselves to planetary healing every single day?

"It's kind of like a wicked huge deal, son," Dad says, handing him a cushion.

"I know," Xavier says, glancing over his shoulder at us, then back at the TV. I remember this moment in the interview. I nailed my explanation of biomimicry's role in cleaning pollution. Now you can see Michelle Zimmerman's eyes go wide as recognition dawns. But Xavier's talking over it. "...you guys talk about this stuff every day. Dad used to read lab reports and data sets as bedtime stories."

I clear my throat. "And you're not impressed."

"I always knew you'd figure it out." He stretches his body long.

How did he know? I didn't know. I think back to our family outings over the years. Any time environmental justice or climate change came up, Celeste and Dad talked about the solutions he was working on or my latest project. Whatever was happening in the world, Dad and Celeste created a little culture of hope around themselves. Sage, Wesley, Aunt Amira and Derek did, too. Lila and I both followed Dad into environmental science. Xavier grew up with hope, despite living in a fearful society.

Like my children, Xavier knows he's basically safe. He's aware, as much as any teen can be, that harm can occur. But knowing dangers exist in the world is entirely different from helplessly watching the world implode. Knowing is nothing like experiencing things get worse and believing no one can do anything about it—which was the world of my youth. I never want my children or my little brother to suffer that level of fear.

Some day, my father will retire. When he does, I'll keep the Albright Lab going. Because I want nothing more than for my children, your children, and all children now and in the future to grow up in a culture of hope.

Discussion

Thank you for reading HOPE. If you enjoyed it, please leave a review wherever you purchased it.

1. What aspects of this story surprised you?

2. Which character did you find most relatable? Why?

3. Before reading HOPE, were you aware of the toxins released into the air when wildfires spread to communities?

4. When you think about the full costs of wildfire, what do you feel?

5. How did you feel while reading about infidelity from the perspective of the partner who strayed and seeks to redeem himself?

6. How did you feel reading the story from the perspective of the partner who experienced betrayal?

7. Do you think Josh redeemed himself? If you were Celeste, would you have taken him back? Why or why not?

8. This book tackles some difficult, potentially triggering topics. Are you satisfied with the way they were resolved by the end?

9. In the last sentence of the book, Satya breaks the fourth wall and speaks directly to you. What's your take on that? How did you feel when the character addressed you?

10. In the final epilogue, Josh says we all need to change our mindset and behavior about buying things, using energy, and that we need to intentionally choose actions that nourish Earth if we want the environment to be safe for us. Do you agree with Josh? Why or why not?

11. Overall, how does this book affect your thoughts about climate change and our potential to overcome it?

Author's Note

I wrote this book to honor:

The scientists—past, present, and future—working tirelessly toward real solutions to the problems caused by climate change;

Those policymakers, brave enough to choose bold, necessary measures;

Anyone else devoting time and resources to making the environment safe again for future generations, and

The people and animals who lost their lives or loved ones in the wildfires that raged in California, Canada, the American Southwest, the Pacific Northwest, Maui, and Greece. In the year I spent researching and writing this novel, the world watched in horror while those communities burned.

I also wrote this book to give hope to anyone who has experienced infidelity and wants to give their partner a chance to make amends and learn how to love well.

Learning to trust after betrayal takes time and enormous effort. Only you know if it's worth it. If you're determined to make things work, you may find the following resources helpful:

♥ Psychologist Esther Perel's books, newsletter, podcast (*Where Do We Begin?*), TED Talk, and interviews. Learn more at EstherPerel.com

♥ Terrence Real's book *US: Getting Past You and Me to Build a More Loving Relationship.* He offers courses online for couples healing from infidelity and other issues at TerryReal.com.

♥ Author bell hooks' *The Will to Change* addresses toxic relational patterns men and women perpetuate.

♥ As I discover more resources, I'll post them in my newsletter at xoxoTara.substack.com

All relationships have their challenges, but abuse, whether physical or emotional, should never be part of any relationship. Sometimes, no amount of therapy and no self-help method can overcome a person's propensity to lie, manipulate, and cheat.

If you are involved with someone who brings out the worst in you, or if you seem to bring out the worst in your partner, please get help. Abusive situations do not improve.

If you have entered a relationship with the best intentions to love and honor your partner, you deserve someone who also holds your best interests at heart. Anyone who offers you less is not right for you.

If your primary goal in a relationship is to "get yours," or to use, manipulate, or coerce, please consider leaving that relationship and working with a therapist to develop healthy relational skills.

If you live in the United States and you feel unsafe at home or in your relationship, please call 211 for help.

Acknowledgements

If this book has any sense of realism in the lab and field research scenes, it is because of the generosity of Professor Eric Appel at Stanford University. I am grateful for our helpful discussions and the materials he shared regarding the research, development and implementation of new wildfire retardant technologies.

Appel's real science created a real solution, which I renamed FireGuard for this work of fiction. Learn about the real wildfire retardant hydrogel at https://www.perimeter-solutions.com/en/fire-safety-fire-retardants/phos-chek-fortify/

I'm always grateful for MacKenzie Coffman and her support. Because she took time away from her busy life, HOPE has a beautiful cover.

I'm indebted to the expert eyes of the New Haven Writers Group and the Connecticut Novelists Group. In many hours of critique meetings, they shared their honest opinions and helped me see what was and was not working. My classmates, mentors, and professors in the MFA program in Writing Popular Fiction at Seton Hill University helped me improve my craft.

Special thanks to my beta readers, who patiently read early drafts of this book and helped me make it better: Christine Rose Elle Blackledge, Eric Epstein, Corrina Lawson, Bethany Miller, David Sepulveda, and Amber Sumner; and to the fantastic editor, Jessica Pryde.

Also By Tara L. Roí

Did you miss Book 1 in the Trilogy?

Doctor Wesley Williams has a reputation for breaking hearts, and artist Sage DesChamps is too busy building her career to risk devastation. But when work and disaster trap them together, they can't ignore their attraction or the feeling they belong together. ***Can love born in a tornado survive?***

Read Sage & Wesley's story in HAVEN: Love & Disaster Book 1.

No flirting. No Dating. No sex.

Derek's female fast is no problem, until Amira strides into his life and New Orleans floods. Now, they're stuck together, unable to deny their growing feelings. ***Can they find safe harbor in love?***

Read Amira & Derek's story in HARBOR: Love & Disaster Book 2.

A standalone Steamy Romance set in Coastal Delaware.

In a small town on the Delaware Bay, Claire is a single mom starting over. Brian is a young widower who moved to town to escape his loss and grow his career. They're on a mission to save threatened wildlife. ***Will they be united by shared passion or divided by fear?***

Fall in love with Claire & Brian in FOR THE BIRDS

About Tara L. Roí

Whether she's indulging her passions for art, music, or yoga, hanging with loved ones, or enjoying a long nature walk, Tara L. Roí is often thinking up meet cutes. You can find her online chatting about romance novels and the writing process. To set up a reading or other author event, reach out at TaraLRoi.com. Get her newsletter, LOVE NOTES FROM TARA, at xoxoTara.substack.com.